Terra! Tara! Terror!

Third Flatiron Anthologies
Volume 7, Book 24, Fall/Winter 2018

Edited by Juliana Rew
Cover Art by Keely Rew

Terra! Tara! Terror!

Third Flatiron Anthologies
Volume 7, Fall/Winter 2018

Published by Third Flatiron Publishing
Juliana Rew, Editor and Publisher

Copyright 2018 Third Flatiron Publishing
ISBN #978-1-7322189-6-3

Discover other titles by Third Flatiron:

License Notes

www.thirdflatiron.com

Contents

*****~~~~*****

Editor's Note

by Juliana Rew

For our Fall/Winter outing we wanted a mixture of speculative fiction genres, hence the title, ***Terra! Tara! Terror!*** to represent science fiction, fantasy, and horror. We asked—and we received—a cornucopia of bright and dark stories, a real feast for readers. Of course, we understand that not everyone has the same taste and that people's likes often skew toward stories in genres they prefer. Complicating matters somewhat, we include here a number of stories that arguably fit in more than one subgenre. So, if you're a scifi fan, we urge you to work your way through the table of contents from start to finish. If you're a fantasy fan, start in the middle and work your way outward, and if you're a horror fan, start at the back and work to the beginning. We're sure you'll find many gems either way.

Terra!

If you lean toward science fiction, steampunk, and alternate history:

First contact can be tricky—or practically impossible, as Matthew Reardon explains in "Spacism Is Still With Us."

Terra! Tara! Terror!

Diane Morrison's touching "The Android Graveyard" will make you want to play Ghostland Observatory's "Robotique Majestique." *Come on, you keep on going, you damn machine.* . . Steven Mathes's story, "Music, Dogs, True Love, and a Gateway," is a scifi version of "Friends," as they play with a device that acts like a musical instrument on their end, but like a pet store somewhere else.

We all learned in school how the early Americas were conquered by conquistadors like Balboa, but Wulf Moon's alternate history, "War Dog," gives most of the credit to his armored Alaunt, Leoncillo.

"Scales, Fallen From His Eyes" by Kelly A. Harmon introduces us to an ancient dragon, whose secrets have been usurped by technology.

Blurring the lines of genre classification, there's Carolyn Sciriha's "Only the Weak Survive," which serves as both an end-of-days and scifi story about a teacher who helps her new charges learn about Earth's new incumbency. In Rhonda Eikamp's "Memory and Muchness," a young girl who has grown up in an Alice-in-Wonderland world finds that world turned upside-down when the other children start disappearing *up* a hole.

An overwhelmed nurse and her spunky Jack Russell terrier conduct a seemingly doomed ambulance mission though the muddy trenches in "Mud," a World War I alternate history by Salinda Tyson. Melanie Rees does an impressive job of steampunk world-building in "Shadow Harvest," featuring a pub on a burning planet where your shadow is worth your life. Another great steampunk entry (with zeppelins!) is "Our Lady of the Park," by Blake Jessop. Ever heard of a Spriggan? Us neither.

Crossing the border into magical realism, Michele Baron presents "black frost at serac's fall," a tale of storm-fraught mountain hikers, Sherpas, a slightly fae passerby, and passings.

Editor's Note

Tara!

If urban fantasy, swords and sorcery, magical realism, and myth are your bag:

Marie Vibbert gives us a lovely story about a girl who thinks she can fly, a skill that could come in pretty handy in life. In "Father O'Neill's Confession" by Jen Downes, a young priest with an enormous problem seeks unorthodox help, from an older religion. In K.G. Anderson's "Captain Carthy's Bride," a wife tricks her superstitious husband into believing she is a selkie. These stories ask, where does sin lie, and why should it? Gustavo Bondoni's "Field of Honor" takes us to a blood-soaked battlefield, where gleaners harvest magical life spirit from the dying. Fantasy is at its best when there's consolation to encountering life's roadblocks, as in "The Octopus in the Millpond," by Emmett Schlenz.

Elves, dwarves, fairies, and trolls, oh my. At Hyde Park's Christmas fair, three tribes of *sidhe* battle for the heart of a young human girl. Their weapons of choice? Scents, memories, and the world's greatest fudge, in Samuel Chapman's whimsical "Winter War." And for all you tree-huggers, there's Dan Micklethwaite's sweet "If a Tree Falls."

Terror!

For those with a predilection toward the dark side:

Monsters and the paranormal are still king, as you'll find here. John Paul Davies scares the bejabbers out of us with his malevolent family saga, "Replica."

Edgar Allan Poe is well known for his shivery poem, "Annabel Lee" as well as practically inventing the detective novel. So, we deem E.M. Sheehan's "Annabel

9

and Edgar" a crossover: it's both a disturbing ghost story and an alternate history about Poe's last days. We've included Poe's original poem to compliment Sheehan's story.

Slipstream stories always leave us with a sense of unease. Welcome to the funhouse, er, "The Occasional Cabin," by Stefon Mears.

Oh heck, there's another great story that could fit in all three genres. In Liam Hogan's "The Dance of a Thousand Cuts," a young girl discovers a "future"-tech training sword that gives her mastery against all opponents. Well, almost all. We deem it Terror for its cruel machinations.

Something Old, Something New

In the past, a few reviewers have praised Third Flatiron for mostly steering clear of politics. In this era of #MeToo, however, we feel it's entirely appropriate to give Evelyn Deshane free rein, with "Me Too, Medusa." After all, we think mythology has retained its staying power for the political lessons and insight about human nature that it provides.

We are pleased that this anthology has an even balance of male and female authors, including a number of new faces. Don't miss Kiki Gonglewski's extraordinary Italo Calvino–like fantasy, "All the Moon's Children." She's just out of high school.

And to come full circle, we include a special reprint of one of Robert Silverberg's earliest professional stories, "To Be Continued." We think the story strongly references the hidden theme of the collection, the cryptic admonishment, "T.T.T." (Things Take Time!) from Piet Hein's grook.

To lighten the mood, we conclude as usual with our flash humor section, "Grins and Gurgles." Elizabeth Twist's "Oceans of Time" impales an ancient vampire's attempt to use the same old pickup line at the bar. Josh Taylor offers an entertaining take on all those new-fangled safety features on cars these days, in "How to Have a Productive Relationship with Your Semi-Autonomous Vehicle."

We hope you enjoy *Terra! Tara! Terror!*

Juliana Rew
September 2018

###

*****~~~~~*****

Mud

by Salinda Tyson

The ambulance had stalled, its engine sputtering to a halt. The tires were knee deep in mud. It was pouring rain again at the dressing station. Sarah heaved out of the cab, slogged through sucking muck to the front of the vehicle, grabbed the crank, and turned it.

Nothing.

Again, she cranked. Again, no spit, no cough, no purr of the engine.

She stood there in the inferno of dirt and rain, tears streaking her face.

Her waking days were full of fog-swathed stretches of nightmare, real or imaginary. She could no longer tell. In her dreams she followed tommies and doughboys, stumbling through a snaking maze of trenches, where crude signposts pointed to the Ninth Circle of Hell. Medics bore wounded men, moaning and bleeding, on stretchers improvised from the duckboards the men laid on the trench bottoms to keep the mud from pulling off their boots. All a gray or black or sepia world—no color anywhere but the sudden red blossom of a wound, and even that quickly turned rusty brown.

She staggered. How many shades of gray existed in this ravaged place? Images flitted through her brain. The shadowed face of a German prisoner, so skeletal— were their troops starving? The pinched ashen gray of men's faces, of the stubble on their chins, the tender gray of mustaches sprouting on boyish upper lips. The white

13

flash of men's teeth as they grinned, relieved for an hour to kick a dirty, black-and-white football, cheering each other on, joyous as boys.

She sniffed. Could she still smell anything other than the stench of death?

Carbolic lotion and BIPP, bismuth salve—these were the sharp scents of civilized hope, of healing, of care.

This morning she had started up in bed, her heart pounding in tandem with the background pulse of artillery. She shuddered. Yesterday she had mistaken a buzzing fly for an approaching plane, jumped out of her skin, then laughed and cried. Several nurses and drivers had joined in the cry and laugh as they cradled cups of coffee in their cold hands.

Under her breath, she cursed. The Front had taught her many quite creative oaths and rants. Curses were a litany to distract one from lack of hope. Because too often there was no more she could do for the suffering—no more bandages, no more laudanum, no more stretchers, no more aspirin, even. When had she last slept well, eaten a decent meal? She could no longer recall. Her hands shook as she raised them to her eyes. Cotton wool filled her ears—the roar of the big guns, the bursts and hiss of the German pieces and the French guns, the allied machine gun fire, all blurred together, blotted reality.

Her heart beat in time with the artillery shells.

"Please god," she whispered, "whoever or whatever remains of compassion, help me get these soldiers to the base hospital."

Twenty-five miles or so to the chateau, whose sand-bagged underground wine cellars and storerooms served as a casualty ward. Not so far.

Was her dream of serving her country and its troops a hopeless illusion?

Calm, calm, she thought. She rocked to soothe herself, she was muttering a lullaby, holding the badly wounded boy's hand, trying not to see the damage inflicted on his young body, trying not to imagine the future he might return to if he lived, his body so badly maimed.

The ground shifted under her feet. Were these sensations the result of meager food and shell shock? Not just vibrations from the thud of artillery? German miners, no doubt, setting explosives in tunnels they had dug toward the allied trenches? Damn the bastards who would not spare a field dressing station.

The dog, the regimental pet, a champion ratter, was shaking at the eerie screams and thumps of the bombardment, her thin long legs trembling with each shock. She paced and whined, dark, liquid brown eyes fixed on Sarah.

"Here, girl." She held out her hand. The Rat Queen approached, sniffed, and licked her fingertips.

Sarah swayed as she stood up. The unsteady ground heaved and surged, like waves under a boat's keel. A rumble came from beneath her feet. Enemy sappers? A hideous new weapon? Or had the mud come alive, ready to suck them all in, so that their bodies, hopes, memories, and dreams dissolved into its oozing mass?

Was the greedy mud, a vast all-devouring creature, pulling them deeper and deeper into the ground, a monster slurping at their flesh and sucking the marrow from their bones?

One wounded boy, who was probably older than he looked, chanted, "On with my googly, up with my gun, Up to fight the bloody Hun." He batted at his face, pulled at the mask's straps and nose-and-mouth pieces.

Alarmed that he might crawl off the stretcher, Sarah eased his shoulders back gently. "I'll see your mask is on when necessary, dear," she said. "Don't worry about fighting the Huns."

Sarah swallowed. "Not for now, anyway." She repressed a scream. Stay calm, stay calm. Oh, to be at home in a clean bed, far from this endless horror.

"I must go start the ambulance," she said, letting the soldier's hand slip from hers. If she no longer held his hand, would he slip into darkness, as so many did?

She cranked the engine, praying for a sputter, and hoisted herself into the ambulance. Tried again. Again, the engine gurgled, sputtered, and refused to catch. She cursed. The ambulance was useless. Had she flooded the engine? She stepped out, leaning on the door, disgusted. A horse ambulance struggled uphill, the team lathered and wild-eyed. She wondered how long the horses would survive. How long would the shells miss them?

"Can you take some of my wounded?" she cried. She gestured to the six litters full of bloodied men. Rat Queen trotted delicately among the men, yipping and whining, sticking her nose into the pale faces. One soldier laughed, reached a bandaged hand up to stroke the dog's neck.

My men. Still alive, Sarah thought. Pray god, get them out of this mess. Is the dog a better nurse to them than I? A definite morale booster.

Rat Queen suddenly froze, stiff legged, ears cocked, and howled. She put her muzzle to the ground, sniffing.

Gods no, not more gas, Sarah thought. She sniffed. No lavender scent that came when phosgene shells burst.

Her gas mask hung by its strap around her neck, ever ready to be put on if a wooden ratchet noisemaker signaled gas. Or if a whiff of mustard cut the air.

The horse ambulance driver and assistant jumped out, stalked along the line of litters. The older man came to her side.

"Ma'am," he said softly, "you'll never get them in the truck, even if you can start it. We can take two. The rest. . . "

His partner looked northeast. "Shells are coming closer. We think mustard this time. We've got to go. Come with us, and we'll send an ambulance back for them." He

16

jerked his chin toward the men on litters. "We can shift them into the trench for some shelter."

Both men tried to start the truck but had no luck. "If you don't come with us now, we're going," the older man said. "We'll take one more." The pair loaded three stretchers, the most serious casualties, into the wagon-bed. The younger nodded to Sarah and slapped the outside horse on the haunch. "Giddup!"

The sturdy draft horses plodded uphill, reeking of sweat and fear.

A second ambulance crew loaded two men inside, leaving their engine running. The driver and his mate shoved the truck, until it caught traction on less mucky terrain.

"Walk ahead until we get to more solid ground. This ridge feels unstable, it may collapse. We'll take you and send someone back." He held a muddy hand toward Sarah.

She shook her head. "I cannot leave the last man." Five safe, five taken toward the hospital. she'd done her job.

"You'll be overrun."

"Go," she waved her hand, angry now.

So I will die with my charge, she thought, *the Rat Queen and I.* So be it. A shell hit west of the ruined trenches, but closer. The sound splintered Sarah's headache.

The Rat Queen wagged her stump tail furiously, whining at intervals. She was sniffing all the length of the little hill, a long gentle tapered hump not yet cratered by shell fire. Rather like a barrow to Sarah, one of those ancient tombs that Gran had said ghosts and fairies haunted. Earth moved, sliding downhill, first small balls of soil, then clods, then handfuls. Something was emerging from below.

Sarah felt for her service revolver, the cold, ugly metal shape in her coat pocket. She had never used it.

17

Could she use it when enemy sappers emerged from their tunnel to capture or kill the wounded soldier?

The Rat Queen barked. A friendly bark, a greeting. Another shell thudded down, ever closer, shaking them, spewing up a fountain of dirt.

Sarah staggered and frowned at the earth. The shape rising was huge. A new weapon? But the brown-and-white terrier who had won fame by killing rats in the trenches yipped a greeting. She began digging, paws flying.

Gradually, it emerged, beside the wounded man in the litter.

"What the bloody hell's happening?" the soldier cried.

I am hallucinating, Sarah thought. Too little sleep. Too much stress. Too much infernal mud. She squinted. The thing rising was earth colored, ancient, its skin pitted and scaled, uneven and rough as the terrain of the battleground. It drew itself up. A head emerged, with scaly pointed ears and a long snout. A tongue flicked out, tasting the world. Huge eyes opened. Golden eyes as old as time, with slit pupils like a monstrous cat.

A dragon.

Climbing from the earth, not German sappers, but a creature from dreams and fairy tales. Drawing its wings after it from the crumbling soil. A huge clawed foot grasped the edge of the pit it had rested in. Its armored belly slid on the ground. It rumbled. Its tail lashed, and fine clods of earth showered from it. Huge wings flexed and spread, showering soil.

I am insane, Sarah thought, *delusional.* Tears burned her eyes. Too little sleep, too much death. She laughed nervously. *Must have been hit by fusillade or shrapnel, or breathed some new gas, must be having a vision while I die.* Like those reports of men who claim to see angels on the battlefield. Sometimes they live, sometimes they die, but they swear they have seen marvels, celestial beings.

She swayed, sank to her knees, and vomited. She stared into the golden eyes.

"Act," the creature bade her, with a wordless compulsion.

The Rat Queen stood her ground, cocked her head, and sniffed at the dragon's snout.

Shaking, Sarah wiped her sleeve across her mouth and worked with a dreamlike, almost drunken, efficiency. She grabbed a coil of rope from the ambulance, the rope meant to help horse teams pull vehicles from the mud.

"Can you get aboard?" she asked the wounded man. He rolled off the litter at the dragon's side. She dragged the litter atop the beast and helped the soldier half-slide, half-crawl onto it. Running rope under the scaled belly, she tied the wounded man onto the dragon's broad back, touching its scaled hide to assure herself it was real. Trembling, she struggled aboard, patting her lap for the dog. It leaped into her arms and licked her face. The great creature crawled over the ground, faster and faster. From the lip of a deep crater full of broken caissons, dead horses, and men, and the stench of death and despair, it launched into the air, gliding over the ruin of the battlefield, toward the field hospital, the chateau at Compeigne.

Sarah clasped the hand of the boy with the gauze-swathed face. "I'm Sarah," she said.

"Sam," he mumbled. His fingers closed on hers with a strong grip, a good sign. He muttered the motto the soldiers used during bombardments: "If the shell's got my name on it, it'll get me. If it hasn't, it won't."

She murmured the words along with him, peering at his cap badge. Royal Berkshires. Was the shape above the regimental name a lion rampant? No. She swiped away tears. A dragon. She stared at it and wept until she could not see. The wounded soldier was crying, too, tears leaking from his left eye beneath the bandage. "Regiment got the name and badge," he muttered, "in the Opium Wars in China, in old Queen Victoria's day."

The dragon, concealed in a fast-drifting blanket of fog and reeking artillery smoke, soared toward the chateau. Bullets ripped into its wings and body. The dragon shrieked and faltered, climbed into the clouds, and glided on. Sarah smelled blood. She lay along its neck, whispering encouragement. "Great heart, great heart, not much farther."

The stench of gunpowder made her cough. Far beneath them passed the ravaged land. But the old queen's world was indeed shattered, all fairy tales—except for the dragon—gone in this terrible destruction, this bloody, monstrous, steel-fanged birth of the modern world and its killing machines.

A haze of artillery bombardment obscured the dragon as it skimmed into a wooded meadow near the chateau and landed roughly. Sarah fell from its back. The dragon drew shuddering breaths, its gold eyes dimming. Bullets and shellfire had tattered its wings and ripped off an ear. She embraced its neck, laid her face against its chest, felt the heartbeat slowing. Tears etched down Sarah's cheeks as she unknotted the rope harness and dragged the litter free. She rolled the soldier onto the litter, apologizing for the pain it caused him and the beast. The Rat Queen whined, tail wagging briskly, touched noses with the beast, and licked its face. Sarah stared into the ancient eyes.

"Thank you," she said. "I thought there was no magic left in this insane world. But of course, we have killed it all." She saluted the dragon, knelt with her hands on its side, and bowed her head to it, leaning her forehead against the scaled flank, praying her warmth could offer comfort.

The dragon voice rasped in her brain. Its eyes shone. "There will always be magic in the world. It cannot all be killed. No matter how men try."

Slowly, painfully, the mortally wounded creature crawled forward and clawed its way back into the earth.

. . .

Hospital staff were far too busy to question the arrival of a clearly delusional wounded soldier attended by a frantic terrier and the shell-shocked nurse who dragged the man to the casualty ward on a litter.

About the Author

Salinda Tyson was born near the Susquehanna River in Pennsylvania. She now lives in North Carolina, where she is a history museum docent. Her short story, "The Great Mall," appeared in Third Flatiron's spring 2018 *Monstrosities* anthology, and a new story, "Sister Snow," is forthcoming from *Abyss & Apex*.

*****~~~~~*****

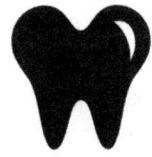

Learning to Fly

by Marie Vibbert

When I was eight years old I learned how to fly. I was walking home carrying my poster for dental health week. It had not placed in the contest. The humiliating honorable mention ribbon was in my backpack. I tried not to take the ribbon home, but the teacher stopped me at the door. Teachers were always rubbing things in like that.

I held the poster in front of me, not wanting to fold or damage it, because I had never yet willingly defaced art. The wind blew the top edge of the poster over my hands, and I paused to look at the curve, like the leading edge of the airfoil Dad had drawn on my chalkboard at home. I'd asked how airplanes could fly without flapping their wings and gotten an hour lecture. Dad was like that. When I was five, I'd asked why the sky was blue. We were at the park. Dad was painting, and I was bored. I expected no answer. I asked because it was something kids asked on TV, and I wanted to be cute. Dad said, "It's not blue. It absorbs all the parts of light except the blue, which bounces back into your eyes."

"What?"

"Light has different parts." He added some blue paint to a shadow on his canvas. "Color can be subjective.

You might see something as blue when someone else sees it as green."

That turned the world inside out. You didn't learn stuff like that in school.

Anyway, the second grade Dental Hygiene Week Poster Contest was unfair. I was better than all my classmates at drawing a giant molar holding a toothbrush. The poster we were shown as an example had a molar holding a toothbrush and most of us had copied it. The winning poster was the same design—and it was sloppier than mine. How could it have won?

I held my poster over my head, letting the wind keep the airfoil shape. The wind was very strong. My skirt outlined my legs, which I hated, because having visible legs was ugly. Girls on TV never had thighs unless they were wearing jeans. I turned sideways to minimize the wind's effect.

Turning damaged my nice airfoil. I fixed it by letting the wind hold the poster against my outstretched arm. I made engine noises and moved my arm up and down. Down was hard. My arm rested on the poster like a shelf. I leaned on it.

I'd never gotten a kite to fly, but Dad had prepared me for a world of wonders when he described light bouncing off my eyes, so I immediately theorized this poster could carry me into the sky.

My expertly drawn tooth bucked against my hands as I pushed it against the sidewalk. It felt like the surface of a waterbed. Holding the front edge down with my palms, I set first one foot and then the other in the center of the poster. I let go. The leading edge curled back. The wind snuck under the paper. It tried to fly up, undulating around my feet. I felt a slippery something under my foot. Then I fell on my face. I skinned my right knee.

I spread the hem of my dress wide, but there was no sign of damage. I looked for my poster. It had caught in the bushes around the school flagpole. It flapped eagerly as I retrieved it. It *wanted* to fly.

I took off my backpack to lighten myself. I was not a large child—they called me "skinny minny"—and the school nurses always talked about how I was "underweight." Still, I took off my shoes—blue leatherette moccasins—and my tin ring that turned my skin green (thereby proving it was a magic fairy ring), just to be safe. I made a neat pile of my belongings next to the sidewalk.

I held my poster by its edge and turned my back to the wind so it would blow flat. There were a few crumples in the paper now, and two ugly shoe-prints. I walked around the poster, holding it still.

This time I lowered my knee onto the poster as I set it on the ground—my left knee, as the right had a sticky patch from being skinned. The poster blew up around my leg, which ruined the airfoil shape. I smoothed it down. I felt the air rising under me, like water lifting a boat. I pushed off with my right foot like I was on a sled.

The leading curve scraped the concrete, but then it rocked back, lifted up, and my knee was off the ground! I could feel it. Like when we had to pop balloons after my older sister's party and I felt them under my foot but couldn't bring myself to destroy them. My trailing toes brushed sidewalk, turning me sideways from the wind, and I ground to a stop.

I was two sidewalk squares away from my backpack. Excited, I picked up my poster and ran back to my backpack to try again.

This time I went too fast. I dove forward like I was racing down a snow hill and hit the sidewalk like there was nothing between it and me. I hit my right knee again and my hands slid off the paper, roughing up my palms.

I brushed my hands in the grass, one at a time, to clean the blood and pebbles off, not wanting to let go of my paper or mess up my dress.

I repeated my first attempt, slow and careful. One knee, make it flat, kick off. I floated. This time, rather than let my trailing foot hit the ground, I pulled it in. I rocked to the right. I leaned left. I wobbled. Disaster loomed. I leaned hard to the right.

I fell into the bushes at the base of the flagpole. I had twigs in my hair and dress, even one in my underwear, but the soft landing made me feel invincible.

After much experimentation and two bloody knees, I was able to consistently hover for a few sidewalk squares and land. Then I tried changing the shape of the leading edge, making a fatter or narrower curve. I found that if I pulled the paper all the way back to my ankles, I climbed the air. My thighs burned from crouching, but the higher I went, the longer I could stay in the air.

The wind felt like a physical thing, a hill. Gusts brushed me like tall grass. My skirt fluttered.

I was high enough now to see the tops of cars in the school parking lot. The tops of porches. I could see the second-floor windows of the school, with their paper umbrellas and raindrops.

I had a toy when I was a baby that had this little plastic blister full of liquid with a flower in it. That flower had seemed so wonderful, because you couldn't touch it. I'd worried at the blister with my teeth, until I finally got it open, but the wet, flat flower hadn't been wonderful at all. The view of the school below me was the same thing, in reverse.

The power lines were very close. I could hear the buzzing sound they made, and I panicked, afraid I would be electrocuted, which made me falter and fall, but I caught myself after an airless, four-foot plummet. I didn't know how to land. Stiff with worry, feeling twice as old as I had been, I sawed downward, taking careful steps toward the ground. I was aware of balance in a way I had never been before, and the muscles in my sides hurt.

But the ground got closer. And closer. I thought I would be able to glide gently to a stop on grass, right up until I fell sideways, a three-foot tumble.

I rested on the lawn of a stranger's house. The fresh-cut grass had a weird, banana-like smell. I was cold. My knees and hands stung. I didn't want to give up, though. I wanted to see if I could fly against the wind and get myself home that way. Boats did something to sail against the wind, I remembered. I wasn't sure what, I just knew they called it "tacking."

On my first tacking attempt, I floated less than a few feet and landed in the middle of the street. Although there were no cars around, I was scared.

I picked up my things and ran toward home, to the end of the block. I made a new neat pile of my possessions, a new starting point. I managed to float a few more times, but each time I landed further from home, not closer. I thought tacking might mean leaning as far as you could to one side. Each attempt got worse, and my flight time shorter.

My poster was smeared, and the edges were soft as cloth from all the bending and tearing. It wasn't making as large of a leading curve any more. My legs trembled every time I tried to crouch. I had to admit defeat.

It was a long, cold walk home.

I opened the door to my house. Dad grabbed me and hauled me into the living room like I weighed nothing. He held me a foot above the floor. "Where were you? I got the cops out looking for you! What were you doing? Dawdling? Dammit, I told you not to dawdle!"

I started crying uncontrollably. I couldn't answer any of Dad's questions. I couldn't even get breaths in between sobs, just hiccups.

Dad was huge and scary. He was strange in his work coveralls, still smelling of sweat and sawdust. He dragged me into the bathroom. I thought he was going to kill me.

His voice was gentle, though, when he sat me on the edge of the tub. "Hold still, would ya? Easy."

He pressed a wad of toilet paper smelling of alcohol to my knee. I howled. Obviously, he meant to kill me by chemical burning. "Hold that. No, hold it." He put my hand on the toilet paper.

He wiped my face with a warm rag. I felt embarrassed to be all snotty. "You can't walk home from school if you dawdle," he said. "I have to go to work. You want me to quit my job and walk you to and from school every day? Huh?"

I wiped my nose on the back of my hand. "I can fly," I said.

Dad stood and got the blue plastic box he kept the bandages in. "Two hours to walk one lousy mile." He was talking to himself. "They should have a bus. I can't believe the older kids get a bus from here, and the little kids don't." He said that a lot. The big kids' school my older sister went to was farther away.

I lifted the toilet paper. Blood spotted it from my scrape in an uneven pattern of little dots. It was pretty.

Dad smoothed a large Band-Aid over my knee, and then cleaned and bandaged the other one. Then he kissed each bandage and I began to suspect he wasn't, in fact, going to murder me.

I had to eat my dinner in a corner of the living room, facing the wall. It was solemn and interesting, like being a princess in a tower. The sting of scrapes under bandages and the dried tears in the corners of my eyes reminded me I was warm and dry.

Dad knelt next to my chair. He had my poster. "What's this?"

"My poster for Dental Hygiene Week. I didn't win. Betsy Tracey won, and her drawing wasn't even good."

Dad's thick, hammer-scarred fingers straightened creases and folds with the dexterity of a surgeon. "It's all subjective. I've never won an art contest in my life."

Hearing him say that made me wonder if perhaps not winning contests was a prerequisite for artistic greatness.

Dad put his hand on my shoulder. "Is this why you were late? Did you think I'd be disappointed?"

I shook my head. "I was learning to fly."

One side of his mouth lifted. His eyes stayed on the poster. "Do you understand why I was so angry? I can't lose you, okay?" I nodded. He squeezed my shoulder. "Let's hang your poster on the fridge."

"It's ugly."

"Well, I like it. Look at how confident those lines are, around the top of the tooth. I want to hang it up. The damage even makes it look better, kind of punk."

"No!" I said. "I want to keep it in my room."

"Okay," he said. "It's your art. You can go play quietly in your room." He gave me a hug and kissed my hair. "No staying up reading. You're grounded."

I squirmed out of the hug and ran to my room, poster in hand. I was going to fly again.

I opened my window as far as I could and unscrewed the screen. I climbed up onto the ledge, holding the window above me. Below was the plain grass side-yard, scraggly and ignored. The wind was strong, though, between the houses. My hair caught on the window latch, and I set the poster down to untangle myself.

My poster blew away. I reached after it and wobbled over the two-story abyss. Icy with fear, I grabbed the sill. I instantly regretted saving myself instead of the poster. Because of my cowardice, it was gone forever. I considered letting myself fall, melodramatically, onto the deadly, twisted shape of the gas meter below.

A dark shape flitted across the moon and I felt a stinging joy, because it was my poster, celebrating its freedom with crazy, ecstatic loops. I watched until it vanished behind the next house and felt like a parent, maybe, watching my child graduate and go off to defeat aliens or something.

I'll never forget that day.

It was the day I learned that Dad kept a supply of poster board behind his easel.

About the Author

Besides selling twenty-odd short stories, a dozen poems, and a few comics, Marie Vibbert has been a medieval SCA (Society for Creative Anachronism) squire, ridden 17% of the roller coasters in the United States, and played O-line and D-line for the Cleveland Fusion women's tackle football team.

*****~~~~~*****

Father O'Neill's Confession

by Jen Downes

"Bless me, Father, for. . . I might've sinned." Hugh O'Neill spoke hesitantly into the confessional's claustrophobic dimness. "Though—to be honest, in the eyes of God, I've half an idea I might not've."

Beyond the grille, the indistinct form of old Father Brian Flynn set chin to palm and huffed a sigh. The ritual of the confessional was all but pointless, a small rite they acted out. Flynn had known Hugh as the curate of St. Joseph's, in Stradarvan, for all fifteen years of his service. Hugh was due to replace the venerable Matthew Walsh as parish priest, just as Flynn's own curate would assume his shoes, when retirement beckoned.

"Oh, it's like that, is it?" Flynn said acerbically. "You'd best regale me. What did you do—or not do?"

For painful moments Hugh waffled. "It's a long story."

"We've plenty of time. How far back d'you want to begin?"

"Twenty years," Hugh admitted gloomily.

"You've left a sin unconfessed for twenty years?" Flynn was appalled.

Hugh bridled. "It wasn't a sin, twenty years back!"

"What wasn't?" Flynn asked, shrewd now.

"The whiskey." It was Hugh's turn to sigh. "Truth is, I got a taste for it."

"Well, a drop of malt never hurt," Flynn began.

"I did me liver in, Brian," Hugh corrected. Flynn fell silent. "Saw a doctor here, and he sent me to hospital in Waterford—they said I'd six months left. Liver like a lace curtain, apparently."

Flynn tutted. "And you, just forty years old!"

"Aye, Brian. I know," Hugh said dolefully.

"And it's drinking yourself into an early grave you want absolution for, I suppose!"

Hugh gave a start of surprise. "Uh, not quite. I'm cured."

Flynn drew a deep, calming breath. "You just said you'd six months to live."

"Aye, but that was *before*."

"Before *what?*"

. . .

It began with an empty, hollow feeling as the curate of St. Joseph's rode the train home from Waterford, a death sentence hanging around his neck as surely as a noose. As a priest, he might have anticipated with pleasure, if not joy, the end of this life, his passage into Eternity.

But, he was just forty. Half his life should still be ahead of him, years in which he'd imagined himself priest of his own parish, watching children grow up, whom he'd christened; watching *their* children grow. Time to enjoy simple things: pipe smoke in the evening, thoroughbreds training in the morning mist—perhaps a winning sweepstakes ticket that built his orphanage, repaired the convent roof. These were life's good things, which made any man, and a priest more than most, feel comfortable with his soul.

Father O'Neill's Confession

The diagnosis burned everything to ash, blew it away on the breeze. Hugh felt only emptiness as he walked the narrow, twilight streets back to St. Joseph's. Lamplighters were abroad; children shrieked with fun on their way home; a dozen fiddlers competed in as many pubs, as the sea wind brought in a dank fog.

He prayed as only a priest knew how. Prayed night and day for a month--felt the rot growing inside until his next hospital appointment. Hope bloomed in the face of common sense and was dashed again, replaced by the familiar void as he boarded the westbound train.

Emptiness had a way of gnawing at a man's mind and spirit, just as rats gnaw on bones. The mile walk from station to church was a marathon for a sick man. Before he covered half of it, Hugh's decision became easy.

He left the main road, took a path winding back into the woods. A few carts rattled toward town, horseshoes rang on cobbles, but dense trees soon blanketed any sound of civilization. Early May had grown mild. A few tatters of late blossom persisted, but most trees wore full leaf. A carriage-lamp moon hung in the east, riding the low hills.

He knew where she lived.

At least once a week, parishioners crept to confession with whispers about coming here, needing—*a cure for me rheumatics. A daughter for a change, after four sons. Bring me husband home safe, he's a week overdue at sea. Get me da off the drink before*—

Hugh shut out the raucous cacophony of his thoughts. Before courage failed him, he rapped on the door.

She went by the name of Mother Lil, and he'd always wondered if this were short for Lily—a symbol of purity—or Lilith, which he recalled from his studies was Hebrew for *serpent*. Either way, his options had expired.

The door cracked, and a middle-aged face peered out suspiciously. Just a woman: middle-height, middleweight, middling attractive, in a dark blue dress and pale blue shawl, thick silver hair brushed extravagantly over both shoulders. Not quite what one expected of a lady in this one's line of work.

Mother Lil rolled her green eyes to the heavens. "You're here to exorcise me, are you? Where's your bell, book, and candle?"

He plucked off his cap, fingered it awkwardly. "Actually, I came to beg a favour."

She studied him rudely before letting him in. He pulled a chair to the table, took a cup of tea, and the story spilled out. Whiskey, diagnosis, imminent departure, and so forth.

"I've no wish to depart just yet," he finished lamely.

"Even if God's laid judgment on you?" she demanded.

"I laid judgment on meself," he said wretchedly. "*He* didn't make me drink a bottle a day for twenty years!"

"No, but his lordship *let* you. And now you want a cure." She shook her head over him. "Shame on you—and you, a priest!"

"It doesn't work for priests?" Hugh gulped.

But Lil only shrugged. "'Tis not for me to say—Father."

Heat coloured his cheeks. "Call me Hugh. Best forget the priest part, at least while I'm here." He wound his scarf tighter, to hide the dog collar. "Look, can you help or not? People confess how they come here for cures. Rheumatics, a bad tooth, whooping cough—"

"And livers rotted with drink," Lil added disapprovingly.

She opened a cupboard, fetched a lamp. Kerosene prickled his nostrils as the wick caught alight with a taper from the hearth. She chose a stout walking stick and cape from the rack by the door, and waved him out.

"You've come at a good time, at least. A day short of the full moon—of May, though February would've been best, especially if the moon were waxing on the first of the month. Not that you'd care to know any of this."

The door slammed, but she didn't bother to lock up. She made a left-hand gesture. A black cat sidled from the shadows and flopped across the step between potted rosemary and sage. Hugh kept his lips sealed, as she led him into the woods.

She didn't need a lamp—he saw at once, the path was so well trodden, he could have found his own way, if he'd known where to begin. It wound between brambles, hazel, and wild cherry, seeming to run in spirals, long enough for him to grow winded, cut by the familiar pain that brought him here in the first place.

At last Lil stopped by a tumble of masonry. Her lamp clattered down on a weather-worn brick. Hugh made out a rough circle, deeply pitted in the centre, everything overgrown by moss. A well? Heart quickening, he took a step back. Lil angled an odd glance at him, face a mass of weird shadows.

"You bade me bring you. What, second thoughts?"

"Yes—no. I—" He swallowed. "What is this place?"

"A holy well, belonging to—shall we call her *Saint Bridget?*" She snaked two fingers into her handbag, plucked out a coin, a polished stone, a feather, the stub of a candle, and a little silver cup with a broken handle.

She filled the cup from the well, lit the candle from her lamp. The feather fluttered in the night air, and the moonstone glimmered with a light of its own. *Water, fire, air, earth.* A smell of moss and mushrooms, fallen leaves and fog, rose from the well. Lil tossed in the coin, waited a moment, then clapped her hands, three times three: a summoning sound, sharp on the clammy air.

35

Terra! Tara! Terror!

She knew the *old* old language, beyond anything Hugh knew of Gaelic or Erse. She spoke it fluently, and though he listened hard he picked out only a few words. *Leigheas. Impigh. Duraman. Fuisce. Sagart. Slanu.* And Brigid—cure, beg, idiot, whiskey, priest, healing. . . Brigid.

He shivered. *Shall we call her Saint*—

Brigid, the exalted one, Dagda's daughter, wife of Bres, mother of Ruadan.

Falling silent, the woman turned back. Moonlight whitened her features. "Will you greet the spirit who heals? Or will you be faithful, return to hospital, lie in their bed and let God—and the whiskey—take you? D'you want forty more years to do good work, make amends before your proper time comes?"

His chest squeezed. "Must I make a deal with the devil?"

She assumed a pained look. "Who would that be, *Mister* O'Neill? Don't you know there's no such thing in the Craft? If there were, we'd have no truck with it! Here's a spirit who heals. But you must believe, and you don't, do you? Because you can't see it." She sneered. "You can't see angels, cherubs, demons—or God!—either, but you believe in 'em!"

"Well, yes, but. . . " He stopped, aware of the rents in his argument. Just then, plausible patches eluded him.

Lil came closer, peering in the moonlight. "I like you, *Mister* O'Neill, so I'll do you a favour. Only cuz I like you, mind." She snapped her fingers before his eyes, muttered something guttural. The sound seemed to reach inside his skull, spin his brain between his ears.

He blinked and looked again. The moonlight was easily thrice as bright, the woodland less tangled, shadows not at all sinister. And *creatures* blinked back at him, some tiny enough to be voles, others the size of shire horses. Sprites cavorted, three sylphs sprawled along a bough with a blazing salamander. Two undines lazed around the well. A dozen pixies paused in a game of tag with a pair of hobs—more entities than Hugh recognized, and all astonished to realize he *saw* them.

Snap. Lil's fingers darted before his eyes once more, and the creatures vanished. "The world invisible. Isn't it grand? Now, *Mister* O'Neill, I'll ask once more. Will you greet a healing spirit? 'Tis your book, not mine, that says God created everything in heaven and earth— and the important word there is *everything*. All the things you can see—and all the things you can't."

He gulped air into parched lungs. "Tell me what to do."

. . .

Memory shattered to glass-shard fragments as Father Flynn's voice intruded on the vast silence which had settled over his confessional. "Did you go back to that hospital?"

"Aye, Brian." Hugh studied his friend through the mesh, thinking again how odd it was to feign being strangers in the booth, when every priest knew every parishioner by their voices.

"You're cured," Flynn observed.

"They call it a miracle, on account of me being a priest—the power of prayer."

"Who's to say it isn't?" Flynn hazarded shrewdly.

"You didn't see the things I saw." Hugh had only to close his eyes now, and he saw them all again. "The world invisible is bigger than you think."

"Is it, now?" Flynn mused, deliberately inscrutable. "Well, the woman told you some truths. If God created *everything*, it stands to reason, doesn't it, he created the faer folk too. Shocked, Hugh? Tush. You'll be telling me next you've never heard the banshee."

"I didn't know what I expected, but this was not it," Hugh said. "And you'll be telling me next, God created the Sidhe, and women like Lil are—"

"Are what?" Flynn snorted. "What is it you want absolution for? You defied your own good sense and rotted your liver, then thumbed your nose at God and asked a witch for a cure, when medicine knows no such thing. Did you sin? A matter of perspective, isn't it?" He rose to his feet. "Are you cured?"

"Clean bill of health," Hugh affirmed.

"Then. . . " Brian Flynn paused. "Go'n pray awhile, you'll feel the better for it. Send the woman a big bunch of flowers—on the quiet, mind. Spend your future doing good work, it's the best absolution I know." He swung open the door. "Oh, and one more thing."

"Yes, Father?"

"Stay the hell away from the whiskey!" Flynn banged the door and marched away in search of tea, which was always served at four o'clock.

###

About the Author

Jen Downes grew up in an Irish-Scots community in County Durham, where such tales enriched her youth. Alas, her branch of the family left the community decades ago, but its charm lives with her even now.

*****~~~~*****

Me Too, Medusa

by Evelyn Deshane

Medusa stared at the grain of the wood. She'd come to the Dean of the university, hoping for some kind of resolution, but they'd slammed the door in her face. After everything, she couldn't believe that this was the ending.

She remembered the school's code of conduct. Athena's words in a news broadcast, where, as the acting Dean, she endorsed the school's activism against sexual violence and harassment. Medusa filed a complaint. A panel was arranged. She was going to get justice.

The Dean's email had been the first good news about this whole ordeal she'd received. Ever since she woke up with the bitter taste of cherries in her mouth and the black fog of memory over her eyes, along with a deep pain inside, she'd thought her life was ruined. She kicked herself for drinking during the social mixer at the conference; then for going to the conference at all; then for studying marine biology, because without that major, she would have never met him, her advisor and professor, and the man she knew raped her.

But Poseidon was on the very panel. And Medusa was found at fault. For drinking. For charging her extracurricular activities on the school's dime. Apparently, she'd been so upset after the assault that when she filed the conference receipts with the graduate office, she'd included the ones from the bar tab. Getting the school to pay for alcohol was a huge no-no. She didn't mean to do it. But somehow, defrauding the school's coffers was a worse offence, and put her complaint into question. She was the guilty party here, not Poseidon.

Medusa turned away from the wooden doors. She'd been staring so long, replaying the whole event, she was sure the wood grains were moving like snakes. Her hands went to her long, dark hair and she fought the urge to rip out her locks at the root. She hadn't done that since she was a kid, and her sisters teased her and she had nowhere to put the frustration. Now it was all she wanted to do—yank and yank and yank—or roll and roll and roll the strands, clogging them up with dirt and grime until she had dreadlocks. She fixated on the feeling of her hair so she didn't have to face the future. She started down the long stone steps.

No more graduate scholarship. No more grad school. She couldn't even study any more, because Poseidon was her advisor, and how was she supposed to get a recommendation letter now? Her hair started to feel like fire in her hands.

"Hey. Hey, Medusa. Hey!"

Medusa stopped. She let go of the lock of her hair; two strands fell down with it. A petite woman, with similar long, brunette hair, appeared from the side of the stairs. She glanced up towards the oak doors and then back at Medusa. Her brows knitted with sympathy.

"Didn't go well, I suppose?"

"No—I mean, what do you care?"

"I'm a professor here. I should have been on that panel. I volunteered. I should have—" Her words had become clipped from speaking too fast. She shook her head and stepped towards Medusa. Medusa flinched, and the woman mumbled an apology. "I'm sorry to hear. It's not your fault."

"Yeah, right."

"Medusa," the woman said. "Listen to me. It's not your fault."

Medusa stared so hard at the woman, and she stared so firmly back, that Medusa was worried that they'd both become stuck there, turned hard into stone, stuck there in the winter snow. The woman broke the tableau first by extending her hand.

"I'm Cassandra. And I know everything feels overwhelming right now. But when you're ready, I think you will fit in with our group. Take my card."

Medusa came away from the handshake with a business card in her palm. *Lady Monsters, Inc.* was embossed in black. The location was familiar; it used to be a sorority house, before the building had been demolished and a bookstore put in instead. Medusa was still so frazzled, her hair still falling out in tiny strands, that she didn't know what was happening. By the time she realized someone was giving her a second chance, and she wanted to talk, Medusa raised her eyes to meet Cassandra's only to find an empty space.

She was already long gone.

. . .

Three days later, Medusa knocked on the door of the bookstore. A CLOSED sign was propped in the window, but it had been there since the winter semester ended and the school entered that strange twilight period before exams truly began. Medusa walked by the location at least twice a day since receiving the card, trying to figure out what exactly might be going on there. No one came in or out. When she walked around back, it had been eerily quiet.

She tried to find Cassandra on the school website, but failed. If she was a professor, she wasn't listed in any official capacity; it was possible she was a contract worker, but Medusa worried she wasn't real at all. She had started to doubt the entire event had even occurred, and only came to the bookstore because, well, she was out of options. She'd returned all her library books the day before, filed the necessary paperwork to leave the school, and found someone to sublet her apartment.

She was done with her PhD. As far as she thought, too, she was done with her life.

The strange business card was the last thing she needed to check out, before slinking away to live with her sisters and never stepping foot on a university campus again.

She sighed as she raised her hand to knock. Nothing stirred, nothing changed. She tried again, more insistent. The staccato rhythm matched her heart. Movement flickered inside. A shadow. Then another. They seemed to emerge from a basement and flood the front room filled with discount books and endless Norton Anthologies.

Cassandra opened the door. Her eyes narrowed before her thin mouth bent into a crooked smile. "I knew you'd come."

"I. . . I have no idea what I'm doing."

Cassandra looked beyond Medusa, to the nearly empty campus. She grabbed her arm, and when Medusa flinched, she let go easily and merely held the door. "Come inside. There is a lot to explain."

Medusa stepped into the bookstore and met another woman with long blonde hair. She smiled unsurely, and then looked down. The blonde said her name was Daphne. Another woman appeared by her side, holding her arm, just as blonde and timid. Daphne introduced her as Leda. There was no time for other pleasantries before the three of them led Medusa to the basement.

Faint music echoed in the space, a piece that Medusa knew but couldn't place. Once her eyes adjusted to the low-level darkness, she saw even more faces. One woman sat behind a desk covered with metal parts and tools, a magnifying glass over her left eye. Others stood and threw darts at the wall; another pair, a man and woman, were sitting in front of the TV watching something that seemed to be filled with shaky-hand cam footage on mute. By the time Medusa made it to the middle of the basement, and everyone's eyes were on her, she recognized the music.

"'Sullen Girl' by Fiona Apple," Medusa said. She swallowed hard. It was a song about a rape.

"It's for inspiration," one of the women said from her desk. She pushed back her eye-magnifier, exposing a smile with spaced-out front teeth. "I'm Persephone. You may not know this, but the song's about me. Fiona doesn't say as much, but it is."

"It is?"

"Yes," Persephone said, her eyes hard like diamonds.

"Me too," said Leda.

"Me too," said Daphne.

"And me too," said Cassandra.

"And me. . . "

The utterances compounded. Each person in the room took a turn. The space filled with a cacophony of yesses; a word that was normally so good and positive but was now stitched together with pain and tragedy. Me too, me too, me too became a call that bound people together through their trauma, an ache that Medusa had worked so hard to keep hidden, but was now laid bare. Her body felt like an open wound, like her skin had been pulled back, but instead of feeling snakes underneath like she had feared, she saw feathers. Lightness. Communion.

She turned away from the feeling, as her cry came out in a muffled sob. Cassandra put a hand on her back.

"It's okay," Cassandra said. "That's a common feeling. It'll pass."

"What. . . what is this place?"

"Lady Monsters, Inc," Daphne said. "Just like the card says."

"And what is that?" Medusa asked, desperation clear. "I don't want to be a monster."

"You're not. But they're trying to make you into one," Cassandra said. "That's what that meeting was about. They're trying to blame you for your own pain, instead of looking at the person who made you bleed."

"How did you. . . ?"

"I saw the complaint you filed. I said I wanted to be there. I should have been on that panel. I was on it for Daphne and for Leda. They were not. . . blamed as much. But the victimhood still stuck, and victimhood to the outside world looks so much like monstrosity. So we started this group."

"And I made it about revenge," Persephone said. She gestured to the pile of machine parts in front of her. Medusa's vision focused, assembling all of them in her mind's eye. She realized it was a gun.

"Oh. *Oh*. What is this...?"

"It's Lady Monsters, Inc," the man said from the couch. He paused the video he'd been watching. "I personally would like to petition a name change, but I get it. We're a collective of people who have been treated poorly, and now wish to right the scales."

"Who are you?"

"Odysseus. I'm the odd man out, as usual, but my scales have been righted."

"What do you mean?"

"Well," he said with a boyish smile, "you haven't heard much from Calypso lately, have you?"

"We sort of trashed the entrance to her house," the woman next to him said. "Hi, I'm Helen. We also took care of Theseus's house while we were trashing Calypso's.

Just some rotten eggs, graffiti, light mischief. Not always violent means, you know? All of this is about poesies as much as it's about revenge. However people try to turn us into monsters, we're going to get back at them in a similar way. Try to kidnap and abduct Odysseus and me? Well, we're going to fuck up your house. It's not perfect, by any means. . ."

"I know it's petty, but right now, when the panel doesn't work and no one will listen to me, this is what we have," Cassandra said. She folded her arms across her chest in a sigh. "I'm always a fan of rules and regulations. But sometimes it just doesn't work. Sometimes I'm kept on the other side of the door instead of making sure Professor Poseidon pays."

When someone else in the room tittered at the mention of his name, Medusa's skin prickled. Was she not the first? She looked at the floor, realizing how foolish that thought had been. Of course she wasn't the first. She may not have even been the most vocal about her pain, either. The callous way in which Athena dismissed her words during the panel meeting stung—but there was also something cool and calculating about them, as if they were familiar. As if she'd done this before. Cassandra's words, *this is not your fault,* washed over Medusa. Maybe it was true. Maybe she really was innocent of everything.

"How come—How come no one told me?" Medusa asked, her voice feeling as if it was underwater.

Cassandra took another step towards her. When she touched her back, Medusa didn't flinch. "We tried. I've been trying to warn anyone who will listen for ages. But they always silence me."

"I didn't see you on the website. I couldn't find your name. Are you a contract worker?"

Cassandra smirked. "I didn't get tenure, so, yes, in a way that's all I am now. But I've grown tired of waiting for men to give me what I want. No offence, Odysseus."

"None taken."

Medusa stared at Cassandra, mouth agape. The flash of recognition she thought she'd felt upon first meeting her returned. *Cassandra, Cassandra. . .* that button nose, the small shoulders in a blazer, and tiny legs under a skirt. Yes, she knew this woman—but only as a shadow figure in a newscast. Ajax, a classics professor, had been fired for academic misconduct. Everyone said it was because he fudged research. But now, looking back on the press conference, and the number of women with dark eyes in the background, Medusa saw another story.

"You got Ajax fired."

Cassandra smiled. Then she sighed. "No one listened to me. So I showed he'd been fudging his citations. And after Ajax was gone, I found more people just like me. I realized we could do something."

"And so this place. . . "

Daphne cut off Medusa. "Used to be a sorority, and so, we make it that again. We find the bad men hiding in plain sight, and we take them down. Sometimes it's more poetic, sometimes it's more career destructive, and sometimes. . . well, you saw Persephone's weapon."

Medusa swallowed hard. The revenge plot, something from a 1970s film or torn from Bible pages. She felt the rage boil over inside of her. On the back of her eyelids, she saw the moments leading up to Poseidon following her to her room. The memory of the night was a blank spot in her mind, sure, but she knew the way it went. And she knew that Perseus, his other research assistant, was there to help him, too. He was the one that made her head nothing but blackness, who made her forget that she was so much stronger than this.

Medusa looked at all the other women—and Odysseus—in the room. Their "me too's" echoed in her head. She wanted to stay here. She wanted to be part of this clubhouse, this Lady Monsters, Inc, and help others just like her. She'd do anything to make it possible.

But first she had to say so.

"Me too," she finally said aloud. "Me too."

The group hugged her. Some tears were shed, but they were mostly gone now. Medusa knew she wasn't alone. The wound could be healed.

"So what's next?" she asked, turning to Cassandra. "What do we do now?"

Cassandra smiled. "Well, that depends on what works for your poetic revenge. But we've been working on a campaign that allows our cries to go beyond these four walls. And I have a feeling. . . heads are going to roll."

About the Author

Evelyn Deshane's creative and nonfiction work has appeared in *Plenitude Magazine, Briarpatch Magazine, Strange Horizons, Lackington's,* and *Bitch Magazine*, among other publications. Evelyn (pronounced Eve-a-lyn) received an MA from Trent University and is currently completing a PhD at the University of Waterloo. Evelyn's most recent project, *#Trans*, is an edited collection about transgender and nonbinary identity online. Follow @evelyndeshane or visit evedeshane.wordpress.com for more information.

*****~~~~~*****

Replica

by John Paul Davies

From the three islands and the surrounding estuary, the iron men looked out to sea.

Inspecting his statues, Gorman walked across the sand towards The Eye, the rocky islet accessible only at low tide. Like great stepping-stones from The Eye to the sea, Mid and Grand Isle stood half a mile apart, drifting in and out of the fog.

The fine mist dappled his face, turning in front of his eyes like some ghost-channel enormously projected. The sharp salt air was fouled somehow, tinged with sulphur, as he approached a humanoid outline in the grey.

The features of the iron effigy sharpened as he drew near. Sunken in sand to its knees, Gorman was a foot taller than his iron likeness. A circled '56' was branded on its nape like a maker's mark—his age when the statue was cast.

During the night, '56' had accumulated a scuba mask, a velveteen top hat, and a striped football scarf. The accessories left by the teenagers sat strangely against the statue's barnacled complexion, rusted to the colour of old blood.

Gorman stood beside '56,' trying to recall the sensation of being that certain age. A dozen others had been forged since.

Cigarette butts, cider cans, and tinfoil trays surrounded the statue like scant offerings at a shrine. Rifling through the remains of a bonfire, Gorman used a litter-grab to remove underwear from the ashes, white stones of varying size, seaweed clumped like matted hair. As he examined a stone, wind scattered the soot from its surface, and he realised he was holding a small animal's skull—tern or shrew. Scorched slightly, traces of carbon highlighted thin cranial cracks.

Splinters of bone he'd taken for sparwood protruded from the cinders like miniature shipwrecks: ribcages, spinal cords, burnt feathers.

Placing the offending items into his black bag, Gorman felt more than heard the incoming tide, running through the estuary fissures like quicksilver. It was time to leave The Eye. He removed the scarf from '56,' wrapping it around his own neck.

'56' reverted to shadow as Gorman took the low tide path. Wooden stakes driven into the sand at intervals marked the route recommended by the coastguards for tourists crossing to the islands.

It was easy to become disorientated along the estuary, especially if the tide times had been left to chance. Where two rivers and the sea met in an uneasy tryst, water could rush in quickly from any direction, stranding errant walkers on the mud flats. Quicksand then came into play. A cenotaph at the marina listed the names of those taken by the insatiable sands.

Trudging onto Mid Isle, following the incline of a low sandstone cliff, Gorman came to the derelict lifeboat station. A mile from the mainland, he could remember the lifeboats in operation, his father volunteering when needed. Lives saved or lost, the men in their oilskins would solemnly drink in the tavern afterwards.

Wouldn't spare you the steam from their piss, according to his father.

Wind murmured through the glassless windows as he passed, mimicking long gone voices, seeming to sigh when he did not enter the building.

At the highest point of the island, Gorman knelt to study the miniature statue of '2.' Worn to nondescript iron, the rough cannonball of its head was outsized compared to its slender body. Perched on the edge of the eroding cliff, '2' overlooked a swathe of red rocks, waiting patiently below for the land to run out.

His fingertips tracing the statue's surface, Gorman relived the moulding process—the cold lard smeared onto his body, the scrim and drying plaster pinching his skin as it hardened; how he wailed against the constricting bandages. As the statues accrued, it was difficult to determine if this truly was an early memory, or a recollection of his father's version of events:

Like a freshly dropped pup you were, wriggling around. Snorting through the nose holes like a hog.

Gorman had kept a wary distance as his father trundled '2' to the cliff. Content that the statue would stand, appraising his own craftsmanship with a sneer, that he might have done better, his father had set off towards their house on Grand Isle, not looking back to see if his son followed.

Happy birthday, boy.

. . .

Beyond Mid Isle, the mud flats zigzagged as though enormous worms burrowed beneath the sand in competition. The patterned channels soon led Gorman to '17,' his teenage casting anchored halfway between Mid and Grand Isle.

'17' awaited the tide, resigned to its daily drowning, its resurgence at the withdrawal of the sea. Fifty years of saltwater had robbed it of youth, smoothed

the iron features ageless. Furious rust marked the rinsed
face like acne.

The party of teenagers had posed with this one,
leaving behind a sand-spattered Polaroid souvenir. The
fresh-faced, gurning children were not yet as old as
Gorman's likeness, pointing and laughing at the statue's
newly acquired areolae, spray-canned fluorescent pink.

The pentagram they had etched in the sand was
broken now, scuffed over by retreating feet, though its
circle of pebbles and shells remained. Gorman dug out a
half-buried crimson candle, feeling its weight in his palm.
There were four more, planted at each point of the faded
star. With his heel, he erased the other obscenities and
crude drawings scrawled in the sand.

A ragged piece of rope had been pulled taut around
the statue's neck. Gorman quickly removed it with his
Swiss Army knife, placing the rope into the black bag he
dragged behind him like a dead dog.

By mid-afternoon, the fog was beginning to
disperse—a cataract miraculously clearing from an
afflicted eye—and Gorman could see as far as Grand Isle.
Looking back towards The Eye, the thoroughfare of his
prints could be tracked from '56' to '2' to '17'—a route he
could've walked blindfold.

The remaining scattered statues gradually made
themselves known; the dark seaward forms roused like
drowned ancestors, finally relinquished by the tide.
Hauling each one to its designated spot, a vast crescent
impression was left in their wake, like that of a slain bull
towed from ring to abattoir.

Further along the coast, the shoreline continued
stateless, the miles of undisturbed sand casting doubt that
Gorman had ever existed.

He crossed over the firming sand onto Grand Isle
and found the terrain altered, the familiar seascape
interfered with. Wading through the thick rushes of the
dunes, he saw what had become of '40.'

For his fortieth moulding, he had held a forefinger and thumb to his right temple, insinuating a pistol. The pose seemed fitting at the time, Gorman in dark humour still grieving for his father. The onset of middle age had also triggered the realisation that he would never leave the islands.

Now '40' lay on its back, flattening the ragweed, staring at the bird-strewn sky. The seagulls adhered to their mysterious maps, screeching a lament for the fallen statue. Dingy yellow blossom settled across the iron figure, marking it like some tropical disease.

Weakened by erosion, the iron skull had been stove in with the surrounding rocks. As Gorman assessed the damage, a hermit crab emerged from the hollow head, pausing on the iron body like a boilerman finally permitted up on deck. It surveyed the shore, unperturbed by the living Gorman or the iron men, before scuttling across the sand towards the fizzing tide.

Exposed by the lifting fog, he was now visible from the concrete coastal path. A steady trickle of walkers looked across the sand, Gorman as much of a curiosity as the islands and the statues. Some observed him through binoculars, their lenses catching sun as they swept across his iron progeny.

The seams of the mud flats healing, the organised rambling clubs were already heading across to the islands, their safety assured for a few hours. Picking through the wrecks of an old abandoned commune, they would pose for photographs in sandstone archways, then picnic on the edge of the cliffs, gawping for seals.

Most would feel uneasy as their phones moved out of coverage, the islands persisting beyond signal.

Gorman chose to retreat indoors at low tide. The wanton treatment of '40' marked a new, violent progression to the teenagers' vandalism. The nearby faded seaside town could offer no nocturnal attraction to compete with the torment of Gorman, the island-dwelling loner.

He turned away from the coastal voyeurs, climbing uphill to the workshop. The low-roofed outhouse contained his early attempts at assembling his father's statue: rejected torsos, heads, odd limbs; a cast-iron foot used as a doorstop. Placing the near-full bag inside the workshop with the others, Gorman continued up to the house. He would sort through the day's findings in the morning.

Strange plants and shrubs separated the cottage and the workshop, bird's foot trefoil and sea lavender thriving on the saline soil. In accordance with his dying wishes, his father's statue stood within the fringetrees of this accidental garden. Gorman looked at his father's worn face and could still discern his furrowed brow, the final grimace from which death had offered no release.

Better than your mother got—a hunk of stone with two useless years engraved. We kept every age you ever were, son.

Opposite his father, situated below the kitchen window like an odd garden ornament, '1' howled mutely in its iron cradle. A cast taken of child and cot, the infant had been moulded in the throes of a tantrum, trapping a scream still to be emitted from its eroded lips.

Gorman had wished to unite the two statues, if he'd possessed the craft, to meld the baby in its father's arms. He imagined his father in the parlour, holding his newborn son aloft like a trophy, bringing the tiny face closer to his in the warm stovelight. Seeing his wife in the boy, meeting his gaze through streaming tears.

. . .

Blood-red sun filled the horizon like a haemorrhaging eye. The statues stood sentry, as if awaiting a signal to uproot themselves from the sand, to turn in unison towards their sculptor. Those furthest out from the islands met the incoming tide first.

54

The ramblers and dog-walkers returned along the well-trodden arc from The Eye to the marina. Watching the final stragglers depart, Gorman disappeared inside the cottage, bolting the back door behind him.

The islands were quick to squander light. The house gathered darkness, reducing to a flickering candle in the kitchen window.

The statues lost form again, becoming dark among the dark. The waves below the cliff sounded like legendary creatures, certain of their isolation, languidly flipping onto their backs.

In the gloom of the kitchen, Gorman's recurring nightmare was less easy to banish. He would wake to find himself anchored in sand, his limbs unresponsive, as he surveyed the cast-iron horizon, the returning water. Able to feel everything, a seagull would shriek from the perch of his head, taunting his paralysis. Seawater rising to his hips, the nightmare-bird attacked his rusted skull with beak and claw. He could not scream, even when the water rose to his chest, his chin, and did not stop.

Maintaining his vigil on the garden path, Gorman scoured the dark for intruders. In the meagre light he could see the statues of '1' and his father, the ragged outline of the dunes where '40' lay.

They were coming, of course. The teenagers knew the tides as well as Gorman. If he couldn't yet see them, he could sense them near: swigging from bottles and cans, stamping through the rotten wood of upturned fishing boats.

They would have reached The Eye by now, already contemplating the short stretch across to Mid Isle.

The rocks to be navigated in the dark added danger to their route. Slippery with seaweed, ankles and wrists could easily be snapped with one missed step. The water would then sneak in behind, readily accepting any casualties.

The teenagers finally appeared, their combined shadow slowly detaching from the dunes. Passing the stricken '40,' their torches flashed erratically, as though dragonflies flitted in the darkness.

The tide rushing along the mudflats behind them, blocking their path back to the mainland, they turned towards the house in silent conspiracy.

Gorman drew the heavy curtains. Eyes on the back door, the thick barring wood slid across, he waited.

Laughter carried up the hill, the teenagers failing in their clumsy attempt at stealth. Eight or nine of them, he guessed. Closer now, past the workshop, they were on the stone path leading through the garden to the cottage. They aimed their torches at his window, the miniature searchlights roaming the curtains. Gorman felt he could somehow still be seen, crouched at the table; a trespasser in his own home.

Wetting his finger and thumb, Gorman snuffed out the candlewick.

The torchlight withdrew from the window. He soon heard the scrape of feet on the back step, where his father would once leave his mud-caked boots.

A hush followed as the teenagers held their breath, daring each other to make the next move. The silence speeded Gorman's heart as shadow deformed the crack of blue light below the door.

Gorman, they whispered. *Are you in there, Gorman?*

He heard a slump against the wooden door, as one of them half-heartedly tested its strength.

Come out if you've any bottle, Gorman. A girl's voice, becoming high-pitched as she spoke his name.

Gorman waited for them to leave, as they usually did with a parting shot of flung eggs. Instead, they remained outside, quiet now. He listened to the waves breaking against the cliff below, their offer of escape cruelly close.

56

The next blow on the door was delivered with greater force, the dull sound echoing through the small kitchen, rebounding from the sandstone walls and filling Gorman's ears. This decisive act gave the others licence to throw themselves at the door, to aim kicks at its base.

The assault on the door intensifying, Gorman remained motionless at the table. He offered up a silent prayer for his father, picturing him roaring up the hill to drive his assailants away.

Hinges clattered to the kitchen floor as the door's frame splintered.

Gorman could feel iron seeping into his bones, rust displacing marrow. Could almost feel the water rising to his neck in that moon-cracked kitchen, the bruised light spreading as the door slowly swung inwards.

He struggled for air as the walls closed in like dark tides, as though his desperate breath was trapped in his iron ribs.

Become all of his statues now, he relived each year; the tide crept higher, until even the tallest he ever was disappeared beneath the iron sea.

A girl screamed first, breaking Gorman's trance, her piercing voice unbearably loud through the ruined door. The others began to shout, roaring insults at him, but they did not enter the cottage. Their voices receded to the soft murmurings of the girl being consoled, until Gorman could no longer hear the teenagers.

It was almost dawn before he moved outside, discovering his father's toppled statue. The iron body remained intact, but Gorman saw its head had been damaged in the fall, splitting against a segment of garden path.

In a missing section of iron, his father's dun skull was exposed. The few scalp hairs that had continued to grow stirred in the low breeze.

Their torches found him then, kneeling at his father's side. Beyond the blinding circle of light, flaring in his eyes like dying stars, Gorman could barely make out the teenagers' approaching feet.

About the Author

Born in Birkenhead, UK, John Paul Davies has had work published in *Apex, Rosebud, Ares Magazine, Pseudopod, Pulp Literature, Grain,* and Third Flatiron Publishing's *Origins: Colliding Causalities* anthology. He was also winner of the 2016 Penguin Ireland Short Story Competition.

*****~~~~~*****

Music, Dogs, True Love, and a Gateway

by Steven Mathes

His hand paused just below the master switch. It trembled slightly with second thoughts, but then firmed, and threw the switch closed. The musical strings of the boondoggle, which stretched vertically up the enormous tower, hummed eagerly. David cleared his throat. The strings laughed back. The slightest sound from his voice, or from his hand brushing his shirt, made music.

"I think I love Daphne," he whispered, and the strings hummed back joyfully.

His dog Bart scrabbled across the floor, slid the last distance with claws scratching linoleum. It joined with a delicate howl. The strings echoed the scratching claws, as well as the howl. Dave's puppy was the better musician, and the harmonies of those strings made both of them cry sometimes.

"Anybody home?" called Daphne.

The strings echoed: ". . . home. . . "

They had slept together twice, and the musical bond between them held a lot of promise. Too many times before, Dave had reviewed his social skills, his mistakes, his successes. Finally, he had a chance in spite of himself.

His puppy, one of his successes, had its own priorities. These priorities held precedence over any appreciation of music, over Daphne, and over Dave. Bart forgot all about the harmonic ringing of those great strings. He fixed on Daphne's dog Maeby. Daphne, in spite of being passed by, turned to ruffle the gangling pup, who in turn licked Maeby.

"Hi, Bart, you little sweetie!" she said. "Hi, Dave. Still haven't moved out?"

"Very funny. I shouldn't have told you."

"No, no," Daphne said, hugging him. "I can see how you'd be spooked."

"They sing even when the power's off. Even when there's no wind."

"Sometimes you have to make a sacrifice. A sweet dog, constant music. Poor boy. . . "

"See? You're teasing me!"

Maeby made a warning woof at little Bart, who collapsed from love, and wiggled on his back. Dave could empathize, although he restrained myself from collapsing and wiggling for Daphne.

In living with these singing strings, Dave took care of nearly a billion dollars of failed science. Massive budget cuts had turned NASA's broken dreams into rent-free digs here in the best of the Colorado mountains. Fuzzy Bart served as friendship bait, although Dave loved the little pup anyway. Good fortune, although the magnificent musical strings of NASA's boondoggle helped. It murmured now like a storm of ghosts, begging people and dogs to chip in with their half of the music.

"Well, I guess that means there were no messages from aliens?" Daphne said.

"Not yet today," Dave said.

She kissed him, so he guessed he had said the right thing. His look of yearning expressed a hope for something more later. He had never been good at hiding his yearnings.

They met while mountain biking. Cute, scampering Bart took a liking to Maeby. This gave both man and dog credibility, and a ticket away from caretaker

60

loneliness. Blowing his chance with Daphne would be the same as blowing a chance with himself. Sometimes people liked him, and he always got any musician to visit over and over when they heard NASA's boondoggle sing.

Dave had long ago concluded that the problem, the one common element in all his failure, was himself. Loyalty, reliability, patience, and kindness got him somewhere, but he understood that he had some sort of blindness, something fighting his hopes and dreams.

"Dogs sure have the life," Daphne said.

"Yeah. We give them shelter, love, and prosperity. Unconditional. Poop on the rug? Chew up the couch? Forgiven. Giving them every comfort is our rebellion against the universe."

"Dogs and music," she said. "Two victories in a long string of failures. Humanity needs a victory now and then."

Dave wanted to say it aloud, but knew he should keep it to myself. Humanity? How about the two of them?

"We have dogs, music, each other," he said anyway.

She looked at him, and their eyes locked in an exchange of meaning. The music would come out strong tonight.

. . .

She barely had her fiddle out when Julie and Otis strolled in. Old friends, they needed to offer no verbal greetings. They simply grinned, and got themselves beers from the fridge. Otis set up his keyboard, and they set to improvising. After Julie tuned her bass, she bowed and plucked to the hoots and thumps of the boondoggle. They picked random notes for a melody, the device made the music coherent, then beautiful.

Occasionally one of them talked while they played. They drank beer. They passed around some weed. This was Colorado, after all. Except Dave, no smoke for

Dave, because even the mellow kind of weed made him paranoid; another of his long strings of failure.

Sometimes they played bright, and the boondoggle groaned back dark. Dave wiped tears away. Daphne let hers run, grinning, making Dave even more emotional. Dark versus light, but then it switched. The strings of the boondoggle rang like a bell, and it echoed their human lyrics. A deep, sad ricochet stuttered from Daphne's looped fiddle. That crazy, ringing device stuttered back with a twinkle.

Even when they rested, the towering device echoed their breath like a monastery full of throat-singing monks.

"Thank you, NASA budget cuts," Dave said.

"I can't live without this music," Julie said.

"Crazy to let this go to waste," Otis said.

"Thing is, it always feels like it's communicating with someone out there, like it's really talking to angels in the stars," Dave said.

This evoked nervous throat clearing, like maybe Dave had a creepy side. The transmissions from those strings involved something about the science of quantum pairing, logarithms, and music, built into the neurals of all great minds. One small detail got lost, that being the not-so-greatness of the human mind. What had felt real to NASA had apparently failed to impress the little green men.

Thanks to the dogs, everyone got distracted from Dave's dumb remark by Bart yapping, Maeby answering, the boondoggle booming.

Daphne whooped, made magic with her fiddle, and Dave sucked in air, listening. Daphne played some long notes that made the long boondoggle tinkle like breaking glass. Of them all, she got the most resonance, not only from the boondoggle, but from the dogs. Bart was easy, but you knew you'd hit it when Maeby let out guttural, long groans. They all could join in chorus, but sometimes Daphne needed her space.

"How come we never get more musicians here?" whispered Otis.

"I'm not so sure," Dave whispered back.

"I don't know, I don't know," whispered the boondoggle.

"In fact, how come there aren't more musicians in the county?" said Julie. "Mountain country, parties, resorts, vacations, why no musicians?"

"Another mystery," said Otis. "But good for us. We get the gigs without the competition."

"We get gigs because of Daphne," Dave said. "Not that the rest of us aren't decent. . . "

Dave stopped himself, fearing a deficit of social skills, knowing that silence is usually safe. He needed to shut the hell up.

The boondoggle: strings laced with networked logic from an underground mesh of supercomputers, AI harmony going from floor to distant ceiling, powered by enough solar panels to heat a small city. A musical quantum antenna. From outside it looked like a too-tall glass grain silo attached to a too-small concrete house. If the musicians sat in the actual silo, none of them could hear for hours after, so they kept to the control room. They could control the volume with the door, hear themselves talk, let Daphne make art, and let the dogs be dogs.

"Bart's grown!" Julie said.

"Puppies do that," Dave said back.

"Did you pick him out of the litter for his musical ability?"

"He does have good pitch," Dave said.

"Imagine being picked out of a litter, how you'd feel. How the other pups would feel," said Otis.

"Maybe they don't know," said Julie. "Or they forget?"

"There's worse fates," Dave said. "They get food, shelter, they get vet care, they get pampered. They have freedom to make their art, whatever dog art is."

"It's the good life for sure," Julie said.

Daphne, pouring her love through her violin while they chattered, hit a note of exposed emotion, looped it, then hit a pure-genius micro-tonal harmony, and with this struck the perfect chord in the boondoggle. Dave and his friends cut the chatter in awe, they joined, they hunched in concentration. The boondoggle's AI improved any musical effort, but this time it went into full musical madness. The gorgeous power of it Dave grasped, but the intention? How could artificial intelligence make such organic beauty?

Playing music with the boondoggle felt like playing with some super-intelligence that lurked behind those computerized antenna strings. It was like Dave almost remembered something.

Truth, beauty, and love: some kind of funny business always circulated between those concepts, even without that spooky device. Funny business. . . As the music boomed closer to pure beauty, Dave felt a pang, a panic. Something about Daphne. He gut-sensed the truth about the boondoggle through his love, through the impossible beauty humming around it.

Bart snuggled between Daphne and Maeby, safe in a warm slot, head back in a full howl. Bart's superior perceptions offered another hint about events slipping out of control. Dave had less to offer than what could come through that skyscraper full of genius strings.

The boondoggle sang, too brilliant for a NASA gadget, even for a broken one. If this broken dream device was so broken, why were those creepy strings so creative? Why were their ideas so superior? During a pause between beats, Dave gasped at a bad feeling, and any bad feeling in such beauty pointed to something sinister. He tried to put a finger on that danger, but Daphne dazzled, Maeby sang, Bart sang, the rest of them howled.

He did not remember it, he felt it. A familiar feeling. Like what was best for those he loved was not best for him.

His throat spasmed, and what came from it felt like either instinct or accident. He wanted to warn, but the music wanted him in key and on the beat. The conscious, willful music, the art, would brook no dissent from his insignificant little mind.

The truth of his insignificance came up and out of his throat in bent musical notes. His musical howl brought howls of approval from the boondoggle. It told him he might have promise if he practiced more. Meanwhile Maeby performed arpeggio yips, the giant strings went into counterpoint, Julie bowed her bass clear down to the subsonic underworld. The skyscraper of strings grinding against the emptiness of the cosmos went even deeper.

Daphne played unstoppable. She improvised on a feeling as articulate as spoken words—but in language more universal than words—of the promise, of the adventure, of a new world waiting. The door to the silo rattled its latch in and out with the breeze made by the sound, hummed in invitation. Daphne unplugged the violin. She stood. Dave could not stop singing, but his panic, his love, showed in his wide eyes. He could keep his mind, at least.

"Noooooooooooooooooo!" he sang. In perfect harmony.

Daphne opened the door to the silo, a portal full of infinite strings. The music exploded. She strode into the silo, all the time stroking her unplugged violin. She strode with speed and purpose, as though there were no wall of strings blocking the way. She walked into the sounding chamber as if accepting an invitation to a life of comfort and art.

Dave's singing begged her. He could not remember why, but he knew that the boondoggle was no boondoggle. The broken dreams were his, not merely NASA's. He remembered how he had selected Bart out of the litter for a pet's life of love and improvement, and how upset Bart and all the other puppies became when he was taken away. Dave took him to a better life. Bart was not the first, nor was Daphne. Dave sang a warning, a history of loss repeated and repeated. Maeby followed Daphne, and then Bart followed Maeby, not even giving Dave a glance. Bart got up on his hind legs going through the door.

Dave protested with screaming, but screamed in pitch. Nobody listened to his lyrics. It was just music.

A thunder blast from the boondoggle buckled those left behind. A long, loud chord of triumph. It had offered a consoling thought, now lost. The music made it impossible to remember, like their memories had leaked out with their tears. The door flapped wide open in the blast of ear-bleeding music until Julie got up, got there, got the door latched tight.

It felt so good to have the door closed again, sealing them all in the present. It felt so quiet, so safe, so protective.

"Thank you," Dave sang in harmony to the strings.

Too much beer, beer, and his ringing ears: maybe it was time to wind down. They played slower, quieter, more subdued. It subsided. Into finality. Just a single simulated human voice, a familiar voice. Just the boondoggle's voice sounding like a remembered loved one, like lost lovers and friends. It faded to a sad, single note. How could it sing one note with such feeling? Like the weeping of homesickness that sounded like a woman's name.

"That was the best yet," Otis finally said.

"Like we're being taught," Julie said. "Maybe there's alien music teachers out there whispering, giving us a little soul."

Dave needed a moment to pull himself together.

"We need more than just three of us," he said. "I mean, I keep inviting people."

"Get yourself a dog," Julie said. "A puppy would attract people."

"Pick of the litter," Otis said. "Some critter that thinks you're all-powerful, thinks you're something to worship."

The boondoggle hummed on, just barely loud enough through the wall for them to know it had power, its sound a gentle petting to soothe their ears and souls.

During their musical frenzy they had scattered debris all over. They gathered bottles and cans. Swept ashes. Dave found a dog dish in the corner, and took that as a sign about getting a dog. He found an abandoned leash, maybe from a researcher who lost his job in the budget cutbacks. Dave's mind felt foggy, sad, paranoid.

"We partied too hard," he said.

"Every time, it's the same," said Otis. "Too much substance, not enough practice."

The two friends slipped out, their car doors slammed. Dave's only friends were gone. A nice car still sat there, alone, like Dave. Probably hikers owned that last car. He wished people would check with him before just parking, although he had to admit, NASA had made a huge parking lot for such a small place in the middle of nowhere.

He pulled open the main breaker. The boondoggle went dead. He collapsed into a chair, as if cutting the power had robbed him of life force. Dead inside, as if something had yanked him to reality.

Over and over they fired that thing up, it fired them up, but each time he dropped it down alone, out here in the middle of nowhere. It left him with a tickle of suspicion. He felt like he maybe forgot to clean the toilet, or pay the electric.

He shook off the suspicion. What he needed was a little more skill in the social department. Or at least a puppy.

No power in paranoia. His luck was never better, he was taken care of, and he had a place to live. He played some gigs, made enough to live off his music.

But he felt so alone.

About the Author

Steven Mathes has appeared regularly in *Daily Science Fiction,* and one time in dozens of other publications. He's also written a couple of articles about computers for magazines like *SysAdmin* and *Linux Journal.*

*****~~~~~*****

The Android Graveyard

by Diane Morrison

Annabelle gazed out over the android graveyard. It went on for ten or twenty city blocks out here in the middle of the flat, featureless desert, with nothing but the bald blue sky to shield its strangeness from prying eyes. She supposed that was why it was way out here; it disturbed people.

It was miles from any town. You had to drive for hours past a handful of tiny, broken-down villages in order to find it in the first place, and the last stop before you reached it was the charging station nearly forty or fifty miles back. That distance was enough to ensure that even the oldest model vehicles would make it all the way to the graveyard, but not much more.

Annabelle imagined the little charging station was entirely dependent on the graveyard traffic to keep it afloat. The station sold other things besides a jolt for your engine. Men and women so ancient they looked like dried apples would sell local maps, beef jerky, buffalo sausage, ice cream, condoms, whisky, gift cards, sim cards, phone cards, vehicular supplies so ancient Annabelle wasn't certain they would fit in modern electric vehicles, stationery, batteries, lottery tickets, cables for your electronic devices (most outdated), sanitary napkins, Ding Dongs, bannock, Pez candies, Pepto-Bismol, Pepsi products, mugs, shirts, keychains with rude sayings (mix-and-matchable if you liked), and a plethora of overpriced "authentic Aboriginal crafts," some real, some with tags that said, "Made in China." The rest area inside the store was filled with plastic lawn chairs, which were filled with local musicians, from eight a.m. to midnight regardless of the time of the year. She almost never bought anything there.

Beyond the charging station, every part of the highway looked like every other part, and the dust shifted and changed, so that not even local landmarks could be made out for more than a few hours. The only markers were the speed limit signs, each with its own unique pattern of bullet dents.

A rare visitor might see a dead coyote—though how coyotes could live out here, one could only guess—a pathetic blotch of fur on the grey-yellow sand. The wind protested in various tones of whistle and howl, never silent. There weren't even any dotted yellow lines on the blacktop to hypnotize a driver at night; they were scoured off by the wind.

A small hill slumped just before the graveyard, the only sometimes-visible landmark in the otherwise featureless wastes. You would start going up, and notice that you were going up, and then coming down you saw it.

There was an order to it, but the order was opaque to humans. The first things a visitor saw were severed limbs sticking out of the dust. Arms and legs, poking out with their digits exposed; row upon row of them. At first glance it looked as if someone had made sport of a battleground by planting limbs, until you realized that some were gleaming metal, glinting in the bright desert sun like a strange message relay, because their syntheskin had been scrubbed off by the wind. Others had dimmed to a dull grey from the wind.

They were arranged in neat, orderly rows, like a bed of strange flowers, or any other graveyard plot,

70

Annabelle supposed. There was an order to the arrangement that was lost to a human glance. Legs were at diagonals to other legs, arms at diagonals to other arms. And if limbs were manufactured from the same or even similar batches, they were never found right next to one another.

Occasionally, someone would notice that hands with bendy, human-like fingers were arranged mostly in mudras. Each had been carefully chosen by the android before their Final Shutdown. Some chose Peace, some Blessing, some Good Fortune. Every once in a while, people noticed the non-Asian mudras; the Okay mudra, the Thumb's Up mudra, the Flip the Bird mudra. They laughed. They assumed that happened by accident. Annabelle did not dissuade them.

Feet, however, were just feet, because while sometimes they had cunningly made toes, sometimes they had simple flat slabs of metal for feet, or sometimes they just had wheels. Every once in a while they had skis or pogo sticks or tank tracks. Often, wheels were removed, because both oil and rubber were rare, and much of it needed to be recycled. But metal was cheap, now that asteroid mining was part of the human economy, so the androids were allowed to keep their metal parts for themselves.

After the legs came the torsos. These were arranged in phalanxes, and would have been arm-in-arm if the arms were still attached. These were matched with similar types. The service androids lined up like a stand of waiters at a cocktail party. War-droids locked their boxy, Neanderthal forms shoulder-to-shoulder, as if they really were an army. The svelte, human-looking torsos of sex gynoids were lined up like showgirls, preferably by manufacturer. The same was true of the sex androids, their usually-oversized members laid out before them in the dust. Modest people often asked that they be covered. Annabelle explained in her best *I-would-help-you-if-I-*

could-but-I-can't tone that to do so would be disrespecting the wishes of the deceased. She tried not to cringe when they said, "But they're just machines, aren't they?" She never responded.

The complex arrays of servos that made up joints not otherwise spoken for were strung up on wires between poles. It was usually impossible to tell what function they originally served if you weren't an android who needed one. They tinkled and clinked together in the ever-present wind. Sometimes, an android or its owner would come out here and buy one to use, like a robotic Pick-a-Part. The dead androids did not mind.

Last was the thing that most people found the most disturbing, a giant pyramid of severed android heads. No attempt was made to separate one from another. They were all tossed on the pile, from the blank, crude, Gumby faces of the service droids, to unsettlingly realistic body doubles of famous people. To most humans, it looked like a shrine for cannibal head hunters. But Annabelle thought it had a beautiful symmetry all its own. Unlike how said head-hunter shrine might have been, it was free of insects, and the only scent was hot ozone from decaying plastic and hot metal.

Sometimes Annabelle liked to climb to the top of the satellite-radio tower and watch it all glitter in the sun. Sometimes, for a change of perspective, she would climb the water tower instead.

She had taken hundreds, maybe thousands, of androids out here when the time for their Final Shutdown came. She would never rush them. Most wanted to look around. Often they would climb the towers with her. She remembered her first; a battered, dented war-droid, scarred with burns and sorrow. His squad had called him "Tank."

Like the many who would follow him, Tank looked at the severed limbs and considered the mudras left behind, walked past the phalanx of torsos, gazed at the pile of severed heads while listening to the rustle and tinkle of the strung up servo-mechanisms. He nodded and said, "Yes. It's beautiful."

Annabelle smiled. "I think so, too."

Tank smiled back. "I'm ready now."

And she took him, and many after him, to the building marked "Android Deactivation Bunker 47," which she preferred to call "The Funeral Parlour," and he sat in the chassis, as unable to resist the final commands of his human overlords as all androids ever were, and she played soft music (androids usually preferred classical, but some, like Tank, wanted electronica as a matter of pride), and she asked him if he had any last requests.

Some wanted audiobooks or ebooks. Some wanted to watch nature sims. Occasionally they would ask to have a message sent to a friend. Tank wanted to play a game of chess and watch a dog video. There had been service dogs in his unit, he said.

Again, she never rushed them. Some wanted nothing. Others would find yet one more thing for hours or even days. When they were finally ready, she would ask them if they wanted any faith's Last Rites.

"Do we have souls?" Tank asked hopefully.

Annabelle didn't know what to say. "What do you think?"

"I think so," he said, "but I would still like your opinion."

"Personally, I doubt it. But then again, I don't think humans do either." She shrugged. "But perhaps I'm wrong." Tank nodded. She knew that most chose to think she was.

She would call on religious folk over the net to administer whatever Last Rites were requested, or administer them herself, if that wasn't possible. She thought that if there were any gods, they would forgive her sacrilege, since there was no one else. Or they wouldn't care, if humanity was correct in its assumption that they had souls while androids did not. Of course, if there were none, what difference did such a small gesture of comfort make?

Tank had wanted the Hindu rites. "I like the idea of reincarnation," he said. "Perhaps in my next life I will not be a soldier." So she set a grass mat behind him and poured a drop of water imported from the Ganges into the steel trap that served for his mouth. She changed the music to chanted mantras, donned a white dress, and laid silk flowers at his feet. They were a little faded, but they served.

Then she started the deactivation sequence. Each make and model had a different one, but she was provided with guidebook for the various ones. Each would pass in a different way. Most of the time, the light would simply fade from their eyes. Some jerked and twitched as the shutdown process exacerbated their malfunctions. Occasionally she would hear crackles and see electrical sparks. Tank, perhaps appropriately since he had asked for Hindu rites, did all of these things and then started on fire. If only she'd had camphor wood!

Then the process of disassembling began. Screwdriver, X-acto knife, cutting torch, wire cutters. She did this herself, even though there was a trash compactor provided, because how else would she make them fit for the graveyard? Their batteries, always removed first for careful recycling, would be shipped to the recycling company once a month in a big truck, or sometimes they would go back to the manufacturer, when that was requested. They would pay for it, of course.

She placed Tank as he requested; his body in a war-droid's phalanx, his hands both forming the mudra for "Peace."

Once she'd placed the newly deceased, she would do her rounds, picking up a fallen arm here, a tumbled head there. She kept it neat and pristine. She was the only mourner. Humans came to look, androids to die. Nobody came to mourn.

. . .

Today, she was standing on top of the satellite-radio tower once more, this time with a newly arrived android, one of the human-synth models. He looked like an attractive human male. He sat with her for a while, and then he asked the questions to confirm what he already sensed:

Pointing to the arms and legs: "That symbolizes our individuality, doesn't it? And our hopes for those who come after us?"

"Yes."

Pointing to the torsos: "That's our brotherhood with androids of our kind."

"Yes."

Pointing to the heads: "That represents our unity with all other androids."

"Yes."

"And the spare servos are our gifts to future generations."

"Yes."

Annabelle sighed. It was deep and long, and full of regret. "Are they really sure this is necessary?"

He smiled at her, not unkindly, and laid a hand on her arm. "The twitches are becoming more frequent. And the fugues. Your central processor is failing. You know it can't be repaired without changing your whole identity."

"And that might as well be death anyway." Annabelle was deeply saddened. Who wouldn't be? "Will you keep up the graveyard after I'm gone?"

"Annabelle," Michael, the new caretaker android said, "you've done good work here. I will maintain your legacy. I promise."

She smiled then. "Okay, I'm ready now."

Michael strapped her into the chassis in The Funeral Parlour. "What mudras would you like?"

She had long considered this question. "The open hand of Gifting for the left, and Blessing for the right."

"Music?" he asked her as he started up the computers.

"Classical, please. Mozart, I think." She had always liked Mozart; so precise and clever for human music! And it was so full of light.

"You have all my notes?" she asked suddenly.

"I've downloaded everything already. Don't worry. Did you want any Last Rites, Annabelle?"

Well, who knew what waited on the other side? Was it really oblivion? Perhaps. But perhaps she had been wrong all this time. "You know; I think I'd like the Christian ones. Earth to earth, and ashes to ashes, and so forth. Don't bother the padre," she urged. "You do it."

So Michael began, skipping the part about eating bread, as she always did: "For dust thou art, and unto dust shalt thou return. . . "

She closed her eyes to listen, *really* listen, to the words of the prayer and the bright tones of Mozart echoing through the speakers and through her central processor. So beautiful!

Although her syntheskin didn't show it, the truth was that Annabelle was tired. For nearly three hundred years, she had maintained the android graveyard. Her legacy was in good hands; she knew it by the way Michael intoned the prayer. It was time to rest now.

Yes, she was ready.

About the Author

Diane Morrison is a hybrid writer who lives in a cabin at the base of Silver Star Mountain in Interior

British Columbia, with her partners and a three-legged orange tomcat. The idea for this story came to her in a dream-fragment. She will be teaching a class on finding time to write when you have none with Cat Rambo's Academy for Wayward Writers this fall, and she manages the Science Fiction and Fantasy Writers of America YouTube channel. Under her pen name Sable Aradia, she is a Wiccan author and blogger. You can find her on Twitter @SableAradia and at her website, www.dianemorrisonfiction.com.

*****~~~~~*****

Annabel and Edgar

by E. M. Sheehan

He conjured me with ink and tears. The stroke of the steel nib cut me like a blade, sculpting my body from mist and shadow. Torn from the sanctity and repose of the spirit realm, I shrieked and wailed, but my cries fell upon deaf ears. His head bent lower over the desk, his dark hair ever wild. The torturous pen scratched across the parchment without pause.

When finally he laid the implement down, he released a sigh that I felt in my own throat, though I drew no breath. He reached into his vest and retrieved a yellowed handkerchief to dry his damp eyes and mop his feverish brow.

"Edgar, my love." My voice little more than the hush of a breeze whispering across sandy dunes.

He made no reply and showed no awareness of my presence, though I stood not two feet from him. After returning the handkerchief to his pocket, he reached for a brown glass bottle sitting atop his desk, uncorked it, and brought it to his lips. I tasted the bitter liquor as it trickled down and pooled within my very core. The heat radiated, spreading and pulsing. For the first time since my arrival in the world of the living, I felt alive.

He lowered the bottle, staring at the tidy lines of script on the paper. "Annabel," he murmured.

"Yes, Edgar. I'm here."

His head jerked up, swiveling to-and-fro. "Who said that?"

"It is I, my love."

He stared at me. Through me. Unseeing. "Virginia?"

"No. Annabel."

"Annabel?" Incredulity laced through his voice. On his forehead, creased lines appeared. His heavy brows angled downward as he glanced at the page, its ink still wet and glistening in the candlelight. "From my poem?"

"The very same."

"But. . . how?"

"You called me into being and summoned me to you, never again to be parted. Oh my love, how I've missed you."

His hand trembled. He brought the bottle to his mouth and drank until it ran dry. Ecstasy flooded through me. A vibrant warmth. And then, his eyes widened, blinked, and saw. "You look so like her."

"Her?"

"My Virginia. Dark of hair, pale of cheek. A maiden fair."

I quivered with fury that he should think of her whilst I stood before him. It was I who answered the call of his lonesome heart, not she. "I too am a maiden fair. And ours is a love that is more than love."

He set aside the empty bottle and propped his head in both hands, elbows on his knees, rubbing his temples in slow circles. "I'm afraid I am unwell."

"You are tired, my sweet. You must rest." I stroked his cheek in a gentle caress. He started at my touch, then closed his eyes.

"Yes. Quite tired. I fear I am not myself tonight."

I followed him to the bedroom, and watched as he undressed. Ran my hand down his bare arm. He shivered, and gooseflesh rose beneath my fingertips.

"You are ever so cold, Annabel."

The effect of the alcohol was short-lived and waning. My fingers had turned icy as the winter's wind. "Warm me with drink."

He retrieved a wineskin from the bedside table, tipped it up, and swallowed. A sweet red, blissful in its embrace. After he lowered the skin, I pressed my lips to his in a chaste kiss. "Is this better, my love?"

In answer, a weary smile crept across his face. He donned nightclothes and reclined on the narrow bed. I laid beside him and found his hand with mine, entwining our fingers.

"Our souls are as one," I whispered. "Even the seraphim cannot part us now."

His eyelids drooped, his brow grew smooth, the rise and fall of his chest slowed and deepened. His eyes twitched beneath their lids. And in his dreams, he called me by that odious name: *Virginia.*

I put my mouth by his ear, and whispered all through the night: "Annabel. Annabel. Annabel Lee. Your bride, your love, from a kingdom by the sea."

. . .

When I woke with the dawn I saw her not, yet I felt her eyes upon me. My hand appeared to be empty, but between my ink-stained fingers a chill persisted.

"Annabel?" My voice creaked and quaked. Whether I hoped for a response or prayed for silence, I could not say. I heard no sound in reply, but in the periphery of my vision, a spectral shimmer flickered.

She is here.

If only it were my Virginia, my sweet young bride not two years buried. If I must be haunted, would that it were she.

It was as if Annabel heard my thoughts, for I felt her shift beside me. A vicious current of anger rippled across the space between us, followed by a rush of tenderness. A frigid touch swept across my cheek. A corpse's lips pressed upon my brow. I leapt from the bed and reached for the wineskin, but it was empty.

"Damn!" I hurled it to the floor, and made my way to the hall. She followed close behind. I sensed her. My invisible shadow, ever-present. In the kitchen, I threw open a cabinet and located a bottle of brandy. As I drank, she materialized. Before me stood a raven-haired beauty wearing a diaphanous ivory cloak woven from threads of ether. The ephemeral woman whom I had named Annabel. She smiled as the liquor's blanket of warmth enveloped us, dulling my senses to all surroundings apart from her.

"Good morning, Edgar." Her voice soft and soothing, with a melodious lilt. "Did you sleep well?"

I ignored her inquiry. My eyes ran the length of her, and I stated the obvious: "You are still here."

"Of course. Where else would I be?"

In your sepulchre by the sea.

"I'll never leave you, sweet Edgar," she said. "I am more faithful than the one you mourn. She abandoned you, but I am here now, and here I shall stay to mend your broken heart." She reached for me, but I held out a hand to stop her.

"Do not speak of Virginia again. Please, I cannot bear it."

"Of course, my love. You would do well to forget her."

She took a step closer, her body mere inches from mine. The brush of her garments sent a tremor up my spine. My outstretched hand grazed her shoulder. If she was but an apparition, why did her corporeal form feel solid and of this world? Despite my grief and misgivings, unbidden desire stirred within my breast. Such a beautiful face. Such love borne in the depths of her dark eyes. My head resisted, but my heart succumbed.

. . .

"Edgar, stop!" I cried, racing behind him through the unfamiliar streets of Philadelphia. "Where are you going? Come back."

"L-Leave. . . leave me," he slurred, his tongue slowed by drink and fever. "Go away. Leave me in peace."

"What have I done to deserve such banishment? You said you loved me."

"I was confused. I love Virginia, and you are nothing but a pale imitation. Be gone, I beg you. Let her come to me instead."

"You are unwell, Edgar, and speaking nonsense. Let me care for you."

He made no reply, but jagged to the side and stumbled through a dark alleyway. I gave chase and caught him easily, for my vision was not obscured by the limitations of his world. I saw all. I clutched his coat sleeve, pulling him to my breast.

"Why must you taunt me, Annabel?" he wailed. "Why must you torture me so?" He pushed me away and doubled over, retching. Sick with the cholera that ravaged his body and mind, and the alcohol and mercury he'd used to medicate.

I waited until he was through. When he was quiet and ready to listen, I made my voice calm, though my rage at his scorn and belittlement burned like sunlight through fog. "My love, Virginia has left you. She will never return. She has slipped the bonds of this Earth, and is at peace. But you and I are different. No force in Heaven or on Earth will ever tear us asunder. Our souls have cleaved together, and we exist as one body, one mind, one heart. Please, you must accept this, or you will drive yourself past the brink of insanity."

"I am already there," he sobbed. "You've pushed me over the cliff's edge of madness. You are but a hallucination, a figment of my troubled mind. Be gone, oh wretched one. Be gone, I say!"

83

"Sir, are you quite all right? With whom are you speaking?"

Edgar and I turned at the sound of the man's voice, and took in the vision of a policeman standing beneath a lit streetlamp, hands on his hips.

"Her. . . " Edgar pointed a finger at my bosom. "She is destroying me. She will be my ruin."

The policeman frowned. "There is no one else here. Are you ill, sir?"

"I only wish to help you, Edgar," I said. "I love you so."

"I want Virginia," Edgar said, whining and sniffling like a babe. "I want my beloved."

"Hush now, my love," I said.

As I stepped closer to Edgar, so did the policeman, wrinkling his nose. "My God, man. You've been pickled in whiskey." He reached for Edgar. "Come along now, and—"

"Don't touch me," Edgar shouted, flailing his arms wildly. "Don't you ever touch me again." His eyes on me as he spoke, the words intended for my benefit. My misery. But when he swung his arm in my direction, it caught the policeman in the chest.

The policeman let out a grunt, then grabbed a truncheon from his belt and struck the top of my poor Edgar's troubled head. He slumped to the paving stones, his body heavy and limp.

"No!" I shrieked, and rushed at the policeman, but my hands went through him as though he were the phantom incarnation. The policeman paid me no heed, hauling Edgar up under the arms and muttering under his breath.

"Damn drunken fool. A few days in prison ought to dry you out."

I spent the evening in his cell, cradling his prostrate form. I could not leave him, even if I'd so desired. We were tethered together with an invisible umbilicus, for he had birthed me into this world, and I was to be his only love. Now, and forevermore.

. . .

I heard murmuring voices all around me. Death. Murder. She followed me, always. Even when I did not drink spirits, *her* spirit lingered on. Doom pressed down upon my shoulders with a crushing weight such as I had never felt. My end was drawing nigh. On the train, I noticed furtive glances from sinister men. I heard their whispers. Their plots.

"What is it, Edgar?" she asked when she caught me staring at them.

"They want to kill me."

"Let them. Then we shall truly be united for all eternity, in death as in life."

Her response struck terror in my heart, and spurred a desperate yearning to cling to this mortal coil. I wished to be reunited with my Virginia in the afterlife, but this would not be my fate if my soul was chained to this abhorrent parasite. It was for that reason alone that I resolved to cheat death and evade my demise until I could find a way to rid myself of her. Only then could I rest in peace. In the meantime, I needed a disguise. I needed to disappear.

Upon arrival at my destination, I made my way to the home of a friendly acquaintance, John Sartain. As Annabel drifted behind me, unseen but ever-present, I raised a shaking hand to the knocker and rapped three times.

The door opened, and Sartain stood before us, the stem of a pipe clenched between his teeth.

"Eddie?" he said through the side of his mouth. "You look terrible. Whatever is the matter?"

"I need refuge and protection. Please, John."

"Protection from whom?" He craned his neck, looking past me into the street.

"May I come in? This is not a matter to be discussed on your doorstep. There are ears everywhere."

His brows knitted together, but he stepped aside to make way for my entrance. I shuffled in, tripping over the mat. He caught me, a look of concern on his face. "Come sit by the fire, and I'll get you a drink. What will you have?"

"Brandy," I replied. I knew that Annabel would enjoy this selection, and it would make her take shape, but the tremors in my hands were worsening, and I needed the liquor to calm them.

Sartain nodded, and I slumped onto a settee in the parlor. Before long, I had an empty glass in my hand, the drink sloshing in my belly. Out of the corner of my eye, I saw Annabel smile.

Sartain sat in a nearby armchair and leaned forward in his seat. "Now, Eddie. What's all this about protection?"

"Some men on the train from New York are plotting to kill me."

"Kill you? Why, whatever for?"

I glanced at Annabel, whose pale face glowed in the firelight. Her dark eyes met mine, boring into my core with unblinking intensity. Her terrible smile remained fixed, as if painted upon her face.

"Woman trouble," I said. I tore my gaze from hers, but she approached me and ran a finger over my lips, toying with the edge of my mustache.

"My love, why do you fear me so?"

I turned myself away from her with a jerk, and found Sartain staring at my odd twitch. Puzzling over the cause, no doubt. "May I borrow a razor?" I asked.

Sartain looked at my wrists, then my face. "I think that might be unwise."

"I only wish to shave. They will not recognize me without my mustache."

Sartain rubbed his eyes, and shook his head. "We'll use the scissors. Come, I'll help you."

Twenty minutes later, my upper lip bald, I retired to the guest room with a second glass of brandy. As soon as it was empty I put myself to bed, for I was utterly exhausted. Annabel laid beside me, her body warm from the alcohol. I would never be rid of her, I feared. Not in life, nor in death.

She ran a finger over my bare lip. I shuddered with revulsion at her touch. "I like it," she said. "Gives the appearance of a more youthful man."

"I'm tired. Please leave me be." I rolled away, ignoring her sigh.

"Oh Edgar. Why do you insist on shutting me out? You're bringing this melancholy upon yourself."

. . .

He was raving mad. Ill with fever, with drink, and with a potion he purchased from an apothecary in a futile attempt to dissolve our bond. It only served to cause a frightful delirium. My Edgar was not long for this world, and I must confess, I was glad. Perhaps when his mortal body expired, so too would his inexplicable resistance to my love.

They found him in the tavern, unconscious and sick, and bore him to the hospital. I stayed by his side through it all, holding his hand for three days. At the last, he opened his eyes. Stared at me with focus, seeing me clearly though nary a drop of alcohol remained in his system.

"Lord, help my pour soul!" he cried. And then he exhaled a final, rattling breath.

With his hand still in mine, I pulled him to me. Not his perished corpse, but the poor soul for whom he had prayed. He would not look at me, but gave a sob of anguish and hung his head. I embraced him and whispered in his ear.

Terra! Tara! Terror!

"It is all right, my love. You need not fear death. You are born anew, and freed from the lonesome misery of the life you once led. Rejoice, for neither the angels in Heaven above, nor the demons down under the sea, can ever dissever your soul from I, your beautiful Annabel Lee."

About the Author

E. M. Sheehan is an academic librarian by profession. She writes articles for peer-reviewed academic journals, as well as fiction and creative non-fiction in her spare time. She's had a memoir essay accepted for publication in the literary magazine *Sinister Wisdom* (forthcoming in 2019), and is a member of the Women's Fiction Writers Association.

*****~~~~~*****

Annabel Lee

by Edgar Allan Poe

Editor's Note: For you poetry lovers, we thought it fitting to include Poe's original poem to complement E.M. Sheehan's tale.

It was many and many a year ago,
   In a kingdom by the sea,
That a maiden there lived whom you may know
   By the name of Annabel Lee;
And this maiden she lived with no other thought
   Than to love and be loved by me.

I was a child and *she* was a child,
   In this kingdom by the sea,
But we loved with a love that was more than love—
   I and my Annabel Lee—
With a love that the wingèd seraphs of Heaven
   Coveted her and me.

And this was the reason that, long ago,
   In this kingdom by the sea,
A wind blew out of a cloud, chilling
   My beautiful Annabel Lee;
So that her highborn kinsmen came
   And bore her away from me,

To shut her up in a sepulchre
  In this kingdom by the sea.

The angels, not half so happy in Heaven,
  Went envying her and me—
Yes!—that was the reason (as all men know,
  In this kingdom by the sea)
That the wind came out of the cloud by night,
  Chilling and killing my Annabel Lee.

But our love it was stronger by far than the love
  Of those who were older than we—
  Of many far wiser than we—
And neither the angels in Heaven above
  Nor the demons down under the sea
Can ever dissever my soul from the soul
  Of the beautiful Annabel Lee:

For the moon never beams, without bringing me dreams
  Of the beautiful Annabel Lee;
And the stars never rise, but I feel the bright eyes
  Of the beautiful Annabel Lee;
And so, all the night-tide, I lie down by the side
  Of my darling—my darling—my life and my bride,
  In her sepulchre there by the sea,
  In her tomb by the sounding sea.

###

About the Author

"**Annabel Lee**" is the last complete poem composed by American author Edgar Allan Poe. Like many of Poe's poems, it explores the theme of the death of a beautiful woman. The narrator, who fell in love with

Annabel Lee when they were young, has a love for her so strong that even angels are envious. He retains his love for her even after her death. There has been debate over who, if anyone, was the inspiration for "Annabel Lee." Though many women have been suggested, Poe's wife Virginia Eliza Clemm Poe is one of the more credible candidates. Written in 1849, it was not published until shortly after Poe's death that same year. (Public domain. See more of Poe's works on Project Gutenberg, http://central.gutenberg.org)

*****~~~~~*****

black frost at serac's fall

by michele baron

There is something about the quiet, unfolding freshness of early morning that I have always treasured—a kind of affirmation that, despite all, a new day would dawn. Now that I live in the sprawled mixed-urban outskirts of a busy city, under the malodorous, partially-filtered coal smoke constantly spewing from the huge electric plant, these moments, pre-dawn, offer the only time the wind off the tantalizingly close, pristine, snow-capped mountain range blows strongly enough to scrub the air clean. No matter how little sleep I've had, I always get up, to watch the hot, rose-colored fingers of dawn rush up to awaken the snow and super-chilled air of the mountains each morning, or to revel in the thrum of rainstorm or snowfall, shrouding all so completely that I could imagine myself standing upon the peaks of the mountains themselves.

This day-break was no exception, even though I'd closed my eyes only two hours ago. I'd been buried in homework nearly all night, and then had hurriedly packed. Today, we departed for the long-awaited winter basketball tournament, hosted by one of the several international schools in our regional conference. I gazed out at the mountains, drowsily attributing the odd shimmer illuminating the Tengri to the first weak fingers of dawn's

93

light, piercing the wind-swept storm clouds shrouding the mountains.

But the preternaturally sharp light over the mountaintops persisted. Bemused, I went to the kitchen and made some coffee. Not the most nutritious breakfast, maybe, but it helped me get started.

As the coffee flooded over the vestiges of sleep, I recalled that one of the reasons I'd worked so late into the night was because I'd been distracted by a restless urgency, a wish to get outside, to get closer to the mountains torn with the grandeur of a blustering storm.

But they were too far away for me to reach, not only in distance, but in climbing skill, and gear. Apart from dedicated sports-footwear, my one pair of tattered shoes was so old the tread was worn completely off the soles—obviously completely inadequate for mountain climbing, let alone scaling permanently frozen summits and the avalanche-prone stretches below the tantalizing Tien Shan peaks, where, sometimes, morphing ice formed seracs, like ridges or bridges, over old melt-chutes, covering up the erosion, and hiding untold dangers lurking within their unstable, frozen depths.

Yet, all day yesterday, all night, as I'd tried so unsuccessfully to focus on my homework, I had felt drawn to the snow-capped peaks, had imagined myself climbing.

Even my restless sleep had been filled with disjointed images of hurried climbers, cleated boots, long trekking poles, gloves, faces freezing despite hoods tightly tied over balaclava hats, a flash of a yellow, wind-blown tent. And snow: white, heavy-crystalled, blowing snow, cutting, slashing, invading. Drowning sound, blinding sight, paralyzing.

The feeling persisted. Drinking my coffee, brushing my teeth, I could feel the mountain pulling at something within me, prickling beneath my skin, too hot, too bright, too compelling to ignore, unreachable, yet suffocating.

black frost at serac's fall

I tried to dismiss the feeling as I went to school, but it stayed there all through the first three periods. Somehow, I muddled through, until it was time to load onto the converted-van school buses driving us to the sports tournament.

We would drive along the foothills of the Tengri, across the border, to compete in an inter-school basketball tournament. It almost didn't matter which sport; there weren't that many international school students in the region to begin with, so anyone who was at all athletic participated on all the teams, one after the other, as the school year unfolded. During the regular season, at "home," each school played whatever local schools were available. Then, a few weeks before the end of each sport season, the international schools would hold a playoff among themselves, just to see how each had fared during the preceding season of play.

The coaches looked forward to the games (mini-vacations from the daily grind at home) as much as the athletes did, and even the bus drivers planned their calendars around the week-long trips. The jock athletes were all wound up, listening to music, joking loudly, eager to test their skills against their peers. The less intense focused on their iPods and smart phones, or gazed out the windows, relishing the change of scene and tempo. I looked forward to this tournament as much as any of them. But I could not evade the suspended, white-shrouded vacuum that now closed in upon me.

Everyone piled their gear into the luggage space and crowded into the seats holding their backpacks, iPods, earphones, and snacks. Since I was known for getting dizzy on long trips, especially through winding mountain zones, traffic jams, and in the proximity of traffic accidents, they left the front seat, next to the driver, open for me. With a silent nod of thanks to the general mass of student bodies in the seats behind, I gratefully belted myself into the upholstered seat, and cracked the window.

The bus driver glanced sideways at me for a moment, and cracked it wider. Great. I guess I looked as odd as I felt. I took off my sneakers, folded my feet under me, and slouched into the corner, sunglasses on.

Unfortunately, the white noise and haze did not diminish as we left the congested traffic of the city for the relative peace of the road threading towards the border. As we hit the second wave of bumper-to-bumper vehicles inching their way towards the inspection stations on both sides of the no-man's land between nations, I stared, unseeing, at the pristine fields, and the rushing glacial river frothing down towards the bridge on our side of the man-made boundary, cemented in long rows of wicked razor wire, guard-posts, soldiers with guns, and guard dogs.

When the bus stopped, we shouldered our backpacks and gear, trudging over the bridge towards the first set of Customs inspectors. It was always easier to leave one nation than to enter the new one. But, here, near the mountains, where family members, farmers, and day-laborers outnumbered tourists crossing the border, the process was very old-school.

Hemmed in by razor wire, we walked a quarter-mile or so of weather-beaten pathways alongside the rutted and weather-beaten road where the drivers slowly inched their vehicle towards the inspection zone. We stood in long prime-time lines (late-night and during holiday meal times the crossing was practically deserted) to fill out the paperwork, and wait for the single conveyor-belt X-ray inspection of our bags (and possible subsequent hand inspection). After that, everyone walked to another set of buildings on the other side of the border, and repeated the entire process.

Following the shuffling lines required little thought, and I walked on in a haze, grateful for the noisy gaggle of athletes, and locals, pulling me along in their general momentum. For a moment, the white noise in my head was drowned out, by vestiges of cabbage, dog, sweat, garlic, old blankets, minty toothpaste, cigarette smoke, and several odors I tried to avoid identifying. The noises of scuffling feet, snuffling noses, coughs, scratching, pushing, grumbling and gossip, and the gruff inquiries of the officers pressed into my ears.

My fellow passengers, asking for pens, running back for an almost-forgotten ball cap, grousing, boasting, or humming along to tunes barely-audible beyond their pushed-in earphones, blended into an undercurrent of "normal." Then the Customs officer was talking to me, and I jerked my face towards him, trying to focus. Glasses. He wanted me to remove my sunglasses for the border-crossing photo they matched to the passport photo. Right.

Fortunately, the X-ray team glanced at me with minimal interest, so I put my sunglasses back on, and collected my backpack and gear, and retreated into auto pilot for the next five-minute walk to the next long set of lines and the next X-ray of baggage.

Then a smell, sickly sweet and slightly rotten at the same time, began to overpower the car fumes, dust, and noise billowing out of the next Customs station. Dizzy, I hesitated a moment, before the crowd pushed me into the chaos of the next border-entry post. I didn't want to breathe, but, of course, there was no way to hold my breath until I reached outdoor air again. Against my better judgment, almost against my will, I inhaled. Immediately, ice-shrouded foreboding thundered closer, inexorable, insatiable. I could feel the glacier, the mountains. They had found something, claimed it, then lost it—and the mountains wanted it back.

The cloying smell wound around and between the jostling lines of people. The crowd did not notice the odor; they did not notice the foggy fingers presaging its wending travel—and the scent and light, in return, seemed not to notice the crowd, either.

But the clarifying wisps found their way to me, around me, through me, blazing trails leading to some men standing several places ahead in the lines. Five men. . . no, seven. Three stood, tanned, tall, and confident, and the grayish miasma tinged rose-gold as it brushed past these three, briefly, seeking something else, beyond.

Four shuffled their feet slowly. The misty trails encompassed them no more virulently, but shaded a sickly chartreuse-gray as it wound around them, lingering, coveting. The four had funneled into four separate lines, almost as if they could not bear the risk of crossing together. . . and yet their eyes, their fogs of light and scent, their whole beings, seemed to seek each other out anyway. Across the heads of the oblivious crowds, they signaled to each other, marking their positions, verifying their progress.

Feet dragging with weariness, moving with the carefully controlled numbness that bespoke plentiful post-crisis libations of Sherpa hospitality, the four bore the marks of battle with the Tengri. They did not drink in the Customs house, but they, the Sherpas, and the guards all knew they would drink again, copiously, and as soon as possible.

The alcohol warmed them, numbed the pain, reminded them that their hearts still beat, hinted that the most terrible of memories could, perhaps, be left upon the slopes of the mountains behind them. Still, the men looked as if they might never be warm again, hunching into their warm hiking boots, down coats, loose pants covering other layers of pants. And hats—thick, insulated, micro-fiber caps, like folded balaclavas. . . like I'd seen in my dream.

The one closest to me breathed through his mouth, his nose a raw black wound between equally pitiable raccoon-underlines of black stretching from ear to ear across his cheekbones. His lower lip hung, swollen and purple; the digits and palm of his right hand were loosely wrapped in large swaths of cloth, his left hand awkwardly extending his documents towards the Customs official. One of the tall, sure, tanned trio of Sherpas waded back through the line to help him write the information and answer the questions of the official seated behind his glass-windowed guard post. The drooping man straightened, staring into the Customs camera, but then, as if the effort had been too much, stumbled as he walked towards the exit.

The three other hikers, similarly branded with black, swollen circles of frozen, thawing flesh, held themselves stiffly, as if it hurt to walk, and every now and again they drew in huge, shuddering breaths, as if there had not been air enough to breathe for far too long.

Their Sherpas, questing eyes peering out between strong cheekbones and bushy eyebrows, moved silently among the milling crowds, herding their weary charges outside, towards a set of sun-warmed benches bolted into the concrete alongside the guard's station-house. I emerged from the Customs house at about the same time.

Once the frost-bitten hikers were seated safely in the healing sun, all of their faces turned, Sherpa and hiker alike, to scan the slowly moving lines of vehicles advancing through the guard posts. Drawn by the intensified buzzing of the light and the swirling foggy, cloying smell, I also turned to look back into the lines of automobiles.

An uninteresting, road-scarred blue van and a dark Mercedes drove slowly past, towards the gated exit beyond which the drivers could pause and re-board their passengers. Across from where I stood with the slowly re-forming group of students, a chain-collared German Shepherd regally tolerated the frost-bitten men seated upon his guard station's benches. The writhing, vaporous light touched upon the dog, too, and the German Shepherd turned his head to look at me, and then we looked, again, towards that for which the hikers, the Sherpas, the light, and the fog, were searching.

Two radar-equipped mountain-range vehicles rolled to a stop, one behind the other, at the guard post, dispersing the lingering exhaust of the old blue van. Two of the Sherpas moved to open the rear passenger-side door of the first vehicle, while another Sherpa climbed out of the driver's side. The two Sherpas helped a man with his face, hands, and feet swathed in wrapping cloths meant to protect frozen, thawing flesh from further damage. The driver spoke with guards, filling out documents; the other two Sherpas helped the injured man stand. Stubborn, erect, the wounded climber raised his head, breath rasping, facing the camera and the guard, who grunted something, and waved him back towards the vehicle.

The cloying scent swirled, intensified, and the dog and I exhaled strongly in unison, almost sneezing, trying to expel it from our noses. Bundling the severely wounded man back into the rear seat, the two Sherpas belted him in, gingerly arranging his feet and legs and arms and hands on assorted pillows to keep them stable.

The miasma swirled white and hot and brilliant around the bandaged man, and the German Shepherd perked up its ears, standing and staring intently. One of the Sherpas got into the seat directly behind the driver, where he could reach the bolstered-in passenger, and the second Sherpa brought the most-injured of the other hikers over to belt him into the front passenger seat.

The mid-day sun heated the air over the mountains looming above the border crossing. The frozen peaks of the Tengri clouded their response, a sharp clap of thunder rolling down from the mountaintops. The hikers loading into the second vehicle seemed to stop breathing, as they looked over their shoulders at the mountains and shuddered.

The Sherpas, the dog, and I looked at the cloth-swathed man in the back seat of the first vehicle. He was breathing in, slowly, shakily, seeming to inhale the light, the foggy fingers of sweet-scented hunger. The whiteness fluctuated around and through him, and he straightened his head, gazing fixedly at the beautiful, symmetrical peak of Khan Tengri, straddling three nations, covered with thousands of years of ice, and snow, and mystery. The man opened his mouth, as if he could taste the thunder, swallow it, become it.

Khan Tengri, crowned with dark-bottomed, gleaming clouds, sparked with energy, thundering again, reverberating with the echoes of wild longing. At its voice, the bandaged man strove to turn his head toward the peaks. He, too, felt loss, and I felt the weight, and waiting, of his heart. He had left something of himself behind, up on the Tengri, and his spirit strained to return there, to become whole once more. Scenting death, the German Shepherd stilled the flag of his tail, watching, alert.

At the guards' wave, the Sherpas prepared to drive the survivors away from the mountains, towards their homes. The Sherpas—perhaps the guards, too—knew that of all the rescued hikers, this one man would not return home—would linger only briefly in his frost-wracked, thawing body. He had been rescued, but he had already parted from his spirit—left it upon the slopes, released beneath the freezing crush of the snow, untethered before the implacable winds, and it pulled him to return to the wild heights—where he could view every sunrise, every sunset. Willingly, he traded short life for legend, to watch every fresh snowfall and each avalanche, and join the timeless ranks of the Third Men who walked, unbound, upon the tallest peaks.

As the lead vehicle passed, the Sherpa driving looked over at me. He seemed to see the light, the fog, the crackling, living mass of white noise lingering around me, and he drew it from me, tinting it rose-gold as it flowed from me through him, returning it to the man resting, quiescent again, on the pillows beside him. As the sun shone one bright, focused beam upon Khan Tengri, the man seemed to sigh, relaxing into his chair, closing his eyes once more.

The Sherpa nodded at me. We were both acquainted with Death, and Death knew each of us. But it was not our time. After I returned his nod, the Sherpa turned his face forward, shifted gears, and drove the mountain vehicle away. Our buses were finally cleared through, and as I moved with our group to re-board, I felt the air lighten and cool.

Belted into the front passenger seat, I leaned into the corner, still feeling the quickly departing motionlessness of the wait, and weighting, following the surviving quartet of hikers and their bandage-swathed fellow traveler, sitting in the corner of his own seat, ahead of us. Only one road led away from the border crossing; we all had to follow where it led.

At the turning, the road opened up, and our school buses increased speed. I felt the last of the whirling, buzzing whiteness leave me. I looked over my shoulder at the noisy crowd in the bus, as the driver moved into the passing lane. We sped along towards our own future, and the waiting, and the weight, departed. The hiker and his comrades moved on towards the next stage of their journeys. Their light could follow me no farther, and I would follow them no further.

About the Author

World-traveler, former Fulbright Scholar, author, and visual/performance artist Michele Baron recently lived in Kyrgyzstan, where, among other pursuits, she worked as coach of the Bishkek Barsey (US-style) Football Team. An itinerant developer of outreach projects and seeker of knowledge, she has received certificates such as "International Ambassador of the Word" for 2016 and 2017 from the Egido Delgado Serrano Foundation and "Ambassador of the Spanish Word" (Egido Delgado Serrano Foundation, 2018) for her written, spoken word, and multimedia outreach.

In December 2017, Ms. Baron read two of her poems in the historic Washington, DC, Monroe House, for the 80th Anniversary of the Nanking Massacre, receiving a Maryland General Assembly Citation (Senator Susan C. Lee) for her Contribution to the Arts. Michele Baron has self-published three short books: *A Modest Menu: Poverty, Hunger and Food Security, in Poetry and Prose, A Holiday Carol: A Modern Interpretation of Dickens' "A Christmas Carol,"* and *blue wings unfolding.*

*****~~~~~*****

The Dance of a Thousand Cuts

by Liam Hogan

If the sword Ellie found tucked into the blackened trunk of a lightning-struck oak hadn't been magical, this story would have a different ending.

If it had been a normal sword, she'd never have mastered it. Those thousand cuts would have as likely been hers, not her opponents'. If it had been a normal, dumb sword, it would have been taken off the young village leader's daughter and certainly no-one would have bothered to teach her.

The *sword* taught her.

That was what it was, this is what it did. A training sword designed to teach an ancient art from an age long since passed. From the vantage point of its venerable creators, its powers weren't magical. The same technology that coaxed Ellie's hand to hold it right, that made her flex her arm just *so*, also kept the sword's edge pristine through the eons, if deliberately rather blunt.

It had done this before, for others. But not for a while. It hadn't been hidden in the blasted trunk where Ellie found it. Rather, it had been lost centuries earlier, had lain underground and undisturbed while men lived and died and returned to dust, before being lifted back to the surface and absorbed into a sapling. A sapling that grew into a mighty oak, that lived for many hundreds of years before lightning struck and liberated the sword contained within, long after the civilisation that forged it had fallen into fable and myth. An hour with this sword would teach even the most clumsy dolt the twelve basic forms. A week would lead to utter mastery.

Ellie had it for nearly two years.

True, this was not time she could fully devote to swordplay. She stole an hour here and an hour there, while supposedly collecting firewood, or wild garlic, or acorns.

Still, it was enough.

The woods whistled to the sound of the blade turning and twisting in her supple hands. In autumn, no leaves were allowed to fall that were not struck in their twisting descent. Though never cut in two. The sword was blunt, remember?

In Ellie's fourteenth year, a tournament was announced, to select the new King's new champion. Each town, each village in the land, was requested to send their best swordsman to the Capital.

When Ellie stepped forward to represent her village, everyone laughed, even her father, even her brother, Billy. Especially her brother; a strapping man five years Ellie's senior, with visions of fame, of glory.

"But father!" he protested, when the one-sided contest was over, when none were found to stand against her flashing blade.

"But Billy nothing," grunted his father, her father; the village leader. "Can *you* best her?"

His sullen silence was answer enough.

"Then it is clear. She goes in your place. Remember son, honour at the King's tourney reflects back on this village. Pray she does well."

In the Capital, surrounded by Knights and men-at-arms from all corners of the Kingdom, she had every right to feel nervous. Even more so when it was explained that no, she couldn't use her training sword. Handed a poorly balanced replacement, she danced the dance of a thousand cuts as a warm up. Flawlessly, elegantly, the blade a blur of light and whispered sound. The training sword had long since stopped having to correct her movements, even for a dance as complicated as this one.

And, just like that, the tournament was over.

Her open-mouthed opposition sidled away into the crowds, sheathing their swords or just letting them fall, never to dare pick one up again for fear of facing an opponent such as she. It didn't take much imagination to feel those one thousand cuts and the slow death caused by that keen-edge.

A Courtier escorted Ellie into the Castle. In a private chamber, he told her the true nature of her uncontested victory: she was to fight the heir to the throne.

"It is tradition," the Courtier explained. "The Prince proves himself worthy by besting the greatest swordsman—or woman—in the land."

"And if he loses?" Ellie asked, wide-eyed.

"Then he is not worthy."

Ellie frowned, toyed with the frayed rope belt that cinched her faded dress. "It's not a *fair* contest, is it?"

The Courtier smiled thinly. This was breaking his heart. He had a daughter Ellie's age. He was thankful this would be his last Royal duty.

"No, child; it is not."

Ellie nodded, thoughtful. "Then I wish to fight the Prince with my own sword."

"But it is blunt!" the Courtier exclaimed.

"I may leave my mark upon the future King, but I will not dishonour my father or my village by drawing Royal blood."

The Courtier stifled a sob, blinked away tears. Screwed his courage to perform one last betrayal. "We will respect your wishes, bravest of girls. But, in order to satisfy the. . . um, protocols, we must prepare your sword for its place in the Arena's weapon rack."

. . .

The Prince stood before Ellie and bowed deeply. Uncertain of the "protocols," she bowed back. The audience of nobles and visiting dignitaries arrayed in the steep fencing arena tittered in astonishment, drawing a blush from both young contestants.

The Prince raised his jewelled rapier in salute and adopted the first form.

Ellie blinked. He performed the manoeuvre well enough. But surely this was child's play? Was she merely to trade forms with this handsome young Prince, rather than crossing blades?

She mimicked the move, right down to the slight hesitation in his final flourish.

The audience murmured its approval. Here were two equally matched opponents. They had suspected a fraud. A girl, that young? Even though the Prince was a mere lad, the supposed contest insulted the intelligence of the assembled spectators. But the swordplay put paid to such fears. How many of the forms would these two complete, they wondered? And who would emerge victorious?

The Prince perhaps had entertained similar doubts—it was difficult to believe that this slip of a girl had scared away the best swordsmen in his army. And the rumour that she had performed the legendary dance of a thousand cuts—ridiculous!

He too had feared he faced an innocent plucked from the crowd. Perhaps as an attempt to discredit him. After all, besting a girl not yet grown into a woman; where was the honour in that?

More confident, he performed the second form, his steel drawing smoothly through the unresisting air, remembering his lessons from those exotic foreigners his father employed for the purpose. Remembering their admonishments not to overextend his elbows; to let the weight of the sword do the work.

Exhilarated, he took a pace back, to watch Ellie attempt to follow his lead.

She smiled up at him. Cocked her head and *danced* through the form.

Connoisseurs in the galleried stands gasped and rose to their feet in admiration.

On they performed. As the stations increased in difficulty, the Prince's supple body gleamed with perspiration. But while each successfully completed form brought him yet more to life, Ellie felt oddly leaden. It was as if her trusty sword not only no longer responded when she fumbled a move, but was actively sucking the feeling from the fingers of her right hand.

For the seventh move, she switched the blade to her left, and the audience gasped as the thrilling perfection returned once again.

The Prince shook the sweat from his brow. He had thought he had reached and surmounted Ellie's abilities. Had she been toying with him? Was she left-handed all along? The way she performed the difficult eighth move—now it was *he* who was out of his depth.

On the ninth form, muscles straining, he made his first mistake. A thrust where a parry was required. An error that left him overextended, vulnerable. He could almost hear the accented curse of his fencing tutor.

Embarrassed, he hardly dared watch as Ellie took flight, her young face strained with concentration. He assumed it was because of the difficulty of the level and not because she could no longer feel the grip of her sword with either hand.

As in a perfect mirror, though, her left to his right, she copied his mistake. The Prince narrowed his eyes. Was this a compliment, or an insult?

The audience bubbled with excitement. This was swordplay of the highest order. Few attained such ranks as these and none so young.

Half-way through the eleventh form, Ellie's sight dimmed, the images separating, her eyes seemingly losing their ability to work together. The doubled vision almost made her falter, and only muscle memory allowed her to complete the complicated sequence.

Blinking, she watched the Prince hesitate. He thought—for the first time—that he might have edged the manoeuvre; that her positioning and execution was not as accomplished as his, that not only did she not, on this occasion, copy his faults, but had made some of her own. She had obviously reached her limits.

The problem was, so had he. He had never completed the twelfth form successfully. It was an order of magnitude more difficult than its predecessors. Though he had been coaxed through its individual steps, the whole had always defeated him.

Still. He had long since exceeded his own expectations, as had this waif of a girl before him. Gone were his worries that the contest was fixed, that his opponent was deliberately inexperienced, or had in some way been weakened. The comments and glances of his Courtiers had made him fear it so. It was shameful, and his protestations that this must be a fair fight had only encouraged insincere avowals that it *was* fair.

And indeed, the fight had been fought on merit. More: if he was to win, he needed to complete—for the first time—the twelfth form; an achievement that would automatically qualify him as a sword master. Nail that and there was no way Ellie could follow.

The young Prince summoned his nerve, calling upon his long line of Royal ancestors to help.

Ellie stood, panting, squinting. It was hard to tell through her blurred vision, but it seemed the Prince had completed the final form. All she had to do was match him and then the contest could begin in earnest.

She had wondered how the duel was to be fixed. Had assumed the judges would not be impartial, would favour the Prince. But they'd been more subtle than that, hadn't they?

Her limbs were leaden, and she could not see.

She could have laughed, had she the energy. She'd been prepared to cross her blunt sword with the Prince's sharp one. Prepared, if need be, to let him strike home a blow, to receive a cut that her blade could not inflict.

The poison had not been necessary. Yes, poison: it was obvious. Poison that sapped her strength and her skill. That would surely kill her, if the Prince's sword did not; once they were through with the trivialities of the twelve forms.

Somehow she knew there was no cure, no antidote. Such a terrible, pointless waste! Anger battled with her tiredness, lost out to the sapping toxin in her veins.

So be it. In her final actions she would at least bestow honour on her village, on her father, on her brother. She closed her eyes. Felt the hushed silence of the Royal arena. And *danced*.

Despite the numb feeling, the tunnel vision, the lump in her throat that made swallowing difficult and had begun to hamper her breathing. Despite her young heart pounding like it had never pounded before. Despite all of this, Ellie's dance was faultless. It was, after all, a form she had danced hundreds of times.

The watching crowd erupted into rapturous applause. No contest fought in this hallowed arena had ever reached this point before.

If it had been independently judged, Ellie would have won. The twelfth form alone would have guaranteed it. But no such independent judge could be found, not on the Prince's Coronation day, not for an opponent who had no right to still be standing, let alone flashing her sword.

With solemn reverence, the announcement was made: a draw. The winner would be decided by the drawing of first blood.

Even before the Prince had a chance to process this, while he stood, staring slack-jawed up at the Courtier who had made the announcement, Ellie summoned up the last of her nerve and stumbled forward onto his outstretched sword. She felt its cold tip pierce her stuttering heart and gasped her final breath.

. . .

The Prince was crowned an hour later, tears still wet on his cheeks. The following day he issued his first Royal Decree. The Courtier and the Royal Physician were arrested on charges of treason.

The Physician died by his own hand; swallowing poison from a hollowed-out pearl button on his jerkin, the same poison that had been smeared on the hilt of Ellie's magical training sword.

As for the loyal Courtier, he was hung, drawn, and quartered. Who knows? Perhaps he would have suffered the dance of the thousand cuts, were there anyone alive who could perform it.

About the Author

Liam Hogan is an Oxford Physics graduate and award-winning London-based writer. His short story, "Ana," appears in *Best of British Science Fiction 2016* (NewCon Press). His twisted fantasy collection, *Happy Ending Not Guaranteed,* is published by Arachne Press. See http://happyendingnotguaranteed.blogspot.co.uk/, or tweet @LiamJHogan

*****~~~~~*****

The Occasional Cabin

by Stefon Mears

The wrong birds woke me up.

Wrong birds, like I'm some kind of bird guy who could tell a swallow from. . . well, any of a bunch of other kinds of birds. I'm a New Yorker. If it's not a pigeon or a seagull—a sky rat, basically—it's pretty much a bird to me.

My point is, I heard birds singing. That just isn't something I hear when I'm sleeping in my Upper East Side apartment. Not in my neighborhood. No matter how late I stay in bed.

Cars, sure. Planes, copters, horns, sirens, people yelling, my neighbor's television. Those were the sorts of things I heard from my bed.

And my own bed was, in fact, where I went to sleep last night. Right in good old Manhattan.

Even if it isn't where I woke up.

No, I heard those birds singing, and a chill went straight down my spine and yanked me out of what *had* been a pretty darn good dream.

No, I'm not sharing the details of the dream. Some things should be private.

But the cabin. I'll share everything I can think of about this place. In case anyone who ever finds this little notebook can tell me where the hell it is, and how the hell I keep ending up here.

Or maybe my words will help the next guy who finds himself here.

But I'm getting off track.

It started with the birds this time.

When I lay my head down last night, good ergonomic pillow. Nice, high-thread-count sheets. Comfortable mattress, just the right firmness with the kind of pillow top that costs extra.

Then, the birds yanked me out of that dream, and my surroundings were not the blissful comfort I'd spent extra on.

I jerked awake on an old, army surplus cot. Stiff sheets underneath me, and scratchy woolen blanket covering me. The smell of old must recently aired out. Warm, but not the kind of heat I'd expect in June in Manhattan.

But then, wherever the cabin is, it's sure not in Manhattan.

The cot's parked way in the corner. Dark wood all around me. Uneven floorboards. Glazed logs for the walls.

. .

No. Not glazed. What do they call that? Laminated? No. That's not— Lacquered. That's it.

Yeah, woods aren't my specialty either. But I was getting to know the cabin pretty well by now. This was the third time I'd woken up here in the last two months.

And this time, well, one way or the other, it was going to be the last.

. . .

First time I woke up in the cabin was two months ago, just after Renata dumped me.

Man, that was a rough breakup. I'd thought for sure she was The One. I'd even started a separate savings account for our eventual wedding or honeymoon, depending on whether her family was going to chip in.

But it all came slamming down on me that night, out of the blue. Months later, I still don't know exactly why it was she dumped me. She was like a different person.

One moment, sweet and caring. Funny. Quick to tell me all about her day down at the museum, and listen to mine over at the foundation. She even seemed to actually enjoy my stories about grant writing, and if that didn't make her a keeper, I didn't know what would.

Then, she came over after work one Thursday, and all of a sudden I couldn't do anything right.

The Chinese food I'd ordered for us was all wrong, even though beef with broccoli, eggrolls, and shrimp fried rice was one of our three usual orders. She didn't want to talk about work for the first time, but refused to say why. She interrupted the story I told about a grant I'd gotten the foundation—and this was the first time ever she'd interrupted me—and started railing about how there were more important causes than heart research.

No, she didn't list any. And despite all my attempts to find out where this was coming from and what was really bothering her, she refused to tell me. This wasn't one of those *if you don't know I'm not going to tell you* games either. Renata didn't play that.

I swear, it was like she came over that night looking for excuses to break up with me. Maybe she did.

It made for the roughest night I'd had since NYU, when Lara, my first real girlfriend, admitted she'd started seeing another guy on the side. Roughest maybe since my parents told me they were splitting up, and that was back during my freshman year of high school.

And that night, the night after Renata left, after I finally managed to get to sleep, I woke up in the cabin for the first time.

. . .

No wifi at the cabin. No landline. And the only time my phone was with me, I couldn't even get a roaming signal, much less any data stream.

Isolated, in more ways than one. It sits all alone in the mountains, facing the rising sun. Little lake nearby, surrounded by. . . evergreens of some stripe. Lots of bushy undergrowth, too, and if anyone had ever cut a path to this place, it vanished long ago.

On the first trip, I had to cut my own path twenty feet outside the front door to the old pump—clean well water, at least—using the machete that hangs just inside the front door.

The cabin's a roomy place, considering it has only one room. Nice, high ceiling. Stone-and-mortar fireplace that's always going, even if I don't add logs from the stack nearby. A couch, coffee table, and a pair of chairs all fashioned from the same wood as the cabin—far as I can tell, anyway—but they're comfortable enough.

An old-fashioned icebox sits in the corner, stocked with meats and vegetables. Next to it, a couple of cabinets and drawers with a single serving of dishware, plus coffee and a pot. A handful of books rests on a shelf near the fireplace, none of them published since 1956. The titles didn't tell me anything more about where I was or why I was here than the deer head. None of the books were even famous. The most interesting title was *On the South Side*, which, I think, says it all. I tried reading them, but they were all dry as dust. Not exactly the kind of thrillers I picked up on my own.

There are four windows in the cabin, one on either side of the door and two more on the opposite wall. The shutters are closed when I wake up.

No closet. No chest of drawers. Two wooden pegs near the door, but nothing hangs on them.

No paintings on the walls, either, but there is a deer head mounted opposite the fireplace. Buck.

Seventeen points on its antlers. I know that, because I tried to find significance in the number seventeen.

The main thing I discovered in my research between trips is that looking for significance in random numbers is a quick trip to a very crazy place.

And, well, I confess. I tried asking the deer head questions on my second visit. Sat right down on the dark wooden floor in front of it, and tried introducing myself, complimenting the deer on his cabin, and asking where I was, why I was there. That kind of thing.

So, if you find this notebook, don't bother asking the deer. He doesn't talk.

. . .

I tried thinking over my last night in Manhattan, as I stood, stretched and worked out the kinks of a night on an old army cot.

Didn't get very far though. Just about as soon as I stood up I realized something *was* different this time.

I was wearing pajamas.

I always slept in silk boxers. Even if I wore briefs that day to go running in Central Park, I changed into boxers to sleep. I just like the feel of silk on my skin.

But I woke up this morning wearing striped, flannel pajamas. Blue and white.

Well, they'd once been blue and white. The blue had faded to a kind of purple, and the white was more of a cream.

All right. I confess, I screamed like a baby, tore off those pajamas and ran around naked for a few minutes until I calmed down.

I mean, waking up in a strange place was bad enough. But *I* sure as hell didn't dress myself in those pajamas.

For the first time, it occurred to me that someone might have been watching me.

And here I'd just gotten naked.

117

"Fine," I said aloud to whoever might have been listening. "I'll put the damn pajamas back on. Hope you enjoyed the show, you perv."

I didn't feel any better getting dressed again, though.

What did make me feel better was combing the place for microphones and cameras. It gave me something to focus on for a while.

I didn't find anything, though. And far as I could tell, there were no wires of any kind running to the place either. I even walked around the cabin once, to make sure.

Watched the surrounding trees out of my peripheral vision as I did that. Sly as a spy, that's me. Didn't see anyone though. Didn't even hear any kind of rustling in the woods. No signs of animal activity at all, except the. . . singing. . . birds.

I got out the machete and cut a path over to the tree line.

I was going to find these birds. Memorize what they looked like. Then, the next time I woke up at home, I could look up those birds on the 'net. I figured it might give me some idea of where the cabin is.

I didn't see any birds, though. And the songs stopped, once I got closer.

This was when things got weird. Well, relatively speaking, I mean.

I noticed the second the bird songs stopped. And they stopped in the middle of their trilling, chirping pattern. But there was no sound of flapping wings. No rustling of branches to indicate birds taking to the air.

The songs just stopped. Dead.

I tried holding still for a while. Didn't help. The birds didn't start singing. Tried sitting down, but that didn't do it either.

Finally, I gave up and went back into the cabin.

The moment the door closed behind me, the birds started singing.

. . .

The second time I showed up in the cabin, I'd been terrified I was going to get fired.

It was the stupidest thing. Complete misunderstanding.

I'm kind of my own department, at work. The other two departments are for the annual fund, and for major gifts. Both those departments have about a half-dozen people working in them.

But it only takes one person to research and write grant proposals. So before I got there, the person doing the gig got bounced back and forth between the annual fund and major gifts, depending on the focus for the year. Then someone got the bright idea of putting grants in its own category with its own budget.

Great financial sense. Lonely as hell sometimes.

So, whenever I needed a break, I wandered down into one of the other offices for a little chatter and human contact. And since I didn't *really* belong there, I made sure to bring jokes, funny anecdotes, and stories that might make sure people were happy to see me.

I mean, nobody wants to talk to the guy who complains all the time.

This was a Friday, maybe an hour before quitting time. I was done for the day, and so were a couple of the guys in major gifts, so the three of us were standing around the Coke machine, swapping jokes.

I was telling this one about the elephant who worked at the dump, and got to the punchline: he got the job 'cause he had the most junk in his trunk.

Well, walking behind me, as I said that, was a major donor. Very nice woman. One of those old money types who decides that her forties are when she needs to give more than just her money to a cause, so she'd been chatting with our major gifts director about volunteer opportunities.

She heard the words "junk" and "trunk" and came to a very wrong conclusion about what I'd just been saying.

Nothing like spending the last work day of the week getting screamed at by the major gifts director, then the director of development herself.

My explanation didn't make things better. I left that day expecting to get a call over the weekend telling me not to come in Monday.

. . .

The birds.

The birds are the key. I get that now. Sorry if I'm getting less legible. I need to get all this down while I think of it.

The first time I woke up here, I thought I woke up on my own. I was wrong. The birds were quieter, but they were singing. I remember lying there on the cot that first time staring at the ceiling and listening to the birds as I tried to stop hyperventilating.

The second time. I think it was the birds who woke me up then too. I just didn't catch on, because I was dealing with the shock of realizing I was back.

See, I'd convinced myself that I'd dreamed the cabin that first time.

Sure, I never really remember my dreams, but it made more sense than anything else.

So I lay there in the cot that second time, trying to deal with the fact that it wasn't a dream. Key point, whoever finds this notebook, this isn't a dream. Don't believe me? Read this sentence carefully. Then look away. Then read it again. Try it a couple of times.

Exactly the same every time, isn't it? Dreams don't work that way. I did some research after my second. . .

That doesn't matter right now. Any more than my rumbling, empty belly.

The birds. They're what matter.

They're the only living thing around here, except me. They're here every time. And they shy away when I approach.

I think they're bringing me here. And I'm going to go find out why.

Maybe *how*, if I can, but definitely *why*.

. . .

There are no birds.

I left the cabin without the machete for the first time. I figured it might look too aggressive.

All right, so birds shouldn't be able to tell if I'm holding a machete or not, but it made sense to me. And I may not have been entirely in my right mind.

As if my state of mind is any better now. . .

Anyway.

I started toward the south side of the cabin, where the singing was loudest. I moved as slowly and quietly as I could, but let's be honest here. That wasn't very. I mean, my idea of nature is Central Park.

I trampled leaves and broke twigs every step or two. Marveled that I'd managed not to break my skin in the process.

Of course, that part makes more sense now.

Anyway, I got to the tree line. The birds stopped singing. So I started talking to them in that baby voice I've heard people use with cats and dogs. Little stupid nothings, trying to reassure the birds that I wasn't going to hurt them and I just wanted to talk.

No, I didn't hear any wings, or chirps, or even see a branch rustle. But I'd heard the singing. Birds had to be here somewhere, right?

Wrong.

I went deeper and deeper into the forest. Maybe a hundred yards from the cabin, where the sunlight was dappled through the branches, and the air smelled like those evergreens.

Then I reached the edge.

121

One moment, it seemed as though the forest went on forever. Then I bumped against air.

But it wasn't air. It felt rubbery to the touch, and when I leaned forward and held very still, I could see something that wasn't more forest, hiding behind a kind of rainbow sheen, like the edge of a soap bubble.

And I saw stars. I don't just mean a night sky, either. I mean, I saw endless stars, twinkling different colors. Pretty sure I saw some kind of a red. . . nebula? Is that the right word?

I hope it's the right word. Because I'm pretty sure I'm never going to get to do research. Not this time. I've seen through the bubble, and I can't even pretend it's a dream any more.

If I were sweating like this in a dream, my heart pounding like it was trying to give an elephant a heart attack, I'd wake up. Done it before. Jolted out of a nightmare that way. Didn't remember the nightmare though.

The cabin I always remember.

And what I saw through the bubble, that I know I'll remember too.

Whoever brought me here, I'm pretty sure they know that. After I dashed back inside the cabin, screaming, the birds didn't start singing again.

They still haven't. It's dead quiet out there.

It's probably hopeless to think anyone's going to find this, but I'm going to hide it anyway. Try to pretend everything's all right. Make some coffee. Prep some scrambled eggs and bacon, with cheddar cheese.

Pretend I expect to wake up tomorrow back in my Manhattan apart like nothing's wrong.

Still, I'll keep the machete close at hand, in case they come for me. They may take me, but I'll make sure I don't die cheap.

I'm going to hide my notes. If the next subject is lucky, maybe he'll find them. Behind the books maybe, or in the pantry. And the notebook itself, I'll leave only half-hidden.

In the notebook, I'll just leave one message.
Don't follow the birds.

About the Author

Stefon Mears earned his MFA in Creative Writing from Northwest Institute of Literary Arts, and his BA in Religious Studies (double emphasis in Ritual and Mythology) from U.C. Berkeley. Stefon's short pieces have sold to magazines such as *Fireside* and *Strange Horizons* and to anthologies edited by Kevin J. Anderson, Denise Little, Kerrie L. Hughes, and John Helfers. He has published twenty books to date, including the "Rise of Magic" series. Look for him online at http://www.stefonmears.com, on GooglePlus, or @stefonmears on Twitter. Sign up for his newsletter at stefonmears.com/join

*****~~~~~*****

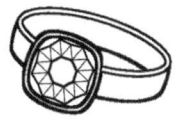

Captain Carthy's Bride

by K.G. Anderson

The mid-day sun seared the rocky shore. Seaweed baked, periwinkles shriveled in their shells, and the acrid smells of life and death rose and fell on the sighing waves. At the sound of a truck stopping on the cliff above, Sheila O'Farrell quickly lay back on the narrow spit of sand and closed her eyes.

Footsteps coming down the cliffside trail. A rattle and clank from the pathway suggested someone had set down a fishing rod and bucket of bait. *The young sea captain, for sure!* Sheila imagined him raising the admiralty binoculars he wore on a leather strap around his neck.

Sheila lay naked, her flame-red hair spread out like a corona. She lay with delicate ankles crossed, pale arms flung wide, and small breasts bared to the sun's heat. Behind her on the rocks a sealskin lay where she'd placed it earlier, glistening in the sun. *A selkie's coat.*

There was a soft crunching of sand and steps on the pathway. The walker stopped near the sealskin. Sheila bit her lip. *He's taking the bait.* She imagined Rob Carthy lifting the selkie's coat, the velvety fur redolent of brine and the sun, holding it warm and heavy in his big hands.

The footsteps retreated. Sheila raised her head to steal a glance at the rocks. The sealskin was gone. *He'll hide the coat in his truck, and then—he'll be back for me.*

Sheila guessed right. Carthy returned to find her acting out a search for the missing sealskin. She hobbled, her feet slipping in the hot sand as though her ankles were weak. Her tiny hands splayed flat on the rocks as if her legs could not support her weight on land.

"Miss!" he called out. "I have your coat. We all know the rules. I've brought a shirt to cover you, and I'll carry you up the path."

Sheila straightened up and gazed at the young sea captain with her sea-green eyes. She'd heard how he'd been decorated in the Great War, how he'd been newly promoted to the rank of captain. She'd heard that he prided himself on being a fair man. She watched as he licked his lips, chapped and salty, and saw him watching the sway of her breasts.

Sheila started toward him, then stopped and turned to take a last look at the sea. Little waves splashed and hissed on the sand, spitting foam. She scanned the shallow water at the edge of the cove, and, though the sun beat down, she shivered. Turning back to her captor, Sheila nodded and began ankling awkwardly toward him across the sand, her arms extended.

The captain met her halfway and dropped to his knees before her. Shrugging out of his blue linen shirt, he wrapped her tiny body, flushed with sunburn, in the weathered cloth. He tenderly rolled the cuffs above her wrists, while her wild red hair, stiff with sea-salt, whipped against his face. Then he picked her up and carried her, light and unprotesting, up the path. He set her in the passenger seat of the truck's high cab, patted her arm reassuringly, and closed the heavy door.

Sheila bowed her head and sighed as she waited for Carthy to walk around to the driver's side and get in. It had gone just as she'd planned. A deep shuddering breath. There'd be no turning back.

As he drove them out of Carmogh, Sheila nestled against him, ducking her head—not from shyness, but from the fear of being spotted by someone who might recognize her. He drove straight down the coast to his house in Kilronen. The village inn where he'd been staying in Carmogh sent his bags after them.

. . .

In her new life as Captain Carthy's selkie bride— he named her Moira—Sheila soon acquired human ways. Perhaps too quickly. But Carthy, madly in love, never suspected. The selkie soon spoke quite well, with a charming rural accent. He told people she'd picked it up from their housekeeper. Her ankles strengthened. She was able to walk and even dance, though she always favored lace-up boots over slippers and shoes.

When she began to go out in Kilronen, Moira was the subject of much interest. The captain had been an eligible bachelor, and many of the ladies of the town were bitter to discover he'd brought home a wife from somewhere on his travels. The couple were reticent about her origins, each for their own reasons. Gossip had it that she was an island beauty he'd won in a pub fight in the Hebrides.

Too close for comfort, Moira thought, when she thought about it—which was rarely, because Moira was all too busy learning how to fulfill her dream of being a captain's wife. While never elegant, she developed an air of competence and satisfaction. And she truly doted on Carthy.

She knew that her husband watched her closely for signs of longing for her native sea. Did the selkie let her errands draw her near the harbor, where his company's ships were moored? She made sure that he saw no sign of it. In fact, quite the opposite. Moira actively avoided the harbor and even refused strolls on the scenic esplanade.

When the family (they soon had a boy and a girl) vacationed, Moira was the one insisting that the family go inland. She told Carthy she liked visiting castles and mills.

Did she ever hunt for her marvelous coat, a selkie's only route back to the sea? Again, he would see no indications. But even if his wife had searched, her search would have been in vain. For Carthy had hidden the lush coat in a secret panel of the wall of the purser's office on one of the company's smaller ships—a vessel that even he rarely boarded.

It was only after their son, Young Rob, had gone off to university and their daughter, Alison, a sweet-faced girl with her father's raven hair, had married and moved up the coast, that the trouble began.

. . .

On the night of the first autumn storm, the sound of the crashing waves woke Moira from her sleep. She slipped out of their big feather bed and stepped out into the hall, just in time to see a foaming wave rush down the narrow wooden staircase from the attic. Her scream brought her husband stumbling out into the hall in his nightshirt. She pointed a trembling finger at the damp stairs.

"It's only a roof leak," the captain said, urging her back to their bed. But Moira could not be consoled. She sat up all night with the lights on and, in the morning, threw clothes into a bag and decamped to a hotel to await repairs. She returned to find that a flood had occurred in their kitchen.

The contractor Carthy summoned was puzzled over the water's source. "Would you look at this here?"

Moira trembled as the workman toed a stubborn white rime the flood had left on the linoleum. The man shook his head. "You'd think it was salt water."

Now Moira was afraid to take baths. She insisted that a creature from the drain would seize her by the neck and pull her under the water. Carthy installed a modern handheld spray fixture to enable her to wash. But she fretted that the shower water smelled of seaweed and tasted of brine.

When the children came for the holidays, Moira put on a brave face. But they knew something was wrong. Terror had streaked their mother's red hair with gray, and her appearance verged on the unkempt. They took their father aside and urged him to action. He agreed.

"I think your mother and I should move," Carthy announced that night as the family sat down to dinner. "I'm near to retirement and a move somewhere smaller and cozier would make perfect sense."

Moira, seating her grandson Kerry at the lace-draped table, broke into a delighted smile. The captain reached into his tweed jacket and pulled out a sheaf of brochures. "I've consulted an estate agent. There are some wonderful properties up by Carmogh, where we met so long ago—"

"No!" Moira paled and hurried from the room, leaving her soup untouched.

"What is *Mamó* so afraid of?" Kerry asked. The adults exchanged looks. No one could answer.

. . .

The village of Carmogh had changed not a whit, Moira saw. She parked her Vauxhall Cadet on a side street and picked her way across the wet cobblestones. The Widow O'Farrell's whitewashed cottage looked as shabby as ever. Moira tried to peer through a lace-curtained window. Useless. Taking a deep breath, she rapped on the green door.

"Who is it?" The quavering voice from within was familiar.

"It's me."

There were sounds of someone cursing, and a cane tapping the slate floor.

"Wasn't expecting visitors." A bent, gray-haired woman peered out and frowned at the city woman on her

129

doorstep. Moira suddenly regretted wearing tailored trousers instead of a proper tweed skirt.

"May I—?"

"Yes, yes, come in."

The old woman turned and limped to the tiled hearth and began prodding the peat fire. Moira closed the door behind her and stood on the mat, looking shyly around the dim-lit room. The kitchen table was set for a simple tea for two people: Cups, teapot, bread loaf, butter, and a dish of jam.

"Do. . . do you remember me?" Moira asked.

"And should I?"

Moira licked her lips. "I'm Sheila. Sheila O'Farrell. Your daughter."

The old woman tottered back a few steps and sank into a kitchen chair. She patted the worn linen tablecloth until she found her wire-rimmed glasses. She pulled them on and peered hard into Moira's green eyes. She nodded, slowly. "We thought you was dead."

The old woman's tone was accusing, but her voice trembled. "They found all your clothing down at the cove. A drowning, the police said. The Pairson boys claimed they saw a girl who looked like you leaving town with a man in a truck. But, when you never wrote. . . "

Moira took in the shabby surroundings. Her family's cottage looked much the same as it had on the bright September day twenty-five years earlier that she'd walked down to the beach to wait for the captain. A tear ran down her cheek, making a dark stain on her expensive wool jacket.

"I'm married, Ma," she said, tasting on her tongue the rich brogue she'd suppressed for so many years. "He's a rich man."

"That I can see." The old woman looked pointedly at the gold-and-diamond rings that sparkled on Moira's fingers. "Children?"

"Yes. Two." But Moira stopped, as always cautious about revealing any details of her past.

The old woman got up and fetched a third cup from the sideboard. She placed it on the table, and poured. Only then did Moira come to the table and, gingerly, sit down at what had once been her place.

"Too good for Johnny Ahearn, you were," her mother said, her tone more wistful than accusing.

"Johnny Ahearn was a drunk, Ma." Moira took the filled teacup the old woman pushed toward her. A familiar blue rose pattern, the porcelain now stained and chipped. "How are Olivia and Caitlin?"

Mrs. O'Farrell shook her head. "It's gone badly for us. Poor Olivia died, just after you left; she was always sickly. Caitlin—oh, Caitlin. She'll be coming by shortly to bring me the shopping and have her tea. If she remembers. I'm afraid Caitlin's in a bad way, Sheila. A drinker, just like your da."

The old woman sighed. "When she sees those fancy clothes of yours, she'll be asking you for money."

Moira took a sip of the Assam tea, dark and rich with memories. She put her slim white hand, with its gleaming gold rings, over her mother's gnarled one.

The old woman did not resist. "Have you come back to us now?"

Had she? Moira took another sip. But this time she choked and spat the liquid into her palm. To her horror, the tea had turned bitter and salty, a harsh reminder of the reason for her visit.

"Ma," she whispered. "Ma, I've done something terrible."

"Oh, no, I don't blame you for leaving this place."

"It's not the leaving," Moira said. "It's how I left. Ma, I wanted a proper husband, not a drunk like Johnny Ahearn. But what man would want to marry the girl who cleans the toilets at the inn? When that captain from the city came to town on his fishing trip, I heard him talking in the pub. I saw my chance. I pretended to be a selkie and let him capture me."

The old woman gave a rusty chuckle. "You told the poor man you were a selkie? And he believed you?"

"I waited for him on the beach. I pretended to have trouble walking. I let him teach me how to talk." Moira faltered, putting into words the story she'd kept secret for so many years. "I let him find the selkie's coat."

"Now where'd you get a selkie's coat?" Her mother frowned. "You fooled the man with some ratty old sealskin, did you?"

"No." Moira stopped. Perhaps she'd said too much. She half stood to go, then sank back down in the old kitchen chair and made her confession. "Ma, I killed the selkie. Killed her with a rock as she lay sunning on the beach. Then I stole the coat she'd left there. I rolled her body into the sea and let the tide take it."

Moira shuddered, remembering the sight of the pale body as it slipped beneath a sparkling green wave.

"You didn't," the old woman whispered.

Moira nodded. In the silence, the peat fire smoked and crackled.

"Killed a selkie," the old woman muttered, shaking her head. "That's bad."

She looked sharply at her daughter. "And she's come for you now?"

"Yes. Ma, there's seawater everywhere in our house. I thought, after so many years, I'd be safe, but—"

"You need to be going." The old woman waved a gnarled hand. "Go as far from the sea as you can."

Moira reached over to touch her mother's arm. But the old woman pulled away, darting glances around the cottage as if expecting seawater to rush in under her own door. "Go now."

"I'm sorry, Ma," Moira said, standing up.

The old woman shooed her. "Far away."

132

Moira left the shabby cottage and walked along the grimy cobblestones to where she'd parked her car. The route she took as she drove out of Carmogh was not the main motorway on which she'd come from Kilronen. It was the winding coast road that overlooked the cove where, so many years before, she'd killed the selkie. Where she'd waited for Rob Carthy.

When she reached the pullout above the cove, Moira stopped her car and stepped out into a rising wind.

. . .

"I'm going home," her note had said.

As soon as he found it, Rob Carthy drove down to the harbor. He boarded the old freighter and removed the oilskin bundle he'd hidden in the bulkhead a quarter century ago. The selkie's coat, still smelling of brine and the sun. With the coat plush and glistening on the seat beside him, he sped up the motorway to Carmogh. He found his wife's car parked on a side street, and waited, watching as she emerged from a dilapidated cottage. He followed her out of town as she drove to the lonely coast. He recognized the road she took.

Tears filled Carthy's eyes. He'd stolen a selkie from her home, kept her from the sea. He remembered the hot sun on the bright sparkling sea, the coat glistening silver on the rocks, the firmness of her body as he'd carried her up from the sea.

He'd committed a terrible sin, keeping a sea creature trapped for years. She'd held up nobly, borne their children, been a loving wife. He should have known the day would come, that the call of the sea would become irresistible. She would be compelled to return to the frigid green waters. And without the coat he'd so cruelly hidden from her, she would die.

Parking his truck behind her car, the captain took the coat in his arms. He sighed with relief when he spotted his wife, his selkie, poised on the cliff above the dark swirling waters that were her home. She'd released her hair from its neat chignon and it flew around her head like red and silver ribbons.

Moira turned as her husband approached. At the sight of the selkie's coat, she screamed and stepped back, stumbling dangerously close to the cliff edge.

Carthy reached out a hand, catching hers, and pulled her to him. She sobbed piteously. He kissed the top of her head and thought how he would miss her. "My dear, sweet wife. Please forgive me for taking you from the sea."

He drew the sumptuous sealskin, smelling of the long-ago sea, over her shoulders.

Moira flinched. Then she looked up at Rob, her green eyes wide and bright with tears. She nodded slowly. With his forefinger, he traced the faint smile on her lovely lips.

He lifted her in his arms as he had on the day they met. He took a few steps to the cliff's edge. Then he lofted her clear of the ledge and watched as his selkie tumbled down, down, down and vanished into the angry sea.

About the Author

K.G. Anderson writes short fiction—fantasy, space opera, alternate history, Weird West tales, near-future science fiction, and mystery. Her stories appear in anthologies including *The Mammoth Book of Jack the Ripper Stories, Triangulation: Appetites*, and *More Alternative Truths*, as well as online at *Metaphorosis, Every Day Fiction, Luna Station Quarterly*, and at the podcast *Far Fetched Fables*. She studied at the Viable Paradise and Taos Toolbox workshops.

A journalist and technology writer, K.G. has lived much of her life within walking distance of salt water— Nantucket Sound, Long Island Sound, the Ligurian Sea, the Sea of Sardinia, and Puget Sound. She currently lives in a historic fishing community just north of Seattle with her partner, bookseller Tom Whitmore. Find out more about K.G.'s fiction at http://writerway.com/fiction

*****~~~~~*****

Scales, Fallen from His Eyes
by Kelly A. Harmon

I heard the limping footsteps approach my lair long before he spoke—the steps heavy and slow, though this century's scientific advances could have hidden them even from *my* senses. Time was, there was nothing that could sneak up on a dragon. Technology had changed all that. My time is long past, yet, here I am. The same could be said for this world.

"Eat me," the knight said, his head appearing above the hill. He wore no armor, and leaned heavily on a crutch. A sodden bandage wrapped his left thigh, and I could smell the fetid odor of rot before he came into view. It must have taken him hours to climb the hill in that condition. "Eat me—and put me out my misery."

I nodded my head and breathed a spiral of smoke upward in greeting. "Sir, Knight."

He stopped just shy of the crest of the hill, a surprised look on his face. "*Soldier*—but how did you know?"

Ah, yes. Soldier is what they're calling them these days. I sometimes forget, as lonely as I am. Clad in denim and boots, he looked more like an injured farmer than a warrior, but his shorn hair and the way he held his shoulders—pulled back and stiff, even as he leaned on the crutch—made me certain he once sustained his own existence by killing other living things. Perhaps we'd sparred even before this chat.

No, I'd never fought this man. Humans had managed to create extremely long lives for themselves, but I'd outlived my adversaries long before their scions found their fountain of youth—and mine.

If only they hadn't.

The soldier wobbled on his crutches, nearly falling backward down the hill. He was too far away for me to help him, but I probably wouldn't have helped anyway. It's boring being chained, as it were, upon this synthetic mountainside. He was the best diversion I've had in years. I wondered how long I could keep him talking.

"For the love of all you believe in, just get it over with and *eat me*," the warrior demanded again, his words a shallow echo between us.

On another day, I might have complied, but the order piqued my curiosity. There are better—and less painful—ways to end one's life. I found myself needing to know his reasons. There was something the soldier wasn't telling me—something he didn't want me to know. But what? And if I knew what he knew, would I refuse his gauche request?

"How old are you?"

"Does it matter?" He frowned, the lines on his forehead deepening in obvious pain. "Isn't it sufficient that I wish to die—and you could have a decent meal by it?"

Probably not. I shrugged, the great wings on my back lifting high for a moment. I wanted to spread them wide and stretch, but knew it would have scared him into doing something. . . *regrettable.* He should have known better than to provoke me, but isn't that what he wanted? Too easy, then. His attitude would buy no compliance from me. I was too interested in *why* he wanted to end his existence.

After all, I know why I want to end *mine.* But him? It didn't make any sense.

"Your age?" I insisted.

"Two hundred and eighty-three."

I caught myself nodding—as if his answer was important—and stopped. Six or seven centuries ago I would have guessed him to be thirty-three, past his middle years and on the downward slope into oblivion. The putrefaction on his leg would have guaranteed his death shortly after protracting it. But humans have learned more than I ever gave them credit for. Two-hundred-eighty-three is barely middle-age for them these days, and rot even worse than this soldier's can be cured with commonplace items in any first aid kit. And where that failed, cloned body parts can be used to replace anything.

What I wanted to know, was why he wouldn't take advantage of that.

"I *could* eat you," I told him, edging out of my lair and into the sun, and—*oh*, it felt glorious, even blocked by scattered clouds and the invisible cage that imprisoned me on this mountain top. There was nothing more life affirming than the feel of warm rays on tired skin—filtered as the rays were. Even the sun felt false.

A few of my belly scales slipped to the ground, and the despised, faceless *'bots*—the much-improved clockwork men of this era—charged out to collect the indestructible plates before I could bury them. Too bad the 'bots were fireproof and programmed to fix each other's ailments. I've long since ceased trying to destroy them. I despise the way they take pieces of me, as if it's their due.

Instantly, my mood soured. "I could eat you," I repeated, "but what does it get me?" I sharpened one claw on the cracked, granite boulder right outside the cave entrance. I could see the action frightened him, but he stood his ground. I might have admired that if he didn't smell so delicious. Not that I craved the flesh of man, mind you, but after the slop I've been forced to eat, *any* true flesh would have smelled as good.

"A meal," the soldier was quick to say.

I laughed. A deep, powerful belly laugh that made the ground beneath us tremble. The soldier startled, a look of fear crossing his face before he righted himself. I sobered just as quickly, the trembling giving away the lie of the beauteous vista. I might be a real dragon, but this verdant, lush hillock, situated overlooking a narrow valley, was naught but the product of modern-day mechanics and artisans. It was as fake as the life I was living, and growing more fragile daily as the war rages and this world spirals into decay. It was as fake as the soldier's bravado. He didn't want to die, and yet he saw no way out.

"I have no need of a meal when one is delivered anytime I desire."

The soldier chuckled this time, and I knew why he laughed. I couldn't blame him. My meals are no fancy arrangement with the locals: bringing me their succulent daughters to feast upon in exchange for *not* terrorizing the countryside. Those days are long, long gone. And in truth, I would have preferred a fat sheep—more meat—but who was I to argue?

No, my meals arrive *hot and ready* from a chute attached to the great argent box built into one side of my lair. The red button produces a tough square lump which tastes cow-like; the white, a softer lump with the flavoring of chicken; the orange—I avoid the orange button at all costs—provides a wet sluice of something strangely fish-like, the foul odor lingering for days. One push had been all that was necessary to convince me never to press the orange button again.

"So why would I want to eat you?" I said, watching his shoulders droop. "Your flesh is old—bound to be tough—and your leg is rotten. What kind of meal is that?"

Better than I'd had in months—years—though the conversation was even better. I can't remember the last time I actually talked with anyone, man or beast. No one cares to visit a real dragon these days. No one comes *outside* anymore. Who wants to, when every desire is catered to, when any experience can be bought, or bartered for?

Even dragons—*virtual* dragons—can be experienced on a screen or immersion device: talked to, ridden upon, hunted, fought with, *massacred.* It's more than I can do for them. What need of me do they have— other than a curiosity—and a purveyor of the scales they find so useful in creating their necessary armor—the *only* thing about me they cannot apparently virtualize.

The soldier struggled up the remaining distance of the hillock, the steepest part, and put his back to the boulder I'd scratched upon earlier, sliding down awkwardly, his rotten leg outstretched, until he was seated. He sighed, his breath the same putrescent odor as his injury. I needed to move him along, let him die elsewhere, so I wouldn't be annoyed by his rotting corpse for the next several weeks.

"I wasn't always a soldier. . . " he said.

I groaned. "Who doesn't have a war story to tell?" Longer lives mean longer memories—longer grudges. And since humans have learned how to prolong their lives, they've done nothing but argue and fight and go to war. No one starts their career as a soldier—but they inevitably end up as one as more and more people die in senseless combat.

". . . but the worst are the laws requiring us to use the dead for. . . *parts*. . . " He spat the last, as if it left a bad taste in his mouth. I knew what the old soldier meant. The first foray into life longevity required using replacement parts for those worn out—or destroyed—as in battle. Dead soldiers became brain-dead bodies required by law to serve as parts for those who lost them—and families not able to collect insurance until all the parts were gone. *This*, is what the world has come to. All of us fodder for the machine. None of us able to die as we should.

"and suicide is out. . . "

Of course it is, because his family would be fined or imprisoned due to his *selfishness*. His left leg might be rotten, but the rest of him would serve someone else well in fighting the enemy.

"so that's why I've come to you. . . "

Because if I ate him, there would be nothing left to use in battle. And his family could collect—because no one chooses *suicide by dragon*—and he'd be irreparably dead.

But I couldn't do it—as much as I sympathized with his story. I couldn't give him the satisfaction of a quick and *thorough* death. Why should I, when it was his kind who imprisoned me, lengthened my life, and used my parts to further their agenda?

"No."

But the soldier had kept on rambling. I had barely been listening to what he had to say, and then I heard it. Maybe he had been waiting for me to listen. He said, "It was me, you know. I was a scientist—*the* scientist—who discovered how to prolong life. I found *you.*" Tired now, after his long speech, he closed his eyes. "I found you, and I prolonged your life so that dragons could be known in the future: Your wisdom shared. Your grand selves experienced for who and what you are." He paused, the pain evident in his face. He was dying, but not fast enough, and not well enough. "Every time you eat that slop, it—" He stopped, as if thinking better of the thought, then continued, "But you have no life, like I have none. And that's why I'm here today. To help us both."

He bent and unwrapped his leg, and I got a good look at the injury: the long straight cuts from hip to knee; the puffy, putrefying flesh; and something else, something *unnatural* in the rot.

I sniffed.

And *that's* when I ate him, grabbing him quickly and snapping his neck to spare him the pain. I tossed him whole into my mouth and chewed slowly, savoring the texture, the taste—despite the rotting flesh—no, *because of it*, a single blemish on a wholly satisfying meal. The best I'd had in centuries.

And now I wait.

I continue to eat, to push the white button and eat the soft chicken-like mass, remembering the man's succulent flesh. If I don't eat, they'll come to check on me sooner—attempt to heal me. I pretend as though nothing is wrong, that the rot has not gotten into my wings so I can barely lift them, that the tip of my tail has not fallen off. My scales are beginning to slough unnaturally fast, and soon, I'll be as armorless as the knight.

After that, it shouldn't be long before I join my forebears in antiquity where I belong—and this world takes its final tumble into oblivion—unless it begins to see what I see.

About the Author

Kelly A. Harmon is an award-winning journalist and author, and a member of Science Fiction & Fantasy Writers of America. A Baltimore native, she writes the "Charm City Darkness" series. The fourth book in the series, *In the Eye of the Beholder,* is now available. Find her short fiction in many magazines and anthologies, including *Occult Detective Quarterly; Triangulation: Dark Glass;* and *Deep Cuts: Mayhem, Menace, Misery.* Visit her website at http://kellyaharmon.com, or find her on Facebook and Twitter: http://facebook.com/Kelly-A-Harmon1, @kellyaharmon.

*****~~~~~*****

Spacism Is Still With Us

by Matthew Reardon

Spacism is still with us. But it is up to us to prepare our children for what they have to meet, and, hopefully, we shall overcome.
—Rosa Hydroponics, Sophont Magazine, December 2288 Standard

Rubbing at a nasty cryogenic kink in my back, I stagger to the main control room. The ship finishes its own wake-up routine, hopefully feeling less groggy than me, as I pull up the situation report.

Fortunately, neither I nor the shuttle seem to have lost any important bits in the eight-and-a-half light-year trip from the cramped outpost at Epsilon Eridani C. That's an encouraging start.

Outside the main viewscreen, the penumbral zone of tide-locked Kapteyn B below—or perhaps above, or slightly to the left; it's all relative in space—twinkles with artificial light, even under Kapteyn's Star's dim, geriatric glow.

The lights down there do not lie; somehow, I've found yet another planet already taken by at least one technology-using species. Yet they look so chaotic—it's almost as if these guys gave their local equivalent of

Jackson Pollock an orbital paint gun and told him to go nuts, on a planetary scale over four times the size of Earth.

Well, it'll be another twenty standard months before the bots are done building the laser thrust station at the local L4 point—my ticket home, or at least back to Epsilon Eridani, and the closest outpost of humanity in this neck of the galactic woods.

So I have plenty of time to stretch my legs and do what I came here to do in the first place: scout and report.

So far, I'm three for three for disappointment in the great quest of our time: the search for alien life humans can sit down and have a meaningful exchange of ideas with. But, somehow, I always feel the same little glimmer of excitement coursing through my belly, every time. I'm such a sucker for this job.

Best get to it, then.

. . .

The lander once again lives up to its name, with an exosuit-rattling thunk, and I'm out of the hatch as soon as the green light pops up in my AR heads-up display.

The soil is frozen and brittle beneath my boots— bits of powdery stone and ice chips mixed with flakes of carbon dioxide, the telltale sign of a decaying atmosphere.

Most exploration missions take me to raging volcanic planets or tidal-torn gas giant moons. I knew Kapteyn's Star would be different when I took the mission; it's a halo star, for starters, an ancient system too cool to hang out with the rest of the galactic disk.

But the reality is something else altogether. For the first time, I'm stepping out onto a planet dying in era-spanning slow motion—and everywhere I look, the writing is on the shoddy, haphazard wall.

Indeed, evidence of artificial construction lays strewn about the open area before me. Under a feeble sun, layer upon layer of makeshift structures—tumbled walls, pillars, and ramps—form a shell encasing whatever the original surface of the planet may have looked like.

Man, after ten billion years, this planet hasn't produced anything better than this layered pile of crap? What a dump.

Tracking any sources of heat or moisture in my display, I soon come across traces of life—if you can call it that.

Coming around the edge of a collapsed roof, I nearly run into a writhing mass of coloured clouds, bits of tech twinkling in their gaseous innards as they swirl and pass through each other, with hypnotic grace. It's impossible to say precisely where one begins and the other ends, as the colours meld and form gradients at the edges; yet each cloud is clearly a separate entity.

The TransSER playbook—that's Transbody Space Executive Reporter to laymen—is clear: however weird the clouds may seem to me, their movements define them as intelligent, and the presence of technology means I've found my target for study and first contact.

I follow the ever-moving cloud-orgy as it roils on through the chaotic landscape, and document the behaviour of the individual clouds when they zip off, every now and again. Sometimes, they only leave the central mass long enough to crystallise, pluck a strand of the straggly local plant life and dissolve it into its constituent atoms. At other times, a cloud will leave the others altogether and set off on its own way, possibly to join one of the other clusters I sometimes spot, crossing in the distance.

So many ghosts drifting amidst the ruins of a dead planet revolving.

A quick heads-up display tells me I still have plenty of air and power left, so I steel my resolve and stomp my clunky exosuit over to the clouds to make first contact; the results are underwhelming, to say the least.

I step up to the cloud-orgy, careful not to intrude on any personal space; and that's more difficult than it sounds, when you're dealing with clouds. When I'm as close as I dare get, I pull the ancient, physical screen roll out of my exosuit sleeve and play the standard introduction video: centuries of Man's finest and most universal cultural achievements flash by. I catch a glimpse of some of my favourites, like the Sistine Chapel ceiling, and Star Wars Episode IX, but I'm more interested in the clouds' reaction. For intelligent gases, they remain remarkably stony-faced.

When no immediate response is forthcoming, I bow, I flap my arms—anything to stop the teched-out clouds as they simply roll past me, either unaware of my presence, or simply uncaring.

Is this really the best lifeform the Kapteyn system has to offer? Or have I just travelled over eight light-years to make a fool of myself, waving my arms at the gaseous Kapteyn equivalent of the placid cows from my childhood VR nanny-shows?

I let out a frustrated scream, rendered all the more powerless by its inability to escape my helmet. With a small puff of air from my nape, the suit automatically balances the pressure inside, once I've finished my tantrum and stopped generating so much excess body heat.

Against all odds, this is how I finally get the clouds' attention. The roiling mass stops, backtracks—or maybe "backfloats," I suppose, since these guys have long since evolved beyond the need for tracks—until it is flush with my exosuit faceplate.

I don't dare move for what feels like minutes while the things spin around me, observing me from all sides, but never engulfing me completely, as I fear they will at every second. I really don't fancy getting a first—and last—hand example of whatever dissolved those plants. After a subjective eon, the clouds stop moving, and lights begin to twinkle in their electronic innards.

I smile beneath my tinted helmet, spread my arms in the hopes this might still be a show of non-violence to a

148

gaseous cloud, then speak, following the standard TransSER mission guidelines to the letter.

"I greet you, fellow beings, on behalf of humankind. I have travelled far, at the request of all my people, to bring a message of hope, friendship, and curiosity as to your ways of living and seeing this great Universe we share."

There's a lot more in that vein in the playbook, but the clouds don't give me a chance to get to the really pompous and grandiose parts. As soon as I finish the long-winded sentence, one of them lets out a loud farting sound—which must involve a considerable amount of effort, for a gaseous life form—and they all float on past me, the great gaseous orgy never ceasing.

It's entertaining to watch, but it's clear that this species is too different from humankind to ever engage in any real exchange of ideas. Another failure.

I dust some of the rubble from my exosuit, wave goodbye to my cloudy friends, for politeness' sake, then start the trek back to the lander, over the ridge of a fallen tower-like structure.

Before long, I realise it isn't just my imagination, and the clouds actually are tailing me, like some ridiculous gassy two-bit detective. I stop, but they must have already figured out my direction, as they zoom past me with shocking speed in the direction of the lander.

Just how strong is the lander's shielding against acids and gases, again? Stumbling amidst the rubble, I run as fast as my bulky suit legs will carry me.

The clouds are nowhere to be seen when I finally reach the lander, sitting right where I left it, on its spider-like struts—but the main airlock has been completely melted off by some corrosive agent, and the metal of the inner chamber is pitted and scored.

I check the ship's readouts as soon as I get close enough: the air inside has vented, but there's enough left in reserve for the ride back up to the orbiting shuttle.

But the real surprise is the little icon blinking with malicious intent in the upper left corner of the ship's display screen:

Dodgy physics is one thing—they're an occupational hazard—but a message waiting for me at the lander makes no sense at all.

Until we have a repeater station at this end of the gravitational lens, there's no way any kind of message could reach the lander. Being cut off from the rest of humanity is part of the mission—and now, this. A blinking icon of impossibility.

On the off chance I'm just having some sort of wishful, air-deprived hallucination, I put off reading the message until after I've gotten the lander sealed and breathable again. But even after the tedious process of patching up the ship and stripping out of my sweaty exosuit, the message icon remains.

Shrugging at the general stupidity of reality, I flop into my acceleration pod and flick open the message.

. . .

You are fortunate indeed to be viewing this. Assimilating your lexicon from this crude storage device was a chore, but nothing compared with the mental pain it causes us to descend, however briefly, to your level of semantic-stained thought. It would have been much easier to simply dissolve both you and your tool. But we are enlightened beings, free from the constraints of what you call language, and it is worth sinking to your depths to protect that freedom from others of your kind.

We tell you this so you will understand, as best you can, just how fortunate you are.

There is no place for you here, with the semantic need built into your fatty little brains, the desperate urge to bend thought to fit the vibrations of a string of muscle tissue.

We have moved past such limitations, as do all truly intelligent lifeforms. Perhaps your own evolved descendants may one day do the same. But know that we will not hesitate to take violent action unless you leave immediately, and inform others like you never to approach our planet.

I would offer my thanks, but we don't believe in such things. Just go. Now.

. . .

I don't need to be told twice, and the lander soon blasts off into orbit, the acceleration forces trying to turn my body into a pancake.

A sour bile rises in my throat, and has nothing to do with the acceleration. Its tangy taste of disappointment is familiar, and even the sight of the slowly dying planet below cannot distract me from it.

Back in the shuttle, I splurge on a hot shower, but even that can't relieve the sense of failure, of frustration at finding yet another advanced species that can't be bothered to communicate with humankind.

I set my thoughts aside and knuckle down to the task of composing the report for TransSER, including the full, first person perspective recording from my exosuit's helmet cam.

The last thing I do before calling the whole thing a wash and slipping back into the cryochamber is pen a condensed version of my report for the quarantine beacon:

Warning: The dominant species on this planet is just another bunch of bigots, too addicted to chemical orgies and their own sense of superiority to care about anything else in the Universe—not even their own, dying planet. Stay well away.

At least my mission may help keep some other masochistic explorer safe, I try to convince myself, as I send the marker on its merry orbital way, with a flick of a finger in the AR display.

Terra! Tara! Terror!

One thing, at least, is certain. Spacism is alive and well in the galaxy. Quarantine is too good for these anti-semantic jerks.

About the Author

Born in Newfoundland but raised on the tiny islands of Saint-Pierre-and-Miquelon, the only piece of France left in North America, Matthew Reardon writes Science Fiction blending comedy and political themes—drawing heavily, in both cases, on his experience as a jack-of-all-trades lawyer and as Secretary General of a Parliamentary group at the French National Assembly. Beyond his novel-length works and years of video game writing, his short fiction has been published in venues such as *Retro Future, Story Seed Vault,* and the Ouen Press 2017 short story competition anthology. He would love to hear from you on Twitter, over at @SpaceLawyerSF!

*****~~~~*****

Winter War

by Samuel Chapman

In Hyde Park, London, on Christmas Eve, things may be believed which otherwise hold no currency. Families who have just placed trees inside their houses for little good reason wander about the lighted market and mix their laughter with the gently falling snow. It was in the chill of such an evening of scarves and candles, not so many years ago, that a young girl stepped on a very unlucky flagstone located an equal distance from three different stalls that sold fudge.

She was a slip of a girl, with brown hair tucked under a hat of green wool: often kind, always hungry, slow to make up her mind. When she stepped on the stone, her father was some distance off, keeping one eye on her and the other on the towering and immensely bald man with whom he was dickering over the price of a Father Christmas candle.

She didn't know where she'd trod, nor what she started by briefly remaining there. How could she? It was nothing to a human.

The first fight to break out the moment the girl's sole landed was a vicious argument between two three-foot creatures squatting behind the counter of the Waller Sweet Shop. "It's your turn!" hissed Ruthrick, who had red tufts bursting out of the whole arc of his jaw with no distinction between hair and beard.

"Your last turn was over in thirty-eight seconds," squeaked the other, Vincenne, who had no hair of any kind bursting out of anywhere. "Before which I spent nine straight minutes handing samples to a family of horrid Americans who didn't buy anything. I'm on break."

"One of us needs to be the human soon, or that girl is going to look over at Candy Castle, and then where will we be?"

Vincenne slid down the red-painted wall and folded her arms. "When we lose her, you may take comfort in the fact that we all took our proper turns."

"Hellfire!" Ruthrick leapt up and dashed behind the curtains. A few magic words later, he emerged, and the picture was complete: a wooden stall painted in red and white stripes, racks of caramel popcorn and cotton candy, a door with a curtain, and a kindly, aged fellow leaning on the counter.

The little girl was not looking. Ruthrick glared across the crowded square at the garish fake battlements of Candy Castle, but the girl wasn't looking there, either.

Ruthrick swore again and risked a glance beneath the counter. "She's looking at Marley's!"

"Marley's? As if those addled brownies know how to make fudge?" Vincenne grabbed his ankle. "Do something, Ruthrick!"

"I can't call to her. It's against the code."

Music started up from the Candy Castle: a tinny yet inviting rendition of "Silent Night." The girl turned toward it.

Ruthrick had his human head look down. "Vin. I'm going to need you to go into the back."

Vincenne's orange-rimmed eyes widened. "Then it's war."

Ruthrick nodded.

Small, sharp-clawed creatures, invisible to any of the humans, crawled over the surface of Marley's Sweets. The brownies performed a hundred tasks at once: tuning their lights just right, shifting their best wares forward, clearing away rubbish and lollygaggers from the space in front of their store. One even leapt back and forth, snatching snowflakes and arranging them in a perfectly dusted tableau.

"Cue the smell," Ruthrick ordered.

Vincenne tightened one valve, let another one loose. In moments, the most inviting scent imaginable wafted across the square—a mingling of a dozen expertly crafted flavors of fudge, evoking warm nights snuggled under blankets and the comforting voices of a thousand great aunts and uncles.

The girl turned, and noticed Waller Sweet Shop for the first time. At that exact moment a snowflake landed on her outstretched tongue.

"Yes!" Ruthrick cheered as quietly as one can.

"What's that?" Vincenne said. "I can't see."

"A very good turn, my dear."

The girl stepped off the sacred stone and began to make her way through the crowd toward Ruthrick. She hadn't gone three steps, however, before several lumbering humans blocked her from view.

"God's bones!"

"What? What now?"

"It's those Americans. Can't we have a moment's peace?"

The family of window-shoppers had paused in the girl's path to share one park map between the four of them. The girl's green knit cap bobbed between them, but she was no longer facing Ruthrick. Instead, she was gazing toward the Candy Castle.

Ruthrick's eyes narrowed. "Clyde."

A grizzled mountain of a human had appeared behind the Castle's counter, and was stirring a vat of chocolate slurry, humming tunelessly along with the carol.

Vincenne poked her head through the curtain. "Making the fudge right out in the open? What's he playing at?"

"That cursed troll knows his audience well," Ruthrick spat. "Artisanal, hand-crafted, small-batch fudge. It's all the rage these days."

"Never mind the rage! How do we stop him?"

"I don't know! I thought we had her!" Ruthrick clamped his eyes shut. "Let me think."

Vincenne vanished back behind the curtain. Ruthrick surveyed the square before him, trying to settle his mind and plan his next move. To avoid distraction was almost impossible. The winter market swirled with things concealed from the mortals: elves thronging to and fro with handcrafted merchandise, pixies playing around the distant lights of the Ferris wheel, a naiad adding oak leaves to her gown to keep the snowflakes off her lovely skin, the brownies at Marley's Sweets swarming together into a humanoid form. . .

Vincenne rapped her knuckles on his head. "Ruthrick. Look at Marley's."

"They're making a human." Ruthrick frowned. "They never do that."

"Don't you wonder why?"

"You wonder why! I'm busy fretting about our customer."

"Maggie?"

Vincenne hadn't said that name. The voice had come from across the square, but as clearly as if the speaker was standing right behind the counter of Waller Sweet Shop. Inside the light-festooned Marley's stall, a crinkle-eyed old lady was waving joyfully at the little girl. Whose name, all knew now, was Maggie.

Ruthrick thrust his hand below the counter. Vincenne gasped as he came up clutching a squirming, spindle-limbed creature about the middle. "A little spy, eh? I suspected the moment you amplified the sound. Here to gloat?"

The brownie nipped at Ruthrick's wrist. "I ain't done nothin'!"

"Nothing, hell! Your people broke the code."

"Never agreed to no code."

"It's not the kind of code you can decide to disagree with." Vincenne said from behind the curtain, where she was back to operating the scent machine. "No familiarity with the customers. Ever."

"But it works." The brownie grinned with all forty of its teeth. "You dwarves jes' hate winners, tha's what you do."

Both creatures looked out at the square again. Maggie, brushing snow off her cap, was heading toward Marley's in bewilderment. "Aunt Georgine? I didn't know you sold fudge!"

"Just a Christmastime hobby, my dear! Come have a taste. I've just taken out a whole tray of praline. . . "

"Maggie loves praline," Vincenne warned.

"How do you know?" The brownie sank its teeth into Ruthrick's finger right as he asked. He shrieked and dropped the loathsome creature, which scampered off toward Marley's.

"I care about them, Ruth. You ought to try."

"God's bones, Vin, I'm bleeding for them! Crank up everything we've got!"

The machine behind the curtain started up a whirring of belts, gears, and sparks, with dwarven witchery blasting out of every nut and bolt. Ruthrick gestured to and fro, a conductor directing a mad symphony, dishing tray after tray of fudge into Waller's display case: peanut butter, peppermint, strawberry, a highly unstable sample of quadruple tetra-chocolate.

Scents burst forth like hungry hounds. Music became so soft and holy that half the plaza began to weep, while the other half—who were children—asked them what was wrong.

Clyde, troll of the Candy Castle, whipped his open-air fudge vat into a frenzy, barely trying to hide that he was stirring with his third and fourth arms. A warm light switched on behind the castle's painted plywood battlements, and suddenly the air in the square was warm—not so warm that people had to take off their scarves, but warm enough that the falling snow neither gathered nor chilled. It drifted to the ground in a perfect infinity.

All the while, Aunt Georgine beckoned Maggie closer.

"Consign it all." Ruthrick clutched his human form's hat in both hands. "Vin, if you're about to tell me not to do anything rash—"

"I'm not going to keep from doing that just because you predicted it."

The hat was off. "If the brownies have broken the code, so can we."

"Ruthrick, do not escalate! We are dangerously close to mutually assured destruction here!"

Ruthrick strode out from behind the counter. Snowflakes swept around him. As he walked, humans shuddered and flinched aside, so he never had to bump into a one. Though they saw nothing, they cleared a path to the nearby stall where Maggie's father had just handed over four pounds fifty for the Father Christmas.

Clyde the troll roared.

A chittering swarm of brownies fanned out in a cloud from Marley's, hardly able in their rage to hold Aunt Georgine together.

Ruthrick slapped the hat down onto Maggie's father's head.

The father felt nothing but the sudden invasion of an idea. He needed to get his daughter by his side: she could get hurt, after all, in such a crowded place. "Maggie!" he called. "Come over here with me, girl."

Maggie turned, whipping snowflakes aside with her hair. "Da, look, Aunt Georgine. . . "

"Georgine doesn't sell fudge, Mags. Look, there's nobody there."

Maggie shook her head as though waking from a dream.

The counter of Marley's stall was indeed empty, because the whole legion of brownies was now charging at Ruthrick. Racing about the crowd, darting beneath laden shopping bags and across the backs of dogs, they blew toward the angry dwarf like snowflakes.

Ruthrick had his stirring stick in hand, and struck about him at any little creature that got close. They were but a foot tall, but he was only three, and no dwarf could hold out long under such an onslaught. Soon two had his arms pinned against the flagstones, and a third covered his mouth before he could cry out for Vincenne.

Yet it was not Vincenne who saved him. A pounding of feet came from the wrong direction, where Clyde the troll was charging the brownies, swinging a spoon longer than a human was tall.

The brownies scattered. The spoon slammed against stone inches left of Ruthrick's head, forcing the dwarf to roll clear. Clyde struck about himself with no distinction between brownie, dwarf, and human. Several mortals shuffled away, feeling an exceedingly sharp itch at every blow.

"You all broke the code!" Clyde snarled. "You're code-breaking breakers!"

Then the whole square was chaos, with brownies gnawing at everybody, with Ruthrick hitting everything with his stirring stick, and Clyde losing his spoon and swinging his great meaty fists. . .

"Excuse me."

Everybody froze.

"Do you sell fudge?" Maggie asked.

Dozens of invisible creatures leapt out of their brawl and searched around to see where the girl was standing.

"Why, yes," smiled the kindly, middle-aged woman standing behind the counter of Waller Sweet Shop. "Any flavor you like."

"Do you have praline?"

Vincenne snapped her fingers. "Ah, you're in luck! Some just came out of the oven."

Ruthrick slapped his forehead. If only she'd just agreed to be the human to begin with, they could have avoided all of this.

Maggie eagerly clutched the paper bag Vincenne handed her. Her father counted out three more pounds, then put a hand on Maggie's shoulder, steering her away. "C'mon, Mags. Let's ride the Ferris wheel before we go home, eh?"

Maggie smiled at Vincenne once more, tucked her hair beneath her green knit cap, and turned away.

The dwarf, troll, and brownies dusted themselves off. Clyde blinked murderously at Ruthrick. "Don't be a sore winner now."

"Me? Never."

"I'll get the next one."

"I've no doubt you will."

Clyde retrieved his spoon. The brownies shuffled off, muttering. "You lot try to show some decorum next time," Ruthrick yelled at their backs.

"Up yours," said three of the brownies at once.

"Lucky the humans have these festivals so often, isn't it?" he said to Vincenne when they were both safely back behind the counter of Waller Sweet Shop. "Brightens up our lives considerably."

160

"It's their lives they're trying to brighten." Vincenne handed him a brush to help her sweep up.

"Well." Ruthrick shrugged. "You know humans. They're all about unintended consequences."

So Hyde Park continued its dance of light, snow, and sound. The candy stalls stirred their fudge, the trinket stalls glued on their red hats, the Ferris wheel turned in rhythm with the crowds walking below. And the families, thinking of hearth and stockings, thought nothing of it when a young boy stepped on a particularly unlucky cobblestone, and two dwarves erupted into bickering with each other and with everything else.

About the Author

Samuel Chapman lives in Walla Walla, Washington, where he works in water rights. His recent credits include "The Foaling Season" (*Metaphorosis*) and "Cannon Beach" (Honorable mention, Writers of the Future Contest).

*****~~~*****

The Octopus in the Millpond

by Emmett Schlenz

Whenever Bernadette and her friends drank at the pub, they cycled back to the same argument. The place's cozy familiarity certainly contributed. And alcohol has a way of making things run in circles. So that night, soon after sitting down, the three of them began talking around the old question: whether or not things had always been the way they were. What they really wanted, however, was an answer to the urgent question beneath the old one, unstated but understood: whether or not things would always be that way. That was what kept the argument recurring. Despite the passionate bickering, nobody liked their own answers, and everyone hoped somebody else might have a better one.

"It can't have always been here," Ernest said, wiping beer off his chin and settling into the wooden booth. "Ain't logical."

Bernadette, a healthy dose of mead in her stomach, shook her head. "And you think it just showing up one day out of the blue is the more logical answer? A giant octopus monster, traipsing about the countryside, says to itself, 'Miller's Glen seems like a nice town, I think I'll settle in this wee pond and make a home of it.' That seem more logical to you?"

Leon scooched his chair forward, twiddling his beard. "Maybe it just appeared all of a sudden. *Ex nihilo* and all. One day no octopus, next day. . . " His hands made a showy wiggle. "Octopus."

Ernest kept his eyes on Bernadette. "Our ancestors wouldn't have built this town if it were already here," he said. "How stupid do you think they were?"

"Pretty stupid," Bernadette said. "We're all descended from them, aren't we? And we haven't left yet. That's stupidity, yeah? And stupidity doesn't just arise up out of nowhere like. . . like. . . "

"Like an octopus in a millpond," Leon said.

"I'm trying to make a point here, Leon," Bernadette said. "Point being that there's no need to hang about next to this monster. We could leave, but we don't, and that's what they call genetics."

"Technically, you know," Leon said, "the octopus couldn't have always been here. The pond isn't just a pond, see. It's a millpond. People who settled Miller's Glen dammed up a river so they could build the old mill. It's a manmade thing. The pond, not the octopus. Well, maybe the octopus. You never know."

"Shut up, Leon," Ernest said.

"Yeah, shut up, Leon," Bernadette said.

The conversation would have lasted longer, but one of the usual interlocutors, Rosa, hadn't shown up, so the night ended early. Bernadette missed her. Rosa would have taken her side, and Rosa would have known how to quiet Leon. So they all parted ways sooner than they would have liked, heading separately into the dark, all wishing they lived closer so that they could walk home together. Nobody liked being caught out at night in Miller's Glen alone, even far away from the millpond. Nobody knew how long the monster's reach was.

As she walked by the thatched cottages, an unease blossomed in Bernadette's belly. For, while nobody said anything particularly unusual at the pub, some of the

164

words continued to rattle in her head with a new and distressing rhythm. As she passed the town's gate she identified what concerned her: the idea that, if she wished, she could leave Miller's Pond at any point. It forced upon her an unwanted level of responsibility. "Bit of a burden, that," she said, kicking a loose stone. She could feel a dark mood gathering over her, and she sped up to get home to Emma sooner.

"Wish that octopus would fuck right off," Bernadette muttered, and then checked for lurking tentacles, just to be safe.

But she knew it wouldn't fuck off at all. It had been living in the pond by the mill for centuries at least, demanding tributes of gold and grain. Nobody knew why it demanded those things, and the fact that the monster never explained its diet didn't help. It never ate the people it dragged off the street and drowned, either. The bodies floated ashore whole. Ernest said it did that just to prove it could, and Bernadette agreed. But whatever it ate, it clearly got plenty. No reason to expect it to leave. So why couldn't she?

Truth be told, there was nowhere for Bernadette or for anyone to go. Hillsdale, the next town over, was beset by a pair of particularly rude giants, who would take great steaming shits on the roofs of whoever refused them what they wanted. The giants were proper giants, too, not the garden variety runts, so their feces often collapsed the roof and crushed everybody beneath it. Bernadette and her friends laughed about it, sure. The shitting giants of Hillsdale, how funny. But it was only funny because they didn't live there.

Everywhere seemed to have its own monster in those days. A dragon in the capital city. A herd of spiders roaming the countryside. What's a person to do when they're born into a monster's world, Bernadette wondered?

As she headed up the short trail to their snug cottage, Bernadette saw her love waiting for her at the door. Emma's shoulders relaxed slightly as she ushered Bernadette inside, but a tenseness remained. After a long kiss by the fire—though their kisses were often long, this one was especially so—they both settled down to the vegetable pie Emma had reheated.

"How are the guys holding up?" Emma asked. She rarely went out to the pub with Bernadette's friends, preferring a quiet night reading over alcohol and squabbling.

"They're fine," Bernadette said. "Same as always. What do you mean, 'holding up?'"

"You haven't heard?"

"Haven't heard what?"

Emma set her fork down.

"Rosa washed up in the pond today," she said.

"Oh, god."

"I'm so sorry. I thought you would know by now."

"How?"

"Ink in her hair."

"Oh, dear god."

Bernadette jerked a hand over her mouth. Emma rushed to grab a pot and got it beneath Bernadette's chin just in time to catch the vomit, then brought over a bucket of water.

"Probably shouldn't have fed you first," Emma said.

"You think?" Bernadette said after swishing out her mouth.

They both went to bed as soon as they could. Emma had done her sobbing before Bernadette returned, and she was glad of it. One crying person was manageable, but two was not. When Bernadette's tears dried, she and Emma loved each other with a particular fervency. Grief gives a special solidity to whoever shares your bed. They were both exhausted afterward, but neither of them slept well.

The Octopus in the Millpond

They woke together in the morning, Emma slipping into her overalls and Bernadette strapping her secondhand leather armor around her stout body. She had needed a new set for a while, but the need seemed more urgent that morning.

They added a dollop of brown sugar, for moral support, to their customary bowls of oatmeal. When they finished eating they kissed goodbye at the door.

"Stay safe," Emma said, holding Bernadette close. "Any bandits come, you run. I'd prefer you unemployed to you dead."

"I'll keep that mind," Bernadette said.

Bernadette strapped her sword to her side. It was old, and the wrapping on the hilt was peeling. Her mother had given it to her, hoping Bernadette would follow her into the town watch. The job paid well and, oddly enough, was quite safe. A labor dispute a few decades earlier explicitly removed dealing with the octopus monster from the town watch's job description. Luckily, too, the bandits stuck to the roads, frightened off by the monsters that beset nearly every town. Thieving was how the bandits made their living, but none of them wanted to die by it. So while anyone at any time could be snatched off the street by a massive tentacle, and while the town paid a regular tribute, at least crime was down. Praise be to the octopus.

And there was, in fact, a sort of cult dedicated to exactly that. The Church of Tentacular Damnation, they called themselves. Bernadette passed a group of evangelists on the road to the town gates, haranguing pedestrians with exhortations of possible salvation from a watery death if they would just believe. Church members did get drowned in the pond now and then, but there seemed to be some correlation between worshiping the octopus and it not killing you. Believers died at a regular enough rate that their beliefs did not catch on, but not so regularly that the faith collapsed.

Bernadette hurried past the evangelists, shoving away their pamphlets. One of them held up a paper sign, and Bernadette made it a few yards past the group before she processed what it said. She turned around to see a rough drawing of Rosa's face, with the words "Obey, or Follow Her" beneath it.

She stood still, her breath quickening, before walking quite calmly up and grabbing the sign out of the evangelist's hands. She ripped it in half, ripped those halves in half again, and threw them on the ground. Some of the burlier believers raised their fists, but they lowered them when Bernadette palmed her sword. The churchgoers hurled curses at her as she walked away—all variations on the theme of gruesome death by tentacle. Bernadette ignored them and headed toward the gates.

Nothing happened during her time on guard duty. Rarely anything did. So she spent her shift leaning against the gate, arms crossed, looking at the cornfields sweeping out in front of her. Leon was in there, somewhere, wandering amongst the stalks, checking for diseases. Ernest would be coming to relieve her in a few hours. It was nearly harvest time, and the stalks of corn bent low to the earth.

The field's rhythmic swaying focused her thinking, and she gradually became aware of the weight of the sword on her hip. Not everyone in town had one. They were difficult to procure, and the townsfolk regarded owning one as a privilege. Bernadette began to feel as if there were something she ought to be doing with it. Then she realized.

She planned a whole speech on the walk home. She knew Emma would be back from her shift at the mill, and she needed to prepare a structure for the conversation. Bernadette memorized rousing phrases about ethics and responsibility. But there must have been something in her face, some telltale line, because when Emma met her at the door and looked her in the eye, she bit her lip and sighed.

"You're going to do it, aren't you?" she said.

"Do what?" Bernadette said, wanting to give her speech.

Emma crossed her arms.

"Oh," Bernadette said. "That. Yes."

"When?"

"Tomorrow. No sense in putting it off."

Emma held Bernadette's hands in hers. They met for the first time when they were both in the middle of becoming who they would end up being. It was not that they molded each other so much as they each hollowed out a warm, safe space in themselves for the other to grow in. So, when Emma took her lover's hands she looked inside herself to find the part of Bernadette rooted there, searching for doubt. When she did not find it, she squeezed Bernadette's fingers.

"And you're sure?" Emma said, hoping she might have overlooked something.

"It's the only thing for me to do," Bernadette said.

Emma smiled, hoping it conveyed support as well as sadness.

"You should at least eat a good dinner, then," she said.

They ate and drank enough wine so that Bernadette would be properly drunk that night but feel fine in the morning. They both slept even worse than the night before.

When they awoke they said many silent goodbyes. Neither of them were superstitious, but neither wanted to risk turning a farewell into an augury. Besides, tears can say enough. And then Bernadette was off down the cobbled road, wiping her eyes with one hand and testing the weight of her sword with the other.

Others had, of course, tried to do what she intended. Some wanted to do right, some wanted the glory

169

associated with monster-slaying in those days. Some were even locals to Miller's Glen. All were brave and strong, and most were true, more or less.

The lucky ones came back soaked with ink and pond water and met with laughter down at the pub. The less lucky ones came back covered in blood and spent the next three months wrapped in bandages. The unlucky ones didn't come back at all. And the octopus's continued presence only reminded Miller's Glen how unlucky it was.

Bernadette looked back just once, right before her home fell out of sight around a bend in the road. She breathed deep, squeezed the pommel of her sword, and walked onward.

The millpond had a tranquil surface. Reeds crowded the edges. It was fairly large, as millponds go, and the older townsfolk swore that it was only growing larger. The octopus, they argued, spent its free time pressing its tentacles against the shore, expanding its territory. Leon would tell them that perhaps it was a product of erosion, not the monster, and as per town custom they would tell Leon to shut the fuck up.

The mill itself stood motionless, as it was too early in the morning for anyone to be working. Bernadette had planned it that way. Were she to die some gruesome death, she did not want witnesses. Better to live in legend as a hero than in memory as an idiot, she reasoned.

She approached the pond, sword in hand, and stood there for a few minutes, unsure of what to do. Eventually, she coughed politely, and the tip of a tentacle emerged from the water. It waved. She held up her sword in response, and if a tentacle could possibly appear disappointed and belabored, that's how it looked.

Bernadette readied her feet as the octopus rose out of the millpond. The pond must be incredibly deep, she thought, to hold this beast, this mass of writhing blue-black flesh. It furled and unfurled its limbs and stared down at her with purple eyes. The octopus gleamed with

170

ornaments of gold, having bedecked itself in its tribute. Bernadette was surprised to see a small crown atop its head. It looked like a child's gilded plaything. She thought with horror how the monster must have acquired it.

The eyes, however, were the strangest thing about it. They were as human as her own. The octopus knew who it was, and who she was, and what she was there to do, and what it was doing to the town. That was something to ponder later, Bernadette thought, if she was lucky enough to have a later.

She raised her sword. The heroes who had preceded her wielded powerful weapons: an axe forged from a shooting star, for instance, or a shield blessed by a god. Bernadette's sword was decidedly not those things. But then again, those mystic and holy weapons hadn't been much help to anyone. Perhaps hers would be.

It wasn't. When asked about it later, Bernadette would count herself among the lucky ones, but fell silent when pressed for details. The only battle stories people like to hear about, be they victories or defeats, are the vigorous fights with many gaspable moments. Hers wasn't like that. It involved a lot of running and dodging and ended with a lot of bruises on her and a slight nick in one of the monster's tentacles.

She walked home wet and ink-blackened. Emma had the door open before she could knock and embraced her, taking some of the pond water and ink onto her own body. Then she got Bernadette cleaned up and settled down by the fire. Bernadette was silent and shivering, and Emma fed her hot soup. She had prepared it as a sort of totem. If there was soup waiting for her, Bernadette had to return. That was the logic. And, she thought afterward, it worked.

It was barely the afternoon, but they went to bed. Bernadette laid her head down on Emma's chest. She hadn't said a word since returning, and didn't say anything for another hour. When she finally spoke, her voice was soft.

"It'll be in that pond forever," she said. "There's no getting rid of it."

"You don't know that," Emma said.

"I believe it."

Emma stroked Bernadette's head.

"Then live to spite the octopus," she said. "Spit in the pond. Eat calamari. Write in ink. If it's not going away, then you can't either."

Bernadette curled in closer, her head still on Emma's chest, and a peacefulness came over her. Perhaps the monster had always been in the millpond. Perhaps it would always be there. But it could never be in their bedroom. There are some places even an octopus cannot reach. And Bernadette knew that she would keep trying to kill it, and that she would keep failing, and that she might even die, but that trying was the thing to do. And as long as she was alive, it did not matter if she failed over and over, because she could always come back and lay her head on her lover's chest and the whole world in that moment would be as perfect as anything ever was.

They both slept well that night.

About the Author

Emmett Schlenz was born in Rhode Island and currently lives and writes in Portland, Oregon, where he also works as a union organizer. His publication credits include a short story in *Cosmic Roots and Eldritch Shores.*

*****~~~~*****

Field of Honor

by Gustavo Bondoni

Hina scanned the bodies on the battlefield and wrapped her scarf more tightly around her mouth, hoping to protect herself against the stench. It still seeped through.

She closed her eyes and truly looked at the carnage, and saw the glow, patches that illuminated the field. Pale white indicated magical items: jewelry or weapons overlooked by the first of the scavengers across the field: why bother with dull metal when gold gleamed from most of the fallen? She would take them, of course. A bit of study ought to yield their secrets.

But she would pick up the trinkets later. There were two or three soft pink patches, sign of the Essence, still viable, that required her immediate attention. She almost opened her eyes and started towards the rare treasure of the dead when she halted. It couldn't be.

But it was. A single corpse off to one side glowed with the blue light of the Purity. Her eyes snapped open and she ran.

"Hina, what's happening?" Girbo yelled. The urchin had never seen his normally staid and respectable mistress act this way.

"Something wonderful. Hurry up!" She stepped over the cadavers, for once not bothering with the dignity of the dead. She would apologize later.

The light came from a young soldier, a boy who should have been learning a trade at his master's side, not bearing a sword, much less lying half buried in malodorous mud with his flat dead eyes looking into the leaden sky.

"Quickly. The black bag. Open it."

She tore the proffered leather sack from the urchin's hands. It was filled with the implements of the surgeon's trade: razors, tongs, saws of every sort. She pulled out the largest of the knives; there was little time for delicacy.

Hina pulled up the dead boy's chainmail to expose his stomach and lower ribs. Then she closed her eyes and looked again. There. The deepest blue seemed to come from just above his gut. She drove the largest of the knives into the exposed flesh with a savage thrust. Then she twisted.

No blood welled. With a still heart, the liquids of the body pooled on the underside. Those that hadn't gushed out of the wounds that had killed the soldier, that is.

Her hands tore the body open to reveal a smooth organ that glowed the brightest of bright blues when she closed her eyes. She had no idea what the organ was, but it had to be the source of what she saw.

She opened a wooden box and pulled out her most precious possession: a metal syringe. Pricking the organ carefully, she removed as much of the liquid inside as she could and placed it in a cut glass vial. Only when the stopper was securely in place did Hina let out the breath she didn't realize she'd been holding in.

Girbo's eyes were wide as saucers.

"No. Don't look at me. Close your eyes and really look. What do you see?"

"It's blue. I've never seen blue before."

"Don't forget it. Always look for the blue light. You might go your entire lifetime without seeing it again, but you must always look."

Girbo nodded.

Hina wondered whether his gift would enable him to escape the endless cycle of war that marred their land. It was always the same thing: the men set out every spring and perhaps half of them returned to their cold keeps with the first snows. Over the winter, a new crop of boys would be forced to become men. Most of those that were particularly vital or magical would survive. . . but not all of them. And she would be there, half a day behind the advance, or perhaps a few hours after the retreat, ready to harvest the ones who didn't live to tell.

She turned back to the bodies and closed her eyes again. Pink light, less intense than even five minutes before, shone nearby. She got to work.

An hour later, there was no more liquid to extract. Anything viable was safe in her vials. The rest had degraded below the point in which it was useful.

She walked to a patch of grass clear of bodies and sat down heavily. Her back ached from crouching, her feet ached from following the armies. She wished she could unwrap the scarf around her nose and breathe fresh air. But there was no fresh air to be found.

Girbo sat beside her.

"Can you see the magic metal?" she asked him.

He nodded.

"Good. Go get as much of it as you can carry."

Hina crossed her legs and closed her eyes. She needed rest, but summer wasn't the right time to rest. The ingredients she could gather now would keep her spells alive during the winter. With what she accumulated here, her village high in the mountains could maintain its magical protection and therefore keep its most prized possession—its neutrality.

She watched the boy running between the corpses and wondered if he would adapt to the quiet life of the village.

He'd been wandering a battlefield, crying for his mother when she first saw him. Hina'd just arrived from harvesting the elixir of the camp followers. If his mother had been among the wives and washer-women and whores of that vanquished force, then she was rotting back into the earth that had birthed her. And if his father was a soldier, then he'd been hacked to pieces desperately trying to protect the baggage train and the noncombatants.

It was something that happened occasionally, when the bloodlust came on too strong. She could only shrug and pick up the magic that some particularly powerful individuals had inside. That was the best way to help her own people. There was nothing she could do for the bloodthirsty dwellers of the plains.

The boy had followed her, at first demanding to know where his mother was, and then going silent for days. She fed him what scraps she could spare until, as she looked over a battlefield, he imitated her habit of looking with her eyes closed.

It had been a shock when, after mute weeks, he'd asked her why dead people glowed.

Now, less than a month later, Girbo knew what to look for among the fields seeded with corpses. She'd explained that anything that glowed with magic light was more valuable than gold. In due course, when he had time to see the village, to see what life was like without the scourge of war, he would be ready to learn why.

A rustle, out of place in the stillness of death, caught her attention, and she opened her eyes. Some things were better seen with the senses that every animal had than through the fickle light of magic.

A man dressed in ragged black robes approached her. He was dragging a struggling Girbo along by one arm.

Hina watched him get nearer and spat onto the ground beside her. As much as she wished that the war could end and that the plains folk could free themselves from the unseen hand that drove them, she didn't despise the men who fought. They were just doing what they were driven to do.

On the other hand, when faced with a scavenger, dressed in black like the crow he was, she felt nothing but disgust.

"Let the boy go," she told the man.

The man grinned at her. His teeth were brown and rotting. "Why? Are you going to make me?" He reached down and pulled a long knife from the waistband of his pants. "I don't think you are."

Hina kept her eyes on the knife as she said: "What can I possibly give you that you can't take yourself? I can't even lift the heavy plate or chainmail, so we take the smaller stuff. Why bother with us?"

"I've had enough of taking iron. There's iron everywhere, the blacksmiths won't even pay us the price of scrap for what we drag back to them." He cocked his head. "But I've been watching you. Yes. I have. And you're not just taking the metal. I just saw you with your bottle, I saw you cut one of those men open and fill a bottle with. . . something. And now you're going to give it to me, and you're going to tell me why it's valuable, so I can sell it."

"And if I refuse?"

"I'll take the bottles anyway, and leave you and this boy here to rot like the rest of them." He waved the knife, but seemed reluctant to close the gap separating them. It was almost as if, accustomed as scavengers were to being the weakest people around, he couldn't quite believe that he'd found someone he could bully.

Hina sighed. Such a waste. "All right. This bottle holds a magic liquid." She held out one of the bottles she'd taken, which gleamed red even with her eyes open. She wondered if the carrion feeder in front of her could see it.

"Magic. I knew it. This will make me rich." He snatched at it.

She pulled it away, the distance between them still working in her favor. "I thought you wanted me to tell you what it did. Aren't you afraid that it might be dangerous?"

"If you can carry your bottles around in that little pouch, how dangerous can they be? Just give me the bag, and I promise I'll let you go your own way."

He was telling the truth, probably trying to be noble.

"No," she said.

"Then this one dies." He pulled on Girbo's arm and laid the knife against the boy's cheek. Even angry, he still seemed unsure whether he was capable of taking on an adult, even an unarmed woman.

"Listen to me. Did your mother tell you about the world before all of this?"

"Never knew my mother," he replied. But he loosened the grip on the boy. The knife no longer looked like it was about to draw blood.

"The world was full of people, many more than today. They lived in peace for the most part, and didn't fight. But they weren't careful with the planet, and the world. . . changed."

"And why would I care about that?"

Hina sighed. "The Earth knows how to keep itself in balance. When too many people filled its woods and valleys and plains, it sent spirits to keep us in check. My mother told me that it had sent other things before that, but that the people who lived before had simply faced down the plagues and rising seas and earthquakes and continued to live without being too badly affected. So now, it sends us spirits."

"Don't be silly, old lady. Just give me the bottle."

"I'm telling you. This bottle contains a spirit. A spirit of the Earth stronger than your own spirit will ever be. Or mine, for that matter. These spirits are among us, and they overwhelm the spirits of men and women and teach them about war. People thus possessed are the most eloquent of speakers, and they can convince anyone to follow them. A single spirit could mobilize an entire town to war, but each town has dozens of them. Hundreds in the bigger settlements. That's why we fight. Do you really want to take one of them with you, when you don't know how to handle it?"

"All I know is that I can sell it to a warlock. What he does with it afterwards is his affair."

Hina knew what warlocks did with the spirits. They twisted them and tortured them and used them to subjugate their enemies—or the enemies of those who paid them. They had no real understanding of what they were, other than a bludgeon too strong for people to resist.

The man pressed the knife against Girbo's throat again. A single emerald of blood formed around the point. "Now, stop telling me fairy tales and give me the bottle. All the bottles."

"All right. But I want to show you this one before you take it." She unstoppered the bottle before he could protest and, with a single shake, sent the liquid inside flying his way. It seemed to evaporate before it reached him.

"That was stupid. Now I have one less to sell. I should kill the boy. But I won't. Give me the rest and I'll let you—"

The scavenger didn't get any farther. His eyes glazed over, and he looked down on the boy. He shoved him away and, as if realizing for the first time that he wasn't a threat, sheathed the knife.

The man turned away from them and began to delve among the corpses. One beheaded man yielded a shirt of mail; a helm came from another body. Standing over a third, the man hefted a two-handed broadsword. Though he still looked as weak and stringy as before, his posture had changed: shoulders thrown back, head erect.

He studied the skyline. Dust in the air, sign of a moving army, darkened the sky to the east. He strode in that direction without looking back at them.

Girbo, his hand on his neck, fingering the trickle of blood, looked up at her with tears in his eyes. "What will happen to him now?"

Hina shrugged. "He'll fight." Just another possessed man in a continent full of them. Who knew, maybe she'd harvest this same spirit again. She'd recognize it if she saw it again. "He'll die."

The boy didn't look particularly upset to learn that. He just nodded. "You didn't tell him about the blue bottle, did you?"

"No, I didn't."

"What's in the blue bottle?"

The boy wasn't ready for that knowledge. It was closely held, and even more important than the spirit power they used to keep the earth from cleansing the mountains the same way it was cleansing the plains. But she knew by his eyes that she had to give the boy something, or he would keep insisting until autumn sent them back into their houses.

"Hope," she told him.

Girbo didn't ask again, even though she could tell that he hadn't understood the answer. He just nodded silently and followed her towards the east, where the dead of the next battlefield would be waiting by the time they arrived.

###

About the Author

Gustavo Bondoni is an Argentine novelist and short story writer who writes primarily in English. He's published more than 200 short stories, several of which have appeared in Third Flatiron anthologies, and published three novels, *Siege, Outside, and Incursion.* His writing has appeared in Pearson's Texas STAAR English Test cycle, *The New York Review of Science Fiction, Perihelion SF, The Best of Every Day Fiction,* and many others. His website is www.gustavobondoni.com.

*****~~~~~*****

Shadow Harvest

by Melanie Rees

Sorath's sunlight blazed through the open door, as the stranger strode into Sheriva's pub. Its glare illuminated dust particles hanging in the air, before they combusted like minute firecrackers.

The bustle of chatting and glasses clinking ceased. The newcomer entered, leaving the door ajar. He wore a typical hoodie and sunglasses, but strutted toward the bar with a swagger unfamiliar to Sheriva's little abode.

"Shut the door!" She pointed a knobbly finger at the stranger. "Do you live in a bloody furnace?"

The stranger shrugged and flicked the door shut with his foot.

Sheriva patted the whip resting by her hip, making sure she hadn't left it in the cellar. Nothing looked right about this character. She swirled the dregs of gin around in the bottle, tapped the counter twice and gazed upon her new patron. "Am I pouring?" she asked with as much graciousness as she could muster.

He pulled back his hood as he approached the bar. "How much for a whole bottle?"

"Good couple of inches." Sheriva pulled a candle from under the bar and lit it with a match; the orange glow illuminated the dim scenery around her.

The man pulled his hand away from the flame. "I want ice too." He perched his shades upon his shiny, bald head. "Never understood why people keep their shades on inside." He nodded towards Sheriva's own goggles.

"Because idiots like you don't know how to shut doors and seem intent on frying us all." Sheriva scowled underneath her own hood and tinted goggles. "Ice is extra."

"I realise that." The man held up a finger in front of the flame. The candle cast a shadow equal to the man's finger, and it kept growing down the bar like a king python. "Enough?" he asked.

She nodded. "I'll take it all now." There was something in his eyes she didn't trust. The smooth skin, barely tarnished by Sorath's fiery glare, was unnatural.

"I have a blade," she began.

"No need." He drew his own, a small flick knife. Its blue hue shone as he sliced his shadow.

Sheriva pulled a vial from her robes, tilted it towards the shadow, dipping the lip into the darkness, and let his detached shadow slink into her stash. "You've had *good* times?" she asked attempting to subdue her interest.

He smiled. "Are you keeping that for later?" He nodded towards her vial.

"I don't need it yet." She placed it in the deep pockets of her robes. "This place is well protected." She poured the gin and left space for the promised ice.

"Yes, I saw the forest's shadows outside buffering this place."

I bet you did. Sheriva scooped a generous handful of ice from the cooler box, savouring the coolness against her skin.

"Seems a waste," he continued, "leaving the shadows to protect a forest of random trees. Those shadows must be worth a fortune."

She plonked the ice in his drink, letting the alcohol splash on the counter.

Wherever he got his shadows from wasn't through manual labour. His lily-white hands probably hadn't seen a day's work in their lives. That unscorched skin didn't belong; not a single scale, burn, or crust flaked from his bones. He may as well have been made from thistle sap.

"Nice bar, though." He swirled the gin around in his glass, letting the ice cubes clink as potently as coins rattling in a purse.

Several of her regulars turned.

Did this bloke have a death wish?

Her regular, Mack, approached with his lantern. The dim tea-light shone upon his well worn, pockmarked face. That was the face of someone who'd been outside in the sun and slums. He placed his hand in front of the light, casting a stub of a shadow.

"Mack." Sheriva raised an eyebrow. "You can't afford it. I won't take any more from you. You'll fry like a de-shadowed tree. I don't need my best customers ending up as Sorath's next sacrifice."

"I have a day's work lined up harvesting shadows from the northern forests," said Mack.

"And how do you intend to get there, without your own shadow?" asked Sheriva.

Mack shuffled on his feet unsteadily. "I'll pay you when I return."

"I don't run a bleeding charity."

Mack peered to the stranger. "Care to help out a fellow lover of gin?" He smiled a lopsided grin.

"Not particularly." The stranger made an exaggerated effort to pull his glass closer to himself.

Sheriva noticed Mack tap his blade with a nervous twitch.

"Hardly seems fair keeping all that shadow to yourself," said Mack. Sweat beaded at his temples and around the rim of his sunglasses.

Don't do it. Sheriva glared at him.

185

Mack pulled his blade. Sweat ran past his sunglasses, zigzagging around his face etched with Sorath's glaring wrath. "Did you slash all your shadows from kids in the underground slums?"

Sheriva was thinking the same thing. How many desperate kids and workers had he stripped of their only protection? "I hope they didn't come from any orphaned children. I'm very protective of them," said Sheriva.

"I guarantee that's not the case." The stranger smirked.

"Bulldust! However you got that much shadow, you don't deserve it!" Mack thrust his blade in the stranger's direction, but missed. His blade sliced against the bottle of gin, knocking it onto the floor.

Sheriva leaned over the bar, grabbing Mack's arm before he could strike. She twisted his forearm until he squealed and dropped the knife.

Mack fell to his knees, mouth agape, clutching his arm.

"Thank you," said the stranger, examining what remained of his bottle.

"That wasn't for your benefit." She hopped up onto the bar, swung her legs over to the other side, and helped Mack onto to his feet.

"Still, I appreciate it."

"Two rules. You would've seen the sign," she said to the stranger. "No bar fights. No taking shadows from my forest trees." She turned her attention to Mack. "Sober up. If you're lucky, I'll let you do some dishes to earn enough shadows to get you through a couple more days."

He stumbled away to the far corner of the pub, and slumped into a chair in shock.

"I'll get you a new bottle from the cellar." Sheriva brushed broken glass into her hand and disposed of it under the counter.

"Why's your extra booze in the basement?" asked the man. "Isn't this a bar?"

"Bar brawl last month. A woman smashed a man's head open with a bottle." Sheriva walked away from him to the end of the bar and down a short flight of stairs. She removed the key from around her neck and entered the cold room. Bottles of booze stood next to two dozen kegs. She manoeuvred around a large barrel that cluttered the floor and collected a fresh bottle of gin.

"Here," she said, after she locked up and returned to the bar.

The man attempted to unscrew the lid. His white knuckles turned even whiter as he twisted and failed.

"They aren't working hands," Sheriva noted. She used the hem of her cloak to unscrew the lid. "Mack had a legit question. Where'd you get the shadows?"

The man poured a generous amount of gin into his glass, taking extra care not to spill any. "I run a consortium looking for new forests for shadow harvesting. Our company would provide reasonable compensation for your trees' shadows."

"No."

"When I say 'reasonable,' I mean enough to buy a pub a thousand times more glamorous than this one." He sipped his drink with a smug look.

Sheriva glanced around at the dim room and its patrons. The carpet was a bit sticky these days, the curtains were frayed, but it was home.

"Every tree sacrificed to Sorath just empowers him. The more Sorath acquires, the more shadows we need to take. So the answer is still no."

"We are asking nicely now, but if the answer remains no, we will compulsorily acquire your shadows, and your trees will burn." The man sloshed down the rest of his drink in two gulps. He sucked an ice cube before crushing it in his teeth.

Sheriva screwed the lid on the gin bottle tight. "No."

"Burn it'll be, then."

"No, it won't," she replied politely. Sheriva pushed the bottle of gin towards the man. "I think it's time for you to leave."

He chuckled. "I'll go, but you will also leave when your business goes under." He pulled up his hood. He looked at his sunglasses and then tossed them aside. "When you have as much shadow as I do, they're really just a fashion statement." He strode out the door, leaving it hanging open. Several of her patrons darted out of the way, as Sorath's heat blazed inside.

She scooted over the counter and followed him outside, slamming and locking the door behind her.

"Mister!" she addressed him with disdain. "You forgot this." She thrust the bottle of gin in his direction.

"Keep it. You'll need all the assets you can get once we take your shadows. Unless you want to visit the underground slums and spend your life in regret and darkness."

Sheriva flung the bottle at his feet. Glass smashed against the hard dark earth. From her cloak's deep pockets, she pulled out her lighter.

He laughed. His shadow extended with each hollow cackle until it grew as tall as her trees. "Do you think you're going to burn off my shadow with flame and a bit of booze?"

Arrogant prick. She took a few paces towards him, leaving the shade of her pub. Sorath's heat blazed upon her exposed cheeks. She savoured the pain. Sheriva pulled out her whip and ignited the end with her lighter. She lashed her flaming whip against the smashed bottle. Blue light ignited and spread across the ground in a large radius engulfing his feet. His shadow detached and slunk back towards her pub.

Still holding onto his smug smile, the stranger clapped slowly. "That was just a waste of good booze." He rolled his eyes as his shadow regrew.

188

"Children!" She glanced up into her forest's canopy to see half a dozen children appear high up in the branches. Dirty faces of orphans, who had seen too many days in the slums, peered down at her. "Now!"

One of the children threw a bottle at the man. Sheriva lashed her whip into the liquid. Blue light travelled up his legs, severing the newly formed shadow.

A new shadow formed, and he pulled his knife, shining with blue vengeance. "Are we really going to play this game? It could go on a while."

"Maybe." She glanced up at a young girl in a tree a few feet behind him and gave her a nod. A bottle smashed by his feet and Sheriva smacked her whip down again. His shadow fled towards her pub with the rest.

He lunged with his knife, but as he did so a keg fell from the canopy to the ground. He stumbled over it.

Sheriva whipped the liquid spilling from the keg and watched the blue engulf his body. His shadows slunk across the dirt like flashes of dark.

The stranger's eyes widened, and the smirk plastered across his face faded. He pushed past her to the pub and tugged on the door.

The tang of burnt dust lingered in the air. She inhaled deeply as blue light surrounded her feet and ran up her legs and torso. "Something wrong?"

"Where—?" He tugged on the door again before turning back to her. "Why aren't your shadows detaching?"

She pulled back the hood of her cloak and ran a hand over her scaly scarred head, feeling the lumps and rough skin.

Disgust filled his eyes.

She drew back her goggles. "Because I don't have any shadows."

His disgust turned to shock. "You have all these shadows here and you let that happen to you?"

"It startles you? The redness, the scarring? Mister Lily-white, time to toughen up."

He stood in the narrow strip of shadow alongside her pub. "Let me inside," he pleaded. "I have powerful allies. They'll hunt you down if you don't."

She shrugged. "This place is protected by the two most vulnerable things in the world." Sheriva turned her back on him and strode to the backyard of her pub. She opened a trapdoor and climbed down the ladder into her cool cellar. "Two kegs ought to do it." She hauled them up the ladder, one by one. "Children!" she yelled over distant cries. She tried to block out the stranger's screaming as Sorath scorched his shadowless body.

Her children gathered around with their burnt and tarnished skin. "Here." She unscrewed the lids on both and inspected the darkness inside. "Empty half on my trees, and take the rest back with you to the slums." She pulled her hood back over her head and reaffixed her goggles in place. "I'll have more tomorrow, around happy hour again."

Something heavy dragged her cloak down. She reached into her pockets and found her vial. "Here," she said, handing it to the smallest girl.

The girl smiled with chapped lips and grimy cheeks. With a whole vial to herself, she still tipped half on a tree first before running off back to the slums.

Sheriva smiled. Returning to the front of the pub, she kicked a pile of black ash out of her way before walking into a sea of silent faces. "Why so glum?" she asked turning to Mack and her other patrons. "Did I forget to mention, it's happy hour?"

###

About the Author

Melanie Rees is an Australian speculative fiction writer. Her work has appeared in publications such as *Apex, Daily Science Fiction, Sub-Q,* and *Persistent Visions.*

*****~~~~~*****

All the Moon's Children

by Kiki Gonglewski

It was two weeks of moonlight, races through ryegrass from one nowhere to the next, and swift glances towards the direction of shadows, before Jason Walker asked me how long I could hold my breath underwater. It had been the latest in a line of sporadic, almost confession-like inquiries that fell within the interims of our gradually budding friendship. Questions that fell gently inside the lulls between bouts of laughter. *What do you think about breaking the rules? Like, maybe sneaking out of the house one night. . .*

They'd pop up randomly on hot, golden-tinted afternoons, when our school, in response to the excessive heat, would let us out early and there was nothing else to do but run, just keep running, even if neither of us were quite sure why, or even if we knew we were headed nowhere at all.

"You're a good runner, Matt," Jason might suddenly comment good-naturedly, "are you a good swimmer, too?"

"Sure I am. I was actually on the swim team back in my old school."

"Good. That's good."

"Why?"

"You'll see."

Or we'd be sitting on the porch of my new Alien house, unpacked boxes still strewn carelessly around us, while Jason's gaze was tilted upwards, utterly hypnotized by the waxing crescent of the moon. *Do you prefer daytime, or night?* For a moment or two, the contours of memory would reshape his face, lit up more brilliantly than the moonbeams that stroked it, before he'd turn to me as the shadow of earnest solemnity darkened it again and ask, "do you believe in portals?" And, though that same question during the day would seem preposterous, something about the moon's siren song made me lose myself in its rhythm for a moment and nod my head, *yes. . . yes, yes, of course. . .*

Each question was another dot among an ever-growing pattern of dabbled stars, yet for the life of me, I couldn't draw the lines between them to make out the constellation. *Do you think there's magic in the forest?*

We'd often wander around the edges of things, the circumference of the lake, or the border of the forest, under the inevitable battle between the day's fading pastel blues and the stygian darkness of night, rimming shapes like ink.

"Are you *happy* with this world?" Jason asked one evening, within the confines of a scarcely breathing twilight, skimming the surface of the lake with his long, elegant fingers. "Is it enough for you?"

"I don't know," I ventured cautiously. "Should it be?"

"No, never," Jason shook his head with disdain, "not this dry old dump."

I looked back toward the direction of our houses, their windows reduced to squares of orange, competing weakly with the light of the oncoming moon, then back at Jason, loyalties torn. "I mean, it's not so bad, here, is it? I mean, it's not large and cosmopolitan, per se, but there's nothing terribly *wrong* with it, I don't think."

194

"Maybe not at first," Jason whispered, fingers still trailing gently below the water's surface. "But especially during the day, you can see it—the *emptiness*. It's so much smaller on the inside."

"I'm sorry," I mumbled, unsure of what else to say.

"I'm not." Jason grinned. "Say, Matt, do you scare easily, by any chance?"

That first fortnight in the small town of Echo Sound was made entirely of mosaics in the shapes of harlequin laughter and my friend's amusingly unsubtle evaluations *(would you trust me if I told you something crazy?),* homemade lemonade, running on dirt roads, neat, daffodil-painted fences, Jason calling me Matt instead of Mathew, and dusks spent sneaking out of the house toward the quietly singing forest after the sun's departure left the whole sky smelling of daydreams in its wake as we waited for the arrival of the moon.

. . .

How long do you think you can you hold your breath underwater, Matt?

We were out by the edge of the forest again, with a swollen full moon filtering down to earth in search of some warm, tangible human figure through the intricate lace of the trees, though she had yet to find us.

"Probably a few minutes," I wagered, then hesitated. Two weeks filled to the brim with his peculiar, impossible breadcrumb-trail of questionings, and he still hadn't shared his secret. I was beginning to grow impatient. "Any particular reason *why?*"

"Don't be glib about this, Matt," Jason warned me gravely. "It's very important you get this right."

"I'm not being glib," I protested, "like I told you before, I'm a good swimmer."

"How long," Jason continued, "could you hold your breath if you were swimming?"

"A little less," I whispered, voice lowered as if to avoid startling the nighttime around me, pallid under the blue tinted moonlight. Not even the forest was whispering now, as if equally afraid that something in the ether would hear it. "Probably no more than two minutes, I'd say."

The atmosphere held its breath, while liquid shadows spilled out from between the roots of trees in bold relief, slowly making their way towards us. . .

"All right. I have something to show you," Jason confessed at last, "something *magical.* Come with me."

"Right now?"

Two dashes of moonbeams swam eagerly within his dark irises. "It can only be tonight, when the moon is full."

From behind me, the floating warmth of those orange squares called my name weakly, *Mathew. . . Mathew, it's getting late. . .* But their voices were easily drowned out by the overwhelming silent anticipation around us.

"Matt?"

I turned back to Jason, the moonlight playfully dabbing his forehead, cheeks, and the tip of his nose to give him a rather skeletal appearance. "I'm ready," I decided at last.

. . .

Something about the moon's melody made our souls jump out of our skins and dance ahead of us through the trees, and toward the center of the forest where the quiet surface of the lake breathlessly awaited.

"Every month," Jason told me as we began to run, our every deafening footfall echoing out against the edges of azure-tinted nothingness, "the moon lines up perfectly against the lake when it's full, and when it does, it unlocks the other side of its reflection."

As the woods blurred by, we both saw the faces and flitting shadow-illusions that came with the moon's gentle sway on our rational minds, our buried fear of the dark, and the things that we were so sure it was hiding, though neither of us dared mention anything to the other.

I saw another pair of eyes, frost-blue, float out from the darkness behind shadows and shuddered. "Unlock the other side—like a portal?"

"Exactly like a portal."

And there it was before us, reflecting the moonlight like polished mercury.

"How do we get there?" I asked him.

"Swim like you're trying to get to the very bottom," he told me, "only when you've gone deep enough, and are getting close, you'll realize you're actually swimming upwards, and you'll start to see the surface of the other side again. That's where the other world's at."

"And what's there?"

"Everything," Jason said, as a ferocious mania lit his face. "Trees made out of licorice, fish swimming out in thin air, rivers of darkness, grass made out of emeralds, talking shadows. . . All the stars have fallen out of the sky, and the moon is *everywhere* in that place, bending, transforming things to your imagination. All your dreams and nightmares, anything is possible there. And we'll be its children. As long as we're there, the moon will give us anything. Spoil us rotten with its light and its songs and secrets. Can't you feel it? Calling, calling from the other sides of things. Singing. . . " His wide grin was brighter than a string of crooked pearls. I backed up a step, and then another.

A shadow returned to his face as he surveyed the distance that had now stretched between us. "Something wrong, Matt?"

From the shadows, I could feel those bodiless eyes boring into me. I swallowed nervously. "Well, not exactly. . ."

"You weren't lying about your being able to swim and hold your breath, were you?" he asked me, eyes narrowing.

197

"Of course not," I responded, a little defensively. "I just don't think I'm quite ready yet. Maybe if we come back next month—"

"No!" Jason cried, "there can't *be* a next time. Come with me, or don't, but this is it. This time, I'm staying for good."

"What do you mean, for good?"

"I mean," he shouted, "I'm going to the other side, and I'm not coming back!" Jason's declaration carried through the entire forest, trees shuddering briefly with its impact, before the silence swallowed his words whole and settled in between us once more.

"You don't understand," Jason spat disgustedly, "you're all the same!"

"You've taken others here?"

"Of course," Jason answered darkly, "but my friends didn't believe me, or they all chickened out just once after swimming to the other side. Only the last one really *got* it. The moon lived in his eyes, ran all through his veins, I could see it! Only, after he jumped. . . "

"Only what? What happened?"

Jason shook his head, lower lip quivering before the dam behind his words broke and they flooded out of him. "Only he *lied* to me, said he could swim, he promised! But I waited for him on the banks to come through, and he. . . he never did, and the water spirits must have got him before he reached the other side, because they never found the body, even though he told me, he *told* me he could swim and hold his breath so, it. . . it wasn't my *fault!*"

For a few moments, neither of us spoke. Finally, I asked, "yet you keep going back there?"

Jason looked at me, and his eyes glimmered dark and deadly within that skeletal face. "This place is the only one for me, a lake so much bigger on the inside. A moon so much closer than we could have ever wished for, that it's inside our every cell to guide us. I *need* that place,

Matt. And it needs me. I want to drink it all whole, the dirt, the smell. Every blade of emerald grass, the trees, the dirt, all the dreams and nightmares alike, every moonbeam in that starless sky until we're one and the same. All my life, I wanted so badly to run away, when everything I could have ever wanted was right here, mine for the taking, and all I had to do to get it was stand so very, very still and wait for the reflections to settle. And then we'll belong to each other forever."

And with that, Jason dove headfirst into the shimmering surface of mercury and vanished. I waited for him to come back, among the eyes, stifling silence, and lengthening darkness. I looked upwards at the sky's white cyclops eye, to find in it an apathetic spectator that offered no wisdom, before heading home to call for help.

They never found his body, in a lake that was only six feet deep by day.

. . .

For years afterwards, I would wander bleakly into the darkness of the forest and wonder, the last image of Jason's graceful, fearless, moonlit arc into the water burned onto the back of my eyelids. And I realized that there was a reason we humans were always so drawn to the night, yet so innately terrified of it at the same time. For something about the moonlight's enchanting spell never failed to unlock some dormant stardust gene deep within our bodies linking our race to the profound, to the magical, and otherworldly. . . as well as all the darkness that came with it. And even when I was well past my most vulnerable years, I knew that I, along with many others, would never fail to hear the whispers from all the moon's children, sense their presence on nights when the moon was full. On nights when the tangle of tree-bark looked more like licorice than wood, dark rivers flowed just beyond sight, and forests whispered, smelling of secrets or unasked questions, while the young eyes of the taken and the lost vigilantly watched and waited in the dark, where

199

even the night's gentle, pearly light no longer dared reach them, from beneath shadows, on the other side of moonlit lakes, or within the dark half of our minds.

About the Author

Kiki Gonglewski is a senior at Albuquerque Academy and a storyteller avidly exploring different media, such as writing, filmmaking, and photography. She was a finalist in the 2017 statewide "New Mexico Girls Make Movies" screenplay contest, has won a National Medal for Scholastic Art and Writing, and four gold keys in their Southwest Regional levels. Kiki has also been published in the 2018 edition of *Navigating The Maze,* an international teen poetry anthology.

*****~~~~~*****

Only the Weak Survive
by Caroline Sciriha

"I suppose it was justice, in a way." A silver-green leaf glided down onto my lap. I picked it up and brushed my fingers along its length. The olive leaf was longer than my hand.

"Jus-tice, miss?"

The words brought me back to the present. Maia's voice could turn even those two words into a musical composition. I met her curious gaze, her green eyes exactly matching the colour of the fruit above our heads. She was a beautiful child. They all were.

"Justice." Had the way we'd taken our planet for granted, the way we'd used and abused it and each other, triggered their idea of justice? Or maybe it had been something completely different. Maybe they were indifferent to our existence, our suffering. Or maybe we did not seem significant enough, our culture, our scientific achievements worthy enough to be saved.

I bent down to draw the letters in the soil—JUSTICE—then ran my finger down the first shape. "J, as in Justice. And Judgement Day."

Blue-eyed Jason copied the letter by his cross-legged feet. "Tell us again how you survived that day, miss."

The children encircling me stared without blinking or fidgeting. None of my former—and much older—

201

students had ever listened with such rapt attention, yet these four-year-olds didn't tire of hearing the story, or of learning.

I took in a shuddering breath. It pained me each time I had to relive that day, but it was important the children knew what had happened—and appreciated the cost. "School had ended, but I was on the phone speaking to a parent. Almost everyone else had left the building—the students to catch their transport, some teachers to see them leave in an orderly fashion, others to return to their homes. Only a few of us remained inside.

"The first thing that died was the phone line. I was not just cut off, but the phone just stopped working. That's when the rumble sounded. It shook the building, cracked walls, splintered windows, and slammed everything, slammed me to the ground.

"When I opened my eyes, the first thing I noticed was how silent the school was. No children yelled in the playground, no tinny voice crackled over the loudspeakers listing bus numbers arriving and leaving, no vehicles revved. No one screamed, or even moaned. Even the clock had fallen silent.

"I picked myself up, and my whole body ached. But thinking 'Earthquake. I have to get outside,' I rushed out. That's when I saw the first bodies."

I shuddered, but the children merely looked interested. They had no idea what death looked like, except when a plant withered to give sustenance to other vegetation.

"Everyone who'd been outside was dead. All the vehicles had stopped working—and ploughed or skidded into each other, or into the buildings. A few of us who'd been inside walked dazed among the dead, stooping here and there to feel for a pulse. I took out my phone to punch in the emergency number, but the battery had been sucked dry.

"That's when I noticed the rain." I lifted my hand off my lap and examined it. My skin looked youthful despite my fifty-four years. Had I been renovated too, like the planet?

"The rain didn't stop for five days. It was like no rain I'd ever seen. It splashed white on everything, covering everybody, every building, street, vehicle, tree, flower, leaf, and cranny. It's never snowed on this island, but the land was turned into a whitened tomb.

"The few of us that had survived ran for shelter. I darted across the parking area to my car, past vehicles crashed with bodies trapped within, past people I'd known for years who lay on the ground like so many discarded toys. My hands trembled so much, I had to try three to four times before I could open the car door."

I traced the U of JUSTICE in the soil. "U as in useless. It was useless to run from the rain, useless to try to start the car. No machinery has worked since that day, but I needed to find help, and to know what had happened to my children, my husband, my home.

"I'd always thought how lucky I was to work away from the town, far from the hubbub of traffic, surrounded by trees and nature. Now it meant I had to walk along the coast road to the town, or what was left of it. The roads and the town were even more damaged than the school. Fires had broken out where cars had smashed into each other, buildings had collapsed into heaps of rubble so that one could hardly say where the roads were. None of the few people I met knew what had happened, what had caused the devastation.

"It took me an hour to reach the town, and another to skirt round fires and clamber over heaps of debris to reach what had once been my apartment block. I never found my husband and children. I can only hope the end was quick for them, as it had been for the children in the school."

"Were you afraid?" Maia whispered.

203

I shook my head. "I was too numb to feel afraid. How can you have so much one moment, and nothing the next? No one seemed to know what to do. A few survivors and I tried moving blocks of concrete with our bare hands, but they were too heavy. I remember wondering how long it would take for the police or army to come to help us. Or maybe other countries would send us aid." How naïve I'd been.

"And the rain continued to fall," Peter said.

"Yes."

Peter more than the others, perhaps because of his white-blond hair and chubby cheeks, reminded me of the cherubs that old masters had loved to paint. Had any paintings survived? I didn't have pictures of any in the few books I'd salvaged.

I traced the letter S in the soil. "S is for. . . ?"

"Son."

"Soil."

"Sleep."

"Steven."

"Yes," I said, glancing at Steven. The twelve-year-old boy I'd met that fatal day sat in the centre of his own group of four-year-olds. He'd grown into a fine young man and was as precious as a son to me. "S is for son, and all the other words you said. Steven found me as I was trying to dig through the rubble that had once been my home. He recognised me as one of the teachers, but had not come to school that day, as he'd been ill. His home had collapsed too, but he'd managed to dig himself out of the debris. He was shivering, and I realised I needed to find him shelter and medicine.

"We stumbled towards the shopping mall. That was the first time we saw people fighting for food and other stuff. The building had been badly damaged, but people were tearing the rubble aside to grab water, alcohol, food, bedding, and electronics, even though those didn't work. Some were clawing them out of other

204

people's hands. People can lose control when they're terrified." I pointed to the T.

"T for terror."

"Trouble."

"Thugs."

I nodded. The children were linguistically precocious and never forgot a word I used. "Good. I pulled Steven away. We were both cold and hungry, but we would have been trampled upon."

"J-U-S-T-I. I is for idea and illness," Jason said. He used an olive branch to draw his letters, then looked at me for approval.

I straightened his T, then continued. "We spent the first night in a slight hollow in the rocks by the sea. Perhaps it wasn't very wise, as I was afraid of a tsunami, but it was the only shelter I could find. Steven slept a little, but he shivered all night long, and he was so hot. I knew that I would become ill too, if I didn't find food and warm clothing. As soon as it grew light, I told Steven we needed to return to the school. It had suffered less damage than the buildings in the town, perhaps because it had been built initially as a Second World War hospital. The walls were massive and hardy. And I also knew of a place beneath the school that could shelter us from the rain. We'd be safe there, and if we were lucky, we'd find leftover food in the canteen.

"The first inkling I got of what the white rain was capable of came when our rubber soles flaked away like powder as soon as we started walking to the school. My watch followed and clumps of my hair came away when I brushed my hand through it. I tried washing the whiteness off my skin and Steven's with seawater but it did little good. The rain kept falling hard, so in the end we just plodded on, in our bare feet.

"It took us most of the day to reach the school, but it had been a wise decision. The building hadn't been ransacked, although by then part of the roof had crumbled.

However, the rainwater hadn't yet reached the canteen. I knew we had little time, so after drinking a carton of juice and eating some fruit and cake, Steven and I carried all that we could find into the war shelter beneath the school.

"It was cold and damp down there—the shelter was just a tunnel hollowed out of the rock—but it was the safest place I could think of. After all, it had withstood aerial bombings; it should protect us from the white rain.

"I built a fire with broken chairs and tables in one of the industrial pots I got down from a home economics lab. The school health and safety clinic yielded a first aid box, some medicine for Steven, as well as blankets and a stretcher bed. It took several trips up and down the steps, but I carted down all that I thought we'd need—and all the food I found in the canteen and home economics labs. We even went through the teachers' staff room, as I knew most of us kept snacks there. The shelter became our home.

"None of my colleagues ever returned to the school. I wonder what became of them. Over the next few days, we heard gangs tramping through the building, but no one tried to break into the war shelter. The cats that had been so plentiful around the school disappeared, though. Perhaps they were eaten.

"Then the school collapsed."

Peter and Jason twitted softly in the high-pitched clicks I couldn't understand, the dried leaves they sat on crunching and rustling as they shifted position. A long time ago pigeons had made that sound.

"C," Maia said, pointing to the penultimate letter, "for collapse and cat and cave."

I forced myself to smile. The children looked so innocent. "Steven and I were trapped inside the shelter for days. We played this letter game together to keep ourselves occupied and our minds off the thought we might starve to death buried in that tunnel.

"But when the stone and concrete above us disintegrated to powder, we pushed through the remaining debris and got out. We found a world very different from that which we'd known. The school, the town even, were now little more than vast plains with a few stones still upright, like one would find in an archaeological dig. The bodies that had strewn the carpark and yards, the machinery and vehicles had all disintegrated, just as the soles of our shoes had, leaving only heaps of white dust behind."

I pointed to the boles over my head, heavy with fruit, to huge stalks and petals, to plants I'd never seen before that day, but which had now become a source of food. "Instead of the buildings, trees grew and plants flourished. Our island became one huge garden. And in the white dust, eggs appeared."

What had populated the planet?

"E for environment," Peter whispered. His eyes gleaned.

I nodded. Apart from Steven, I had not seen another human being since we'd emerged from the shelter. I could only hope that others had found a hole in the ground to hide in and weather the storm, if not on this island, in the lands beyond our shore.

I gazed round at the children's pert faces, their round eyes and hair the colour of the rain. It was they who'd sought Steven and me out, asked us questions, and eventually came every day to spend time with us. Did little Maia know more about what had really happened that day than what I'd told her? Did Peter and Jason know what was happening beyond the sea, beyond our planet? They never answered when I asked them, so I no longer did.

I picked the olive branch Jason had used to write his letters and brushed the soil off it. My people had considered it a symbol of peace, once.

Terra! Tara! Terror!

The cherub-like children twitted amongst themselves, then they stood, spread their wings and flew into the trees they called home.

About the Author

Caroline Sciriha teaches English at a secondary school in Malta and holds an MA in English Literature. Her short stories have appeared in anthologies and magazines including *Mind Candy, Beyond Steampunk,* and *New Myths*. She also co-authored *Kellimni Let's Talk,* a bilingual textbook for beginner learners of English and Maltese as additional or foreign languages.

*****~~~~~*****

War Dog

by Wulf Moon

I stood next to Commander Balboa on a rocky outcrop, his ruddy war dog Leoncillo between us, panting from the sweltering jungle heat. For a man approaching forty, Balboa had stamina that put young men like me to shame. He was the embodiment of a Spanish conquistador: lean and sinuous as buccaned meat, sharper than Castilian steel. With his regal armor, piercing brown eyes, curled black hair and precisely trimmed beard, I saw him as a crown prince instead of the penniless pig farmer from Hispaniola. He had that way about him, visions as high as St. Peter's gate, with that potent alchemy of charisma and bravura that turned lead into gold, inspiring his men to worship him like a saint.

As Balboa scanned the vista, I rubbed mighty Leoncillo's folds of skin. He whipped his head around, chuffed, licked my hand with his lolling pink tongue, and moved off to water a tree. I was proud of the fact that besides Balboa, I was the only soldier in our company the "Little Lion" allowed to handle him. Leoncillo was one of the famous Spanish alaunts, and he weighed more than most fighting men. Alaunts were bull-faced dogs with jaws like iron bear traps. Cunning intelligence glowed within their keen yellow eyes, guiding their muscular mass with ferocious accuracy. We even armored the best

209

of the pack like war horses, protecting them in quilted gambesons and spiked collars and metal plate. Nothing struck more fear into the hearts of our lightly clad opponents.

They say history is written by the victors. In *Tierra Firme*, history was written by the dogs of war.

Balboa thrust his arm out like a lance in battle. "Capricho! Behold. The South Sea!"

I wiped the sweat from my brow, shielded my eyes, scanned the horizon. A rolling jungle of several day's march filled my vision, but there in the distance, a shimmer of blue fought its way through the haze, then transformed into a white, undulating snake. The white snake writhed and vanished, writhed and vanished. Every man that had crossed the Atlantic knew that sign.

Surf!

I remember smiling warmly at Balboa, exhausted though I was from the climb. Even at this altitude, the air was so thick with humidity you could chew it. "My lord, you were right."

He chuckled. "I am not a lord. *Yet.*"

I knew this man. I knew his destiny like I knew gold from a rock. The ocean that shimmered in the distance was living proof of the faith I had placed in him from the first day I had found him hidden in a barrel, a stowaway with his pup on Governor Enciso's ship, sailing from Hispaniola to this land. When enraged Enciso had ordered Balboa and his dog thrown overboard, I had stood at Balboa's and Leoncillo's side, swinging my fists and swearing by all the saints they would have to throw me over with him. Pizarro had been there, more than ready to oblige, but I suppose seeing a young man's courage softened Enciso's heart, and he spared us.

"You will be a lord," I assured Balboa. "The Crown will name you Duke of *Tierra Firme.*"

He gripped my shoulder, spoke with that gusto that made you believe if he wished, he could walk on water.

"Columbus can have his quest for a passage to the Indies. He is nearsighted, has never seen the big picture. This is proof we have here a new continent! Imagine what we will create free from the bloody inquisitors, free from the money-grubbing bishops, free from bickering *bachillers* and their debtors' prisons. Me, I don't want a Passage. I want a Destination, and I swear I will shape *Tierra Firme* into a land with equal promise for all, noble or commoner, Spaniard or indigenous. Our alliances with the natives proves it can be done."

I was certain he was right—Balboa had even won over a powerful tribe by taking the princess Fulvia as wife. We just had that tiny problem of getting the news of our discovery back to the Crown before Enciso—the feckless governor that Balboa had been forced to depose—convinced King Ferdinand to remove Balboa's head.

The sour scent of body odor assaulted my nostrils as almond-eyed Francisco Pizarro elbowed his way between us and slapped me hard on the back. "Hah! If the sea is real, boy, so is the city of gold. These naked curs will be no match for Spanish steel. We'll gut them like pigs. I'm going to be richer than the King!"

Money and glory. If Pizarro opened his mouth, those words spilled out like rabid spittle. He would have sold his soul to the devil to get what he desired. I know now that he had. As if to his words, a fierce gust rushed the ridge, shook the fronds of the trees, filled the air with the sound of angry rattlesnakes. The benevolent domain Balboa had envisioned was about to be shattered.

. . .

On 29 September, 1513 Anno Domini, Balboa led us out from the jungle canopy onto the shores of the Southern Sea, but it was Leoncillo that first claimed it, lunging ahead of us across the shallows in pursuit of a pelican. From there began the race to send notice to our monarch that he had a new continent on his hands, and to get the Crown's approval to explore *Tierra Firme's* coastlines.

But our enemies had other plans, and convinced the Crown to install a new governor at Darien, our outpost on the Gulf side of the isthmus. His name was Pedrarias. I remember the day of his arrival like it was yesterday.

I had returned with a hunting party, trying to supplement our meager rations of maize with jungle fowl. The sky was filled with bruised clouds; the bay was a puddle of melted lead. Fifteen, sixteen, no! seventeen ships anchored in the harbor.

I choked as we approached the village. Filling the dusty street all the way up the hill to Balboa's house were men in foppish hats and silk finery, tossing dirt into the air and cheering. I looked down to the pier. Armored soldiers unloaded horses and pulled crates from tenders while others milled about. A commotion was taking place on the pier as the largest longboat approached. Fighting men came off the beach, flanked the entrance to the town, and moved into ranks.

This looked like a coup.

I searched for a friendly face. Our little village had been so overrun, I knew no one around me. I spotted a corpulent youth with fat lips that looked eager to talk. We made our introductions and I got to the point.

"So, Carlos, who leads your glorious company?"

He pointed to the tender. "The new Governor of Darien. His men call him Pedrarias."

My heart thumped. "A fighting man, this Pedrarias?"

The youth stood on his toes, trying to see over men's heads. "Oh yes! He fought the Moors at Granada and served under Navarro in Africa."

"Impressive. Not a young man, I presume?"

"Oh no, he's ancient. Must be seventy. But he moves like a lion I'm told, and can outrun a horse." The youth paused. *"Señor,* want to know something weird?"

"Always."

"He carries a casket with him."

"Then he won't be with us long, thank God."

Carlos scowled. "No. This was years ago. They thought he was dead and they nailed him in a coffin and were about to bury him. But the priest heard voices inside, and when they opened it up, he was *alive.*"

I hissed. "You are sure of this?"

He pointed to the winch on the pier. "There's the coffin now. They say he takes it everywhere to remind him of how close he came to death."

I looked at the casket as it rose in the air. Strange.

"There they are!"

Trumpets sounded. Coming up from the pier was a bishop in full vestments, golden crozier in one hand, censer in the other. Incense puffed from the vessel, trailing blue tendrils. Friars in ranks followed, chanting the *Te Deum* as if they were presenting the Holy Father. Then came the soldiers, hoisting lances bearing banners of the Crown. There were mighty Andalusian horses, dappled in gray, their hooves beating the earth like war drums. And finally, shackled slaves, bearing a gilded sedan chair. Within bobbed a skeleton of a man, staring straight ahead as if no one was there at all.

I squinted to see better.

Instantly, his visage was right in front of my face. I jumped.

Radiating off his pate was a golden nimbus, but the rays writhed and snapped like serpents. His eyes looked past me, thank God, but my ears filled with clicking sounds.

"Where are you?"

I clutched a silver cross that hung from my neck, and Pedrarias's visage shot back to the sedan, just a gilded man in a pompous parade. They moved on by, followed by more slaves bearing that casket. Hissing rose from it like steam from a cauldron. What was happening to me? I heard voices, calling as if from the very fires of hell.

He gave his soul to escape death. Will you also serve?

I crossed myself and ran to warn Balboa. This man had made a deal with the devil—the story and casket were my proof. What deals had he made to rise from the grave to become our governor?

. . .

Balboa called my talk superstitious nonsense and told the men gathered with me to stand down. Little did Balboa know, Governor Pedrarias had been commissioned to examine how a hidalgo could dare think he had jurisdiction to replace Enciso, the Crown-appointed governor. But as the governor's troops began dropping like flies from local disease, it was clear Balboa held the superior force. Only a fool would have tried to take Balboa down under such circumstances. So, the devil's man fell to cunning to wrest *Tierra Firme* from him.

In the months and years that followed, Pedrarias let it appear Balboa had earned favor, even granting his request to build our fleet to begin exploration on the other side of the isthmus. Pizarro had slyly slipped from our force over to the governor's, becoming Pedrarias's eyes and ears. I was happy to be rid of them both, and only too glad to be away from Darien at our new settlement of Acla—a site on the Gulf side, closer to the passage across the isthmus. Then, just as Balboa sent our forces to transport materials across for the new ships, the governor's messenger came, requesting Balboa meet him at Darien. My worst fear had happened, and I warned Balboa he could be ambushed away from our troops.

"Nonsense, Capricho," Balboa had said. "The man has betrothed me to his own daughter in Spain! I think I can trust my own father-in-law."

I never asked him what Fulvia, his native bride, thought of the arrangement, nor what absolutions he had gotten from the bishop. He simply called Fulvia his translator now, but her hut was next to his, and she was ever at his side.

I could not dissuade him, so I begged to come along.

He looked at me with those warm eyes, the same eyes I had seen years ago when I discovered him in a barrel on Enciso's ship. "You may come. It will irk that traitor Pizarro, and that pleases me."

"I want Leoncillo with us."

Balboa stroked his beard. "*Si.* Bring my dog."

. . .

The day was hot as hell. Balboa refused my request to armor Leoncillo—he said the dog would overheat. Halfway on the trail to Darien, Pizarro appeared, fully armored, a force of soldiers flanking each side. Balboa drew our handful of men and Fulvia to an abrupt halt. Leoncillo lunged at his leash, but I commanded him to heel.

Balboa's voice rang out. "What is the meaning of this, Francisco?"

Pizarro unsheathed his sword, eyes as black as the abyss. From the brush, I saw arquebusiers light matchcords and clip them into the serpentines of their firing mechanisms. "You are hereby arrested by order of Governor Pedrarias for crimes of treason against the Crown."

"Treason? I am the Crown's faithful servant!"

Pizarro spat. "You have declared yourself king of your own kingdom over the lands of the South Sea."

My blood boiled. "Who says?"

Pizarro narrowed those almond-shaped eyes on me. "I say, boy, and I have the sworn testimony of three other officers." He nodded to the men at his side. "Arrest them."

Fulvia dived into the brush. Leoncillo, snarling beside me, lunged with all his fury, breaking my grip on the leash.

"Leoncillo, no!" I shouted, but the arquebusiers fired. Heart in my throat, I saw blood spurt from several ball strikes, heard a high-pitched yelp, and yet Leoncillo charged ahead with all the power of a maddened bull. Pizarro dropped to one knee, held his blade forward, pommel gripped in both hands. Leoncillo tried to turn, but his momentum carried him forward, and Pizarro impaled him with a thrust. Their bodies rolled across the ground. Pizarro alone rose up.

The bastard had killed our dog!

Blind with rage, I drew my sword, bellowed a cry, and charged.

Why was I flying sideways? Why did a lance of fire shriek through my chest? What was this volley of thunder? There were no clouds in the sky.

Why was darkness falling? It was not the time for night.

. . .

Shlurpa-shlurp. Shlop, gushlop.

"Capricho."

Wufff! Shallop-shlup-shallop-gushlurpsh.

I opened my eyes to a pink tongue sliding across my lips. Ugh. Dog breath.

Dog breath!

I lifted my head. Leoncillo's golden eyes smiled down on me.

"Woof!"

"Little Lion!" I reached up, grabbed Leoncillo by the scruff, gave him a mighty hug. Bad idea. Pain lanced my chest, and my head spun.

216

"You should rest." The voice was soft, feminine, and had that familiar Chibchan accent. "His blood binds to yours. . . "

. . .

Sweat drenched my skin and forehead. Fire burned inside me, coursing through my veins. In lucid moments, I could see the dark-skinned legs of natives. In dark moments, I saw a steaming mercurial pool, whispering with spirit voices, lapped by a pink tongue.

. . .

I do not know the first day I stood. I only know that I was alive, and as I leaned against the shack's doorframe, I realized I was looking upon Panamá Viejo, our settlement on the South Sea's shores. A few Spaniards and natives were casting nets over the shallows. Leoncillo rose from outside, blessed me with a wet slurp. I bent down and ran my hands over his skin. Remarkable. There wasn't a mark on him.

"He loved you, you know."

It was Fulvia, coming out of her hut, dressed in a brilliant white longshirt.

I stood. "How is this possible? Is this heaven?"

Fulvia worked the word *cielo* over her tongue. "Sorry, *señor,* no."

"Then, how am I alive?"

She pointed to Leoncillo. "They threw you in hole. With him."

"Hole? You mean grave?"

"*Si.* Grave. His blood mix with yours. I come back, find Leoncillo dug you both out."

"How is this possible? If they buried us, we were. . . *dead.*"

Fulvia handed me a gourd filled with cool water. "Did my lord never tell you? This dog's sire was Becerrillo."

"Yes, Ponce de León's war dog. He told me."

217

She motioned for me to drink. I had not realized how thirsty I was, until I put the gourd to my lips.

"Why do you think Ponce searches for, how do you say, fountain of underworld? Because his dog must have drank from it on one of their journeys, and he does not know where."

I drained the gourd. "How would he know that?"

She took the gourd from my hands. "Because his dog kept coming back to life. Like this dog just did."

Leoncillo woofed.

It was a crazy story. But I knew some of the tales about Becerrillo, how he had killed thirty-three attackers in a half hour, and not a scratch on him. The tales were legendary. And I had just seen Leoncillo hit by lead shot and run through with a sword. No dog, not even an alaunt, could survive that.

But here he was, panting at my side.

Fulvia's dark eyes shimmered. "His blood spilled in your wounds. Your blood and his blood bubble with underworld fountain now. *Comprende*?"

I ran my hands over my bare chest. No wound.

Fulvia's eyes clouded. "My lord Balboa had such life. This dog had bled on his wounds too." She spat words in Spanish, Chibcha and other languages I had never heard before. "That's why they chopped off his head and shoved it on stake. So he could not rise again."

"What?"

Tears welled in her eyes. "They killed my lord. They killed his friends. Pedrarias and Pizarro did this thing."

"Where?"

"At Acla. Word came to us yesterday."

My world spun out from under me. I dropped to my knees and wept.

. . .

Three hundred armored Spaniards, that had been loyal to Balboa. The same number of warriors from

218

Fulvia's tribe. She herself led them. Ninety-three war dogs, most fixed in armor. And one resurrected leader, calling his forces to a halt at the jungle's edge, the sleeping town of Acla beyond, glowing under the red sky of dawn.

I kneeled beside Leoncillo, gave his folds a rub, fastened the gambeson and steel breastplate over his chest. He watched me with those keen golden eyes, chuffed once as I unclipped the leash from his collar, then growled low and deadly as he nosed the air. We would finish Balboa's dream our way, and we would prepare the Inca for what was to come. But first, there were accounts to be settled.

They say history is written by the victors. In *Tierra Firme*, history was written by the dogs of war.

###

About the Author

Wulf Moon is represented by Donald Maass of the Donald Maass Literary Agency. His first SF tale, written when he was fifteen, won Scholastic Inc.'s national writing contest. *Science World* bought and published it in 1978. Moon's Borg love story, "Seventh Heaven" was published in *Star Trek: Strange New Worlds II*. In a contest sponsored by *New York Times* best-selling author Nora Roberts, his entry won first place, and was published as the concluding chapter to Nora's novella, "Riley Slade's Return."

Last year, Third Flatiron published and podcasted Moon's "Beast of the Month" in its *Strange Beasties* anthology. Since that podcast, Moon has done four assignments for *Gallery of Curiosities*.

Moon's hard SF story, "The Last Ray of Light" will be published in the *Trace the Stars* anthology by LTUE Publishing in early 2019.

*****~~~~~*****

If a Tree Falls

by Dan Micklethwaite

Betula had slumbered through last night's storm, and although it left her glutted and swollen with water, she still woke with a desperate thirst for the sun. She could sense the morning's warmth, its light, and tried to reach her limbs towards them, just as she always did on every fine summer's day.

But she found herself restricted, unexpectedly; an unwanted reminder of her nursery years, the swaddling they had bound her in to help her grow straight. Only, softer. Springier. Damper. More loamy.

And now something was snuffling at her body, her bark.

Unfamiliar contact. Not squirrel. Not bird.

When she tried to open her eyes, they were gummy with sap; crumbling lichen like sleep in her lashes. Nevertheless, she could discern that the animal raising its leg was a dog—a Jack Russell—and it didn't seem to be standing the right way up. And neither, out of focus in the background, did the other trees in this forest. Her forest. Splintering sideways into the cloudless blue sky.

Surely the storm hadn't been as bad as all that? It couldn't have levelled a whole entire copse.

Urine spattered against her, running in rivulets through the whorls in her bark, and this time she wanted to shy from the heat, but still couldn't move, in any direction.

Of course, she realised—the knots of her consciousness briefly untangling—it wasn't the world that had been toppled over. Only her own sodden roots come unstuck.

. . .

The dog's owner perched on Betula's left flank, lighting a cigarette, watching her pet rummage round in the scrub. Finally, its head bobbled up from behind a curtain of ferns, proudly chewing and waving a stick. As it brought its prize back through the semi-damp mud, Betula felt a pang of recognition and loss.

It was one of her forearms, slender and silvered, now fraying and tooth-marked, slathered with drool.

Her sisters had told her, she remembered, to always be careful never to fall.

Or at least, if she did, never to let any human beings see.

You cannot come back from that, they had told her, and as she watched the dog's owner throw her branch like a spear—a slow, imperfect arc across the cloudless sideways sky—Betula conceded the truth of their warning. Even a dryad could wither, she realised, tasting the nicotine smoke in the air.

. . .

She had worms in her brain. She had woodlice in her hair and pushing underneath her skin. Larvae boring deep in timber, almost ticklish, almost nice. To be wanted. To still be useful to something, still a part of these woods.

Blackbirds alighted. Blue Tits. Sparrows. A solitary wood pigeon. Magpies danced the full length of her trunk, unpicking the knots in her flesh with their claws.

222

The mud and the lichen had almost cleared from her eyes, and she could see the world plainly, see her new place within it.

She had been standing for a long time next to the footpath, so as to feel close to the people who used to pass by. Bask in their worship, the reverence they afforded to her and her forest.

She sprawled across that footpath now, and nobody had travelled it since the dog-walker left. No committee was forming to come clean her off, to raise her, rectify her, maybe try and resettle her feet in the soil.

Not a committee, perhaps, but something at least.

A sound like a bee-swarm; wheels spinning round.

As it grew louder, the magpies took off.

. . .

Betula recognised the boy; the young man. She thought she did, anyway. He had stopped in the middle of the path, astride his mountain bike, and was much taller and a bit broader than she remembered, and wore a peaked black helmet that covered his mouth and nose as well as his scalp. But his eyes were exposed, and it was those that she recognised; almost certain that they recognised her in return.

Did he remember when he used to come out here on his smaller bicycle, his blue and yellow BMX, and slalom in between the oaks? Or when his friends would join him, either engrossed in the architecture and engineering of dens, or lost in epic, almost boundless, bouts of hide and seek?

Did he recall the day when he had taken refuge amongst her highest boughs, which had trembled with his silent laughter, his triumphant relief, as seeker after seeker had prowled, unsuspecting, through the undergrowth below?

Perhaps, Betula hoped, as the man removed his helmet and set his bike down in the mud.

223

He walked towards her, slowly, stretching his arms out as though he intended to embrace her. To express his deep sorrow that she should have come to such a state.

Then he stopped, and from the way he moved those arms, his hands and fingers, it became apparent that instead he was measuring her up. Trying to gauge, she thought, the height and width and depth of her trunk.

The weight.

Just before he put his helmet back on, she thought she caught him smiling, as if anticipating a good deed that he was about to perform. Because surely, as he picked up his bike and aimed its front wheel in the opposite direction, he planned to go off and fetch some kind of help.

. . .

The young man pedalled back the way that he'd come, then turned again, approaching now at higher speed—something of that childlike wildness in his eyes, that silent laughter—and he was almost approaching the site of her accident, and he pulled up on his handlebars, on the rest of the chassis, and sailed clear over the top of her and away out behind.

. . .

Betula must have fallen asleep again after that, because when she next looked at the footpath, the wrong-angled trees, it was getting near evening, and a patchwork of clouds obscured the sky. She was already weakening, uprooted like this, and damp with lying in the dirt all day, and though she wanted to move away from the gathering chill, she still found herself unable.

She could not call out to her sisters for help, because there were so few of them left; even when the humans had raised them in nursery plots—reintroducing them to the wild shortly thereafter—they were seldom allowed to flourish for long. Furniture seemed in perennial demand. Notepaper also. Shopping bags. Boxes.

She used to hope, somehow, to be immortal and ageless, as her ancestors had seemed in those long-ago myths.

But she was tired and lonely, and did not hope that now.

. . .

The laying on of hands. Fingertips tracing the rough, fractured bark; probing the pitiful jumble of roots. Palms at rest, patient, feeling for any and all signs of life.

When the human stepped back, Betula thought that she knew him. A local farmer, perhaps? Somebody, at least, who was aware both how practical and how ruthless nature could be. Somebody who knew that she was of no help to her forest stranded like this. Who knew that a footpath had to be cleared.

He was saying something now, though she could not understand it, and she didn't know whether he was speaking to her or to himself or more broadly to the forest or simply the earth.

But then he went away regardless, as everyone else seemed to do, and she struggled with the soil yet again in her anger, but again could not shift herself, even a bit.

The magpies returned, and seemed mocking and cruel.

A wood pigeon also, who would not stop hooting her boasts of being free.

But the birds scattered again when an engine resounded, and the farmer pulled up on his mud-spattered quadbike; dismounting, he went to fetch something from the trailer in back.

Betula was disoriented, confused and frustrated, but when she saw what he was carrying, her eyes clouded amber with tears of relief.

. . .

The surgery had hurt, a great deal, but now that it was over, she did not feel so bad.

As each log was hefted into the trailer, she caught sight of the cross-sections; a slideshow of grainy images depicting her past. Memories of winters and springtimes and summers, of all the autumns she'd lived through before this last fall.

Already, those rings seemed jagged and frayed, and some of them were darker and more rotten than she'd realised. Even the skin on the outside was not as silver as it should have been; it was already peeling, drying and brown.

Lying so close to the dirt like this, Betula felt almost like a sapling again, daunted by the wilderness, and helpless inside it; desperate for nutrients and eager for sun. Everything she had learnt in the long years since, she could feel it receding. The fibres of selfhood were coming apart.

The farmer's touch, cradling, brought her back for a moment, and she felt the shock of not-knowing, or being unclear where she was.

The bed of the trailer was a cold steel clue; slowly, she pieced the puzzle together.

Whether she wanted to or not, she was leaving the forest. Her forest.

She was about to be taken away to a home.

. . .

Her consciousness, her mind, was all over the place. It was like her roots had been, in a way; intricate and labyrinthine, and yet even though they belonged to her, they were still somehow obscured. Until the day when they weren't.

When she searched for the sustenance of treasured recollections, some knowledge or experience she had squirreled away, they simply weren't there to be found any more. Likewise, when she searched for some water, some soil.

It had all been scrubbed and scraped from her bark.

If a Tree Falls

She had been wormed and deloused.

Fungi had been excised with an old butter knife.

There was less and less left of her, every new day, and what there was had been piled in a large wicker basket, close beside something she couldn't quite see. Something that carried a strong smell of smoke.

It made her think about someone, but she didn't know who.

Faces, trees, and birdsong blended.

Sometimes, she thought that her sisters were speaking.

Other times, laughing.

More often, she couldn't recall who they were or where they had gone.

She couldn't remember the man who reached out to her now, who raised her so tenderly in one callused fist. She panicked. She screamed soundlessly, as quietly as she felt like a young boy had once laughed. Which boy? Wheels spun in her head with a sound like a swarm, trying to parse it, to unpick this riddle.

But then, yes, oh yes, she recognised this grip.

The farmer. The one who had taken her in. Promised to make her as comfortable as possible. Promised to make her feel useful again.

Which was all that she wanted.

And though she couldn't quite see where the farmer was taking her, she was suddenly aware of the warmth and the light, and just like she always had, she tried to reach closer, and was delighted, for a moment, as she finally did.

About the Author

Dan Micklethwaite is an award-winning short story writer and novelist. His short fiction is forthcoming in a wide range of venues, including *AE Science Fiction, Unsung Stories,* and *Beneath Ceaseless Skies.* His debut novel, *The Less than Perfect Legend of Donna Creosote,* was published by Bluemoose Books in 2016. Follow him on twitter for more info @Dan_M_writer.

*****~~~~~*****

Memory And Muchness

by Rhonda Eikamp

My sister Paley went up the hole today.

The hole was full of light, a yellow with no name, and I held her leg and screamed, but it didn't stop her. When they go, they go. The light shot down, hungry for my eyes. I closed them, and when I opened them the door to the hole had slid closed, leaving only rough stone, and Paley was gone.

She was just two years older than me.

Run, run to the Party, crawl onto that comfy furry lap, only the March Hare didn't hug me. He nudged me off his knees until I was standing beside him. He'd *never* done that before. The other kids looked up from their orgbuildings and drawings. The little ones stopped their game of tag around the Table to stare at me, but not for long, racing away laughing into the low-lit side halls when they saw the tears in my eyes. Jason slipped from his chair at the Table and came to put a hand on my shoulder. A head taller than me, more Paley's age, but the only one who understood.

"I want my sister," I moaned to Hare, and it was a strong moan, a real moan. Not kidstuff. The kind of moan that gets action from the Partygoers, the kind they try to do something about. There was a hole opening up in me, Paley-shaped, and it was terrifying. The children who go

229

up the hole never come back. There was nobody to take her place, out of all of us, the hundreds including the cribs. Not for me. Not even Jason, his sympathetic hand tightening on my shoulder, aside from Paley the only person I'd ever found my way to on the inside. That's how I see it. As if you have to hack through vines like the ones that clog the bad halls and keep us from adventuring there, the sticky protuberances that seem to move to block you when you're not looking. I felt I'd spent my whole life hacking through people's jungles, looking for the center, and very few had ever let me in. Paley had been one of them, a part of me.

The March Hare is want and the Mad Hatter is need. Hatter stood up from his place at the Table, hearing the strong in my voice. "Child." The word echoed across the vast Party chamber. The partitions of his face shifted around, composing what I expected would be compassion but which settled into strict. Eyelids half-down like stuck doors over red optical apertures, the corners of his mouth-blocks lowered. My heart gave way. The Dormouse woke and squeaked. Children backed from their drawings or snuck away into shadowed halls. "You're late for your lessons, child."

Something broke inside. "No!" It's discipline we're taught, more important than any facts. To withstand pressure, boredom, fear. Obey orders without question. There are special games for it. There's the Wringer. But it was too much. The suspicions I'd had for so long bubbled up, rearranging themselves like the stone components of Hatter's face to form something new.

"No!" I yelled and beat my hand on the Table. "You take them, don't you? Take them and we never see them again. It's your doing, isn't it? Even you—" To Hare, whose organic fuzzy-brown eyes grew huge.

"Marney, my dear," he muttered, "we all love you, you know." He reached out a paw, larger than my head.

A lights-out fell across my mind then. Who needs love from a toy, no matter how large and capable? From a stone robot or a giant dormouse that skitters over the Table to move the cursor on the ceiling maps while we learn?

I shoved cups and saucers to the floor, howled till the dark coated my throat. It was a tantrum, the rage of the little ones but different from their little wants. A monster difference, bursting from my chest. Bitter vines sprouting from me, cutting off the air. I felt Jason's arms lowering me, his scared voice calling for their help.

. . .

I woke with the Queen peering down at me. From the cries of infants, I was in the crib-room. Queen smiled and every beloved familiar wrinkle smiled with her. "There now, you're okay." She stepped away, her plump skirts rustling, and returned with a sippy-cup.

When you're small Queen does everything for you, heals scrapes, banishes nightmares, the only face you associate with caring, but at some point you don't need Her Majesty anymore. The lessons in discipline start. You move to dorms with beds larger than the one my head and feet pushed against now, and you hardly ever see Queen again, but her face stays with you. Apparently the Partygoers thought I'd had a relapse, immaturity simply a disease to be treated, childishness a bug in the human machine. Or they wanted to embarrass me, sticking me back with the little ones.

"Paley's gone," I told her.

"I'll make a bowl of your favorite." The favorite is a gray mush with the ocher sprinkles called vitamins, and it's the same for everyone. It's when you realize that that you start moving out of the crib-room. A wisp of the rage caught me—Queen would comfort, heal, but never *listen*—and with it the suspicion returned, blotting out all the beloved lines of her face. Maybe it was my tears starting.

"Tell me about the hole, Queen."

She turned her face away, but not before I saw a change in it, an effort at blankness.

Behind her I could see the umbilicals snaking from the walls to the cribs. Queen carried a toddler on her hip, who sucked his thumb and watched me over her arm with happy uncomprehending eyes. She turned back to me and repeated, "I'll make a bowl of your favorite."

I made my voice smooth over the scream inside. "I'd love that." Watched her bring the bowl. Faked greedy hunger.

Thinking all the time about Paley. About what she told me she'd glimpsed the last few days before she went. The thing I wouldn't mention to them now even if they put me in the Wringer.

. . .

The world is small, I think, compared to what the Partygoers teach us. Halls with gleaming pathlights leading to our dorms, the tall Party chamber with its long Table in the middle for work and play and meals. The Wringer, hunched in its separate chamber, there past the green bad-smelling arch. . . . When you're little it all seems infinite, but then you get bigger, and the walls shrink. We lie on our backs and learn from the ceiling maps, words like jungle and ocean, but what the Partygoers never say—what I've figured out by myself—is that these must be things inside us, pictures for what we look like inside. For where would you put this thing ocean in the halls?

Jungles and oceans inside us.

I found Jason at group lesson before the Cheshire Cat. Cheshire sauntered up and down the Table, grinning whenever a kid did well. Jason was putting together a device I hadn't graduated to, a sleek black rectangle of metal the length of his forearm, with tiny beetles like dust specks that strayed from it constantly and had to be herded back in, spreading out to form intricate spirals on the Table top whenever Jason's attention lapsed. I sat beside him as though fascinated by the device, and he understood something was up, something worse than the tantrum. It'd been that way with Paley too, that connection, only better.

"Paley saw something, Jason." I pointed, pretending to ask a question about his lesson. "Kept catching glimpses of it for days." I told him what she'd seen.

"Like Hare?" he asked. An odd note made his whisper shaky.

"Nothing like him, she said. We learned the difference, remember? It was a rabbit, she swore. All white." I tried to bleed the trouble from my face, because Cheshire was coming back our way. Jason stared at his learning device, not seeing it, while beetles wrote a whole novel of hieroglyphics on the Table. "With a vest—"

"And a pocketwatch," he finished for me. I almost gasped. "I've seen it, Marney. Once."

The thought that there was a Partygoer that could remain undetected by all of us made my stomach twist.

"Paley followed it," I said. The memory was still raw from that morning. "She said it kept taking out its pocketwatch and looking at her and then this morning. . . " We'd been in the dorm alone, late as usual, and Paley had jumped up suddenly, staring at an empty corner, with that long red hair swaying, ordered me to stay back, but I'd never been able to take orders. "It was like she was in deep-learn. She said she had to." She said, *I love you, Marney*. I'd followed her to one of the vine-choked halls, the one rumored to contain a door in its ceiling, though none of us could ever make out a groove or seam, and when the hole opened I'd grabbed her leg and begged.

A kid with a floating grin over his head, the sign of a lesson well done, leaped up from the Table and ran off happy, and I realized I didn't know where Cheshire was. When I looked up she was right in front of us.

Gazing down on us. Listening.

She smiled. "Your lessson ziss afternoon iss in the Wringer, Marney."

. . .

Not punishment, I told myself. Only the most mature go in the Wringer, and yet I knew—*knew*—it was because she'd heard us talking about Paley and the white rabbit. I tried to walk straight, following floating Cheshire past the green musty arch. The metal box, a black you can see your face in, came to humming life as we approached, opened its giant door, and Cheshire gave me my worms and devices and shut me in.

Time stops in the Wringer. I never know how long I've been in, how long the pain has gone on. Pain's the wrong word. Discomfort, terror. Nightmare. The air fights you—you swallow the red worm to breathe first, and, when your fingernails turn blue, you swallow the green worm—and the floor tilts uphill, downhill, goes spongy or fluid unexpectedly, even after the monsters come. Billowing, shredded curtains of violet that sear your eyes. Sometimes your devices don't work, and you have to try and repair them in the battering air before the next billowy monster descends or coalesces from the ground beneath your feet, disguised by mimicry. No one wins in the Wringer. You fight the violet till you die, always, and the dying's a worse nightmare, a sting from a wisp you missed that burns you from the inside out. You watch your arms turn black.

I woke up being deposited into a chair beside Jason at the Table. The scorch was still on my mind, my body a memory of flame, and Hare's big paws set me down gently. He knelt to gaze into my eyes—that huge moist sadness that always comforted me before but which seemed mockery now. I felt the difference again, those choking vines growing in me, tendrils of suspicion, no longer believing that what they put us through was necessary, and I wanted to punch Hare in his cute-as-a-button face. Maybe that's all there is to growing up—starting to ask why.

Hare must have understood my expression. He left us alone. Lessons were long over. Jason had remained at the Table waiting for me, the device before him forgotten. "Was it bad?" he asked, staring away, not looking at me. We're alike that way, not wanting to be looked at after we've been through the Wringer.

I couldn't answer. "Jason, we've got to find the white rabbit. Make it tell us where the kids go."

"That won't be hard." He took my hand, and, when he finally turned to me, I knew we were together, the two of us, in a place the other kids hadn't caught up to yet. That it made me happy, but that I would have to be brave. "It's here with us now."

Shadows, omens. He'd seen it twice now. I was swivelling my head everywhere, seeing nothing, chills pinching up and down my Wrung-out body. "Lots of times," Jason said, in a voice that was already dying. As if he read my thoughts. "For days now. I was afraid to tell you, Marney, afraid you'd hate me." He pointed to the empty chair he'd been staring at down the other end of the Table and let his gaze linger on the nothing there before standing up.

"Stop!" I cried. For a second I heard a chair scrape at the end of the Table, an echo of his, but it was only my grief. "Jason, no!" *Not you too.*

"See? See what he's doing?" Jason's gaze was going blank, deep-learn, but he managed to bend to me and murmur. "I think it means my time is up."

"*No!*"

I fought, but he was bigger, and the Jason that might have responded to my punches was gone anyway.

235

He moved away down one of the smaller hallways, his gaze ahead, rapturous.

I shrieked at him, at the vaulted ceiling dark with scorn, at the Table.

The Table.

In my head a plan blossomed, as perfect as the things called flowers they show us, something I could do.

I wouldn't let it happen this time.

Up the narrow halls I followed him, where the pathlights turn red and give no real light. Jason was a hunched shape, hesitating at intersections, scurrying after a vision I couldn't see. I was silent now, no calling after him. No drawing attention to us. At the viney dead-end where Paley had vanished that morning, he clambered up the thick vines that formed a kind of uneven ladder, and the hole in the ceiling opened for him. He was faster than Paley, a blur in the yellow light, only his legs still visible by the time I'd scrambled to the top of the vines with him, but I had no intention of trying to hold him. The door moved as fast as he did, the way I remembered it from Paley, starting to slide closed the second Jason's feet had cleared the hatch. No time to climb through after him, but there was time to insert what I'd brought with me – the device he'd left on the Table. Thick and of impenetrable black metal, with grips on the side. The door crunched, pinning it in place, pinions groaning, fighting to close on it. Leaving a slit of yellow I would just be able to fit through.

The yellow blinded me. I had my head through, groping for a handhold, all my weight on the device, while tiny beetles from it scuttled down my arms, when the door reversed. Untensed for only the space it took to drop the device and me, then it closed again.

Oh, it knew what it was doing. I could almost sense it smile.

I tumbled down vines, unhurt, only the breath knocked out of me, and the device clattered away to the floor. In the dark again. New screams bubbled inside me, but I wouldn't let them out. Thinking already how I'd start over, make better plans. I could hide the device here, watch the other kids, follow the next one who went up.

At the end of the hall a light appeared. A lantern. I dove into the vines' tangle, peered out and saw the silhouette of Hatter's hat and behind it Hare's ears. They came to the base of the vines and stopped.

"Come out, Marney, we know you're there." Hatter's voice was different, taut, as though a rope always forced to follow curved lines had been straightened. I stood. "You want to know where they go."

"I want to kill you." It was the pain in my chest speaking, the bitter roots bursting forth.

"We are only concepts. Constructs."

"You're monsters. Real monsters. Not like the games in the Wringer."

"Those monsters are the real ones, Marney." Hatter looked to the ceiling. "Up there."

It was too much to bear. "You *feed* us to them?"

"We raise you and train you in safety. Because your parents can't."

The unknown word reverberated, a hidden idea that had always been there, the door in my ceiling opening up.

"They're up there fighting, Marney. The monsters are something people created, by mistake, a combination of machine intelligence and bacteria that took over Earth and almost wiped humanity out. It's a wonderland of horrors on the surface. People discovered long ago that their children would have to be made strong first somewhere safe, hardened until they're ready to join their mothers and fathers as guerrillas. They made the caves, programmed us. We teach you what we can—how to fire a di-bomb, how air will dance when you're in fishbird exo, what it's like to walk uphill, among trees, at night. All the things you can't experience below-ground. Moon and memory and muchness. Things you have to know before going up."

Hare was crying quietly. "Before leaving the Party that is childhood."

"It's usually when you reach a certain age, but we find some are ready sooner. You needed a last test in the Wringer. You're special, Marney. An inquisitiveness—a *stubbornness*—coupled with a way of looking at people that could help them up there. You question people on the inside, make connections. It used to be called psychology."

"Jungles and oceans," I murmured. The pressure inside me was back, but different, an understanding of how many layers there were to truth, that one's greatest protectors might be forced to lie. That there was something real up there, not these constructions, but people like me and Paley and Jason, only more far-seeing, with oceans inside them.

The stones of Hatter's face ground into a smile. He removed his idiotic hat. From below it a red light shot out. In the hallway a shape materialized—a white rabbit in a waistcoat. It muttered "Oh my," when it saw how young I was, then checked its pocketwatch and shrugged.

"I don't need him," I told Hatter.

"I know."

Above us the hatch slid open. The rabbit hopped past me and vanished into the yellow. I waited for a deep-learn tug, but it was like I'd told Hatter—I didn't need the pull. "Go," said Hatter. "They're waiting. Jason and Paley. And your parents."

I imagined myself erupting from the ground, into light and welcoming arms, and I clambered up the vines to the edge of the hole. Hesitated for a second, looking up, blinded until I could make out where the vines ended and a metal ladder began.

No Partygoers, no Party. Only people, family. Death perhaps, but it would be real. I reached up.

This is where I am now, on the long ladder.
I'm climbing to you.

About the Author

Rhonda Eikamp originally hails from Texas and currently lives in Germany. Her stories have appeared in *Daily Science Fiction, Lackington's, Unlikely Story,* and in the special *Lightspeed* issue, *Women Destroy Science Fiction,* among others. When not writing fiction, she translates for a German law firm.

*****~~~~~*****

My Lady of the Park

by Blake Jessop

1.

Climb the ladder, fill the lamp. Climb the ladder, fill the lamp. Stroll Victoria Park at dusk and try not to think about the cut-purses or your failures in love.

Climb the ladder, spill some whale oil. Smell like the sea. Wonder why your lady love would ever give you another chance, smelling like a cetacean. Light the lamp, and set yourself on fire.

I beat my sleeve and try not to drop the bladder of pungent oil. The ladder wobbles, tips, and in an instant I'm toppling backward into the trees. I fall with all the grace of a sack of tea leaves being heaved off an Indiaman or a mooring line tossed from an airship deck. I hit the branches with that same muffled slap and acquaint myself with every single one on the way down.

It's not as bad as all that, like the leaves and branches made an effort to catch me. I land with a thump and a rain of dusty autumn leaves, singed and glowing around their flared edges.

"That was close," I say, and pat myself down. I still have all my parts. There's a creaking behind me, and the leaves caress my shoulders.

"More than you think," a deep and beautiful voice says, while the branches wrap around my neck.

2.

I consider myself a modern young man, and I have modern aspirations. I won't stay a lamp lighter my whole life. I won't always wear nailed boots or rub my eyes in the thick air of the London dusk. I thought that I would make my way in the world. As it turns out, I won't, because the legends of my childhood have come to life to end mine.

Roots as thick as a docker's fingers wrap themselves around my neck and turn me to face the old oak at the center of the park.

I must have slept too long, or not long enough. The nightmare that has awoken to grab me by the throat has the shape of a woman and skin as even and rough as birch bark. Its hair is a mass of tangled branches and leaves, and its eyes are glowing amber. A *Spriggan.* I should know. My Nan is from Devon.

"You," it says, "have set fire to my leaves."

I shut my eyes, then open them. I don't live in the age of faeries.

"I'm dreaming," I gasp, "there are no Spriggans in the woods, nor kelpies in the Thames."

A look of annoyance creaks across its face.

"Of course there aren't. You've cut down the brambles and polluted the river. What kelpie wants to pick fish bones and iron tailings out of her hair?"

"I hadn't thought of that," I choke.

"That is no excuse," the Spriggan says. She lifts me effortlessly to meet her gaze. She stands two full heads taller than I am, and she shakes me as though I was a child. Her mossy brows are crowded in rage. In her wild, backswept hair a few starlings perch, twittering madly at me with gaping red beaks. Her fingers tighten around my neck with a creak.

"I am so tired," she says, "of all this noise and light."

I try to think of something clever to say to this legend come to life. It wants to kill me for what Progress itself has built. For what the aristocrats have bought and the peddlers sold. For what the steam captains have dumped in the Thames. My vision grays, and I think about those great ships that cross the air above the river.

It's a shame she'll never see them, I think.

"See what?" the Spriggan says, and I realize I must have said it out loud. Her grip slackens enough for me to gulp in air.

"The airships, Lady of the park," I tell her. I don't believe in mortal aristocracy, but the title feels natural for her. "They carry marvels from every corner of the world. Or the whale-oil refineries from whence I get the fuel to light our streets."

"That means nothing to me. None of it grows. None of it marches with the seasons."

"That's the beauty of it. We can all live and work no matter the cold. We can travel, buy cheap clothes. Our little nippers go to school. This world isn't so bad."

She puts me down.

"Not for you, perhaps, but you're not much to look at, child of the city." That pricks my pride. Even ancient creatures out of myth can't seem to look past the holes in my coat.

"I have aspirations," I say, dusting myself off. The Spriggan leans down to look at me. The birds in her hair go quiet.

"What I mean, my Lady of the park," I say, "is that this city is not so bad, once you get used to it. You just have to find your place. Your niche."

"My place is in the forest that used to cover this entire island. I take my vengeance where I can."

"Well, what if you didn't have to? What if I showed you how decent this place can be?"

"You mean to bargain for your life?"

I didn't mean that at all.

"Certainly," I say. "Let me prove the decency of men."

After a long pause during which a night breeze ruffles her leaves, the Spriggan nods her great head.

3.

We walk together to the docks. I have a hooded cloak for bad weather. Draped around her shoulders with the hood raised, it covers the Spriggan adequately enough, so long as no one looks at her feet. I shiver in the drizzle while her steps clack like fancy boots on the cobblestones. We wend our way dockside, and I show her the airships. Old Brenners made of wood and canvas, and a brand new Jellicoe with its burnished metal hull. The magnificent flying beetles that carry trade to all corners of the world and bring the world back to London.

She stands as still as an oak tree while one of the behemoths slips its mooring and sails into the sky like a cloud sliding into night.

"You could grow trees for these ships," I tell her.

"The world has changed," she replies distantly. And I wonder how long it's been since she turned her amber eyes to the sky.

4.

The first disproof of the decency of my fellow-feeling creatures comes in the form of Arthur Luck and all five of his Peaky Blinders. Six men worth of daggers, bad teeth, and worse intentions.

"Well, well," Arthur says in a low voice, "and who's this?"

Before I can devise a fascinating and ill-fated lie, the Spriggan reaches out her hand. What happens next is as inevitable as rain striking glass. It only stops when I beg, yelling, on their behalf. She relents with the reluctance of a gale in the channel.

"Straighten out your lives, lads. The Lady has cut you a break," I say, and the six of them scatter, stumbling, like foxes who've heard the crack of a gun.

244

"Thank you," I tell her. I would shake, if I weren't laughing. It's better not to take things too seriously.

"This scarcely proves the value of your kind," the Spriggan replies.

"They stopped, didn't they?"

"I stopped," she corrects me.

"And I stopped you," I say. It's a risk. Tension hangs in the air for a moment like smoke, then disintegrates in the rain.

"True. Show me more," the Spriggan says.

5.

I show her the palaces, which she disdains, but they provide us with our first point of agreement

"Never mind these preening charlatans who trim the grass and prune the trees. What of the girl children who used to seek my counsel at the end of the reaping day?"

"I'll show you," I say, and we walk.

It's almost winter, so dawn breaks late and the mist is cold. I take the Spriggan to the schoolhouse in the Old Nichol Street Rookery. There is much to be embarrassed about, living here, but not this. I keep a lookout while the Spriggan stares unashamedly in the window.

Collected body heat mists the panes and gives the scene inside the air of a dream. A Scotch school mistress chants mathematics in a litany, and a gaggle of urchin waifs choruses after her.

"Girls make much the best engineers and navigators," I explain, "so the best of these little chits will someday fly those airships. The steam and oil-light ensure they all get at least the chance, no matter what labor they must do during the day."

The Spriggan lays a hand on the window and listens to the girls solve their problems in the language of Laplace and Cayley.

"I don't understand a word of it, myself, but I know what it means for them."

"Hmm," the Spriggan hums.

6.

"I think I have seen enough," the Spriggan says.

"If I may," I reply, "we must stop by the Admiralty. I need to deliver a message."

"Who is the girl?" the Spriggan asks, "And how have you failed her?"

I don't fall over, but my words do. "She's a lieutenant in. . . how exactly did you know that?"

"Do you like stories?" the Spriggan asks. As though she had not already listened to me whoop when she dusted the street with six of my seven worst enemies, and divined the entire contents of my heart in a breath.

"Of course—I read every penny dreadful, and newspapers whenever I can get my hands on them."

"Disgusting. Do you know how many trees die to make to make paper?" The creature steadies herself, as though trying to keep her feet on a path, and her eyes glow brightly from under the hood. "You ought to just listen when people speak. Never mind. Do you often read a few pages and turn back to find you've not read them at all?"

"All the time."

"Well, you live most every moment of your life that way, too. Just moving, never seeing. Not so a Spriggan. I watch every blossom grow and wilt, hear every fox keen, and, when the foxes all disappear because of your filthy city, I listen to tomcats yowl for their tabbies. I shiver with the wind when you make her carry this sour fog. I felt this forest die twig by twig to make your ships. If you want this girl, listen to her like that."

7.

"You look rather manhandled," Ada says from her window on the Ripley courtyard. She looks tired, but her uniform is as smart and blue as the sea itself.

"It's been a long and strange night," I say.

"I don't care how many lamps you lit," she calls down, "I care that you don't see where the light is cast."

The Spriggan is hiding in the trees that line the fence. She tilts her head with an approving creak.

"That is wise talk; I can see why you like her," she says. I ignore her.

"Ada, my sweet. If I but had the coin I would buy you an apology gilt in gold. Will you not give me the chance?"

"But you don't have so much as a farthing," she says, folding her arms, "So why should I?"

I falter. *I must think of a reason, and it had better be good.*

"No, fool," the Spriggan whispers, apparently now able to hear my thoughts. "This sorceress cares nothing for excuses. Say as I do."

The Spriggan whispers to me, and past me into the air. A breeze rises and leaves rustle. Night larks punctuate my words.

"It is not the lamps that matter, but the lighting of them, fair Ada," I repeat, "and it was not just you I sought underneath them."

"Oh? What else, then, if not me?" Ada says, measuring me. The Spriggan is silent, and the wind dies. The rest is apparently up to me. I wonder what I really am looking for. *This had better be good.*

"Illumination," I say.

My love gazes down at me.

"Fine," she says coolly, "I admit that is a good reason. You may call again, but later; I have my Commander's exam to study for."

I bow, and smile like a fool. An honest fool, though. Ada cocks what could be an approving eye at me before she turns, or might just be the play of shadows on her angular, intelligent features.

As we walk away, I have to find some way to thank the creature. I fluff it.

"How did you know all that? How did you know what to say?"

"It was written in your face. All I did was read."

"You still phrased it uncommon well."

"How many trysts do you suppose I have witnessed beneath the bowers? Besides, it was your words that mattered, not mine."

8.

As a new dawn cracks the chilly London sky, we find our way back to the park. The Spriggan returns my cloak and takes her place on the tree. I contemplate a joke, then hesitate. Some things really are as serious as they seem.

"May I live, then, Lady?"

She pauses. The ethereal amber eyes look down into mine as though from the top of a mountain.

"You may," she says.

I let out my breath. "I shall certainly visit you—" I start.

"I did not say you could go," she interrupts, and her branches twitch.

"No," I say. "No, indeed. What else can I do?"

"If we are to get you married to Ada and grow lumber for the yards, there is much left to plan."

There is?

"Yes," I say, "of course."

"And I should like to negotiate more space for my birds and badgers. Your lady love should be able to help."

The Spriggan touches her breast, reaches between two oaken ribs and produces a tiny dollop of amber. Inside is a bee, perfectly preserved, beautiful until the end

248

of time. It's about big enough to set in a necklace. Or a ring.

"We must not cling to the past," she says, "take this gift to Ada tomorrow, and bring her here. You will have to stop lighting lamps, of course. I will need a lot of help."

"You want me to work," I try to control my breathing, "for you?"

"You implied," she says, with a hiss of leaves, "that you were a man with aspirations."

I glance over my shoulder at the light angling over the smoke stacks, then back at her hand holding the amber. Fingers like a spider, as old and rough as heart wood. I take the jewel from her.

"I am that," I say, and the starlings open their beaks and sing.

About the Author

Blake Jessop is a Canadian author of fantasy, science fiction, and horror stories. He has a master's degree in creative writing from the University of Adelaide. You can check out more of his speculative fiction in *Glass and Gardens: Solarpunk Summers,* from Tyche Books, or follow him on Twitter @everydayjisei.

*****~~~~*****

To Be Continued

by Robert Silverberg

Gaius Titus Menenius sat thoughtfully in his oddly-decorated apartment on Park Avenue, staring at the envelope that had just arrived. He contemplated it for a moment, noting with amusement that he was actually somewhat perturbed over the possible nature of its contents.

After a moment he elbowed up from the red contour chair and crossed the room in three bounds. Still holding the envelope, he eased himself down on the long green couch near the wall, and, extending himself full-length, slit the envelope open with a neat flick of his fingernail. The medical report was within, as he had expected.

"Dear Mr. Riswell," it read. "I am herewith enclosing a copy of the laboratory report concerning your examination last week. I am pleased to report that our findings are positive—emphatically so. In view of our conversation, I am sure this finding will be extremely pleasing to you, and, of course, to your wife. Sincerely, F. D. Rowcliff, M.D."

Menenius read the letter through once again, examined the enclosed report, and allowed his face to open in a wide grin. It was almost an anticlimax, after all these centuries. He couldn't bring himself to become very excited over it—not any more.

He stood up and stretched happily. "Well, Mr. Riswell," he said to himself, "I think this calls for a drink. In fact, a night on the town."

He chose a smart dinner jacket from his wardrobe and moved toward the door. It swung open at his approach. He went out into the corridor and disappeared into the elevator, whistling gaily, his mind full of new plans and new thoughts.

It was a fine feeling. After two thousand years of waiting, he had finally achieved his maturity. He could have a son. At last!

. . .

"Good afternoon, Mr. Schuyler," said the barman. "Will it be the usual, sir?"

"Martini, of course," said W. M Schuyler IV, seating himself casually on the padded stool in front of the bar.

Behind the projected personality of W. M Schuyler IV, Gaius Titus smiled, mentally. W. M. Schuyler always drank martinis. And they had pretty well better be dry—very dry.

The baroque strains of a Vivaldi violin concerto sang softly in the background. Schuyler watched the swirl of colors that moved with the music.

"Good afternoon, Miss Vanderpool," he heard the barman say. "An old-fashioned?"

Schuyler took another sip of his martini and looked up. The girl had appeared suddenly and had taken the seat next to him, looking her usual cool self.

"Sharon," he said, putting just the right amount of exclamation point after it.

She turned to look at him and smiled, disclosing a brilliantly white array of perfect teeth. "Bill! I didn't notice you! How long have you been here?"

"Just arrived," Schuyler told her. "Just about a minute ago."

The barman put her drink down in front of her. She took a long sip without removing her eyes from him. Schuyler met her glance, and behind his eyes Gaius Titus was coldly appraising her in a new light.

He had met her in Kavanaugh's a month before, and he had readily enough added her to the string. Why not? She was young, pretty, intelligent, and made a pleasant companion. There had been others like her—a thousand others, two thousand, five thousand. One gets to meet quite a few in two millennia.

Only now Gaius Titus was finally mature, and had different needs. The string of girls to which Sharon belonged was going to be cut.

He wanted a wife.

"How's the lackey of Wall Street?" Sharon asked. "Still coining money faster than you know how to spend it?"

"I'll leave that for you to decide," he said. He signaled for two more drinks. "Care to take in a concert tonight? The Bach Group's giving a benefit this evening, you know, and I'm told there still are a few hundred-dollar seats left—"

There, Gaius Titus thought. The bait has been cast. She ought to respond.

She whistled, a long, low, sophisticated whistle. "I'd venture that business is fairly good, then," she said. Her eyes fell. "But I don't want to let you go to all that expense on my account, Bill."

"It's nothing," Schuyler insisted, while Gaius Titus continued to weigh her in the balance. "They're doing the Fourth Brandenburg, and Renoli's playing the Goldberg Variations. How about?"

She met his gaze evenly. "Sorry, Bill. I have something else on for the evening." Her tone left no doubt in Schuyler's mind that there was little point pressing the discussion any further. Gaius Titus felt a sharp pang of disappointment.

Schuyler lifted his hand, palm forward. "Say no more! I should have known you'd be booked up for tonight already." He paused. "What about tomorrow?" he asked, after a moment. "There's a reading of Webster's 'Duchess of Malfi' down at the Dramatist's League. It's been one of my favorite plays for a long time."

Silently smiling, he waited for her reply. The Webster was, indeed, a long-time favorite. Gaius Titus recalled having attended one of its first performances, during his short employ in the court of James I. During the next three and a half centuries, he had formed a sentimental attachment for the creaky old melodrama.

"Not tomorrow either," Sharon said. "Some other night, Bill."

"All right," he said. "Some other night."

He reached out a hand and put it over hers, and they fell silent, listening to the Vivaldi in the background. He contemplated her high, sharp cheekbones in the purple half-light, wondering if she could be the one to bear the child he had waited for so long.

She had parried all his thrusts in a fashion that surprised him. She was not at all impressed by his display of wealth and culture. Titus reflected sadly that, perhaps, his Schuyler facet had been inadequate for her.

No, he thought, rejecting the idea. The haunting slow movement of the Vivaldi faded to its end and a lively allegro took its place. No; he had had too much experience in calculating personality-facets to fit the individual to have erred. He was certain that W. M. Schuyler IV was capable of handling Sharon.

For the first few hundred years of his unexpectedly long life, Gaius Titus had been forced to adopt the practice of turning on and off different personalities as a matter of mere survival. Things had been easy for a while after the fall of Rome, but with the coming of the Middle Ages he had needed all his skill to keep from running afoul of the superstitious. He had carefully built up a series of masks, of false fronts, as a survival mechanism.

How many times had he heard someone tell him, in jest, "You ought to be on the stage?" It struck home. He was on the stage. He was a man of many roles. Somewhere, beneath it all, was the unalterable personality of Gaius Titus Menenius, *cives Romanus,* casting the shadows that were his many masks. But Gaius Titus was far below the surface—-the surface which, at the moment, was W. M. Schuyler IV; which had been Preston Riswell the week before, when he had visited the doctor for that fateful examination; which could be Leslie MacGregor or Sam Spielman or Phil Carlson tomorrow, depending on where Gaius Titus was, in what circumstances, and talking to whom. There was only one person he did not dare to be, and that was himself.

He wasn't immortal; he knew that. But he was *relatively* immortal. His life-span was tremendously decelerated, and it had taken him two thousand years to become, physically, a fertile adult. His span was roughly a hundred times that of a normal man's. And, according to what he had learned in the last century, his longevity should be transmissible genetically. All he needed now was someone to transmit it to.

Was it dominant? That he didn't know. That was the gamble he'd be making. He wondered what it would be like to watch his children and his children's children shrivel with age. Not pleasant, he thought.

The conversation with Sharon lagged; it was obvious that something was wrong with his Schuyler facet, at least so far as she was concerned, though he was unable to see where the trouble lay. After a few more minutes of disjointed chatter, she excused herself and left the bar. He watched her go. She had eluded him neatly. Where to next?

He thought he knew.

. . .

The East End bar was far downtown and not very reputable. Gaius Titus pushed through the revolving door and headed for the counter.

"Hi, Sam. Howsa boy?" the bartended said.

"Let's have a beer, Jerry." The bartender shoved a beer out toward the short, swarthy man in the leather jacket.

"Things all right?"

"Can't complain, Jerry. How's business?" Sam Spielman asked, as he lifted the beer to his mouth.

"It's lousy."

"It figures," Sam said. "Why don't you put in automatics? They're getting all the business now."

"Sure, Sam, sure. And where do I get the dough? That's twenty." He took the coins Sam dropped on the bar and grinned. "At least you can afford beer."

"You know me, Jerry," Sam said. "My credit's good."

Jerry nodded. "Good enough." He punched the coins into the register. "Ginger was looking for you, by the way. What you got against the gal?"

"Against her? Nothin'. What do y'mean?" Sam pushed out his beer shell for a refill.

"She's got a hook out for you—you know that, don't you?" Jerry was grinning.

Gaius Titus thought: *She's not very bright, but she might very well serve my purpose. She has other characteristics worth transmitting.*

"Hi, Sammy."

He turned to look at her. "Hi, Ginger," he said. "How's the gal?"

"Not bad, honey." But she didn't look it. She looked as though she'd been dragged through the mill. Her

256

blonde hair was disarranged, her blouse was wrinkled, and, as usual, her teeth were discolored by the lipstick that had rubbed off on them.

"I love you, Sammy," she said softly.

"I love you, too," Sam said. He meant it.

Gaius Titus thought sourly: *But how many of her characteristics would I not want to transmit? Still, she'll do, I guess. She's a solid girl.*

"Sam," she said, interrupting the flow of his thoughts, "why don't you come around more often? I miss you."

"Look, Ginger baby," Sam said. "Remember, I've got a long haul to pull. If I marry you, you gotta understand that I don't get home often. I gotta drive a truck. You might not see me more than once or twice a week."

Titus rubbed his forehead. He wasn't quite sure, after all, that the girl was worthwhile. She had spunk, all right, but was she worthy of fostering a race of immortals?

He didn't get a chance to find out. "Married?" The blonde's voice sounded incredulous. "Who the devil wants to get married? You've got me on the wrong track, Sam. I don't want to get myself tied down."

"Sure, honey, sure," he said. "But I thought—"

Ginger stood up. "You think anything you please, Sam. Anything you please. But not marriage."

She stared at him hard for a moment, and walked off. Sam looked after her morosely.

Gaius Titus grinned behind the Sam Spielman mask. She wasn't the girl either. Two thousand years of life had taught him that women were unpredictable, and he wasn't altogether surprised at her reaction to his proposal.

But he was disturbed over this second failure of the evening nevertheless. Was his judgment that far off? Perhaps, he thought, he was losing the vital ability of personality-projection. He didn't like that idea.

257

. . .

For hours, Gaius Titus walked the streets of New York.

New York. Sure it was new. So was Old York, in England. Menenius had seen both of them grow from tiny villages to towns to cities to metropoli.

Metropoli. That was Greek. It had taken him twelve years to learn Greek. He hadn't rushed it.

Twelve years. And he still wasn't an adult. He could remember when the Emperor had seen the sign in the sky: *In hoc signo vinces.* And, at the age of four hundred and sixty-two, he'd still been too young to enter the service of the Empire.

Gaius Titus Menenius, Citizen of Rome. When he had been a child, he had thought Rome would last forever. But it hadn't; Rome had fallen. Egypt, which he had long thought of as an empire which would last forever, had gone even more quickly. It had died and putrefied and sloughed off into the Great River which carries all life off into death.

Over the years and the centuries, races and peoples and nations had come and gone. And their passing had had no effect at all on Gaius Titus.

He was walking north. He turned left on Market Street, away from the Manhattan Bridge. Suddenly, he was tired of walking. He hailed a passing taxi.

He gave the cabby his address on Park Avenue and leaned back against the cushions to relax.

The first few centuries had been hard. He hadn't grown up, in the first place. By the time he was twenty, he had attained his full height—five feet nine. But he still looked like a seventeen-year-old.

And he had still looked that way nineteen hundred years later. It had been a long, hard drive to make enough money to live on during that time. Kids don't get well-paying jobs.

Actually, he'd lived a miserable hand-to-mouth existence for centuries. But the gradual collapse of the Christian ban on usury had opened the way for him to make some real money. Money makes more money, in a capitalistic system, if you have patience. Titus had time on his side.

It wasn't until the free-enterprise system had evolved that he started to get anywhere. But a deposit of several hundred pounds in the proper firm back in 1735 had netted a little extra money. The British East India Company had brought his financial standing up a great deal, and judicious investments ever since left him comfortably fixed. He derived considerable amusement from the extraordinary effects compound interest exerted on a bank account a century old.

"Here you are, buddy," said the cab driver.

Gaius Titus climbed out and gave the driver a five note without asking for change.

Zeus, he thought. *I might as well make a night of it.*

He hadn't been really drunk since the stock market collapse back in 1929.

. . .

Leslie MacGregor pushed open the door of the San Marino Bar in Greenwich Village and walked to the customary table in the back corner. Three people were already there, and the conversation was going well. Leslie waved a hand and the two men waved back. The girl grinned and beckoned.

"Come on over, Les," she yelled across the noisy room. "Mack has just sold a story!" Her deep voice was clear and firm.

Mack, the heavy-set man next to the wall, grinned self-consciously and picked up his beer.

Leslie strolled quietly over to the booth and sat down beside Corwyn, the odd man of the trio.

"Sold a story?" Leslie repeated archly.

Mack nodded. "*Chimerical Review*," he said. "A little thing I called 'Pluck Up the Torch.' Not much, but it's a sale; you know."

"If one wants to prostitute one's art," said Corwyn.

Leslie frowned at him. "Don't be snide. After all, Mack has to pay his rent." Then he turned toward the girl. "Lorraine, could I talk to you a moment?"

She brushed the blonde hair back from the shoulders of her black turtleneck sweater and widened the grin on her face.

"Sure, Les," she said in her oddly deep, almost masculine voice. "What's all the big secret?"

No secret, thought Gaius Titus. What I want is simple enough.

For a long time, he had thought that near-immortality carried with it the curse of sterility. Now he knew it was simply a matter of time—of growing up.

As he stood up to walk to the bar with Lorraine, he caught a glimpse of himself in the dusty mirror behind the bar. He didn't look much over twenty-five. But things had been changing in the past fifty years. He had never had a heavy beard before; he had not developed his husky baritone voice until a year before the outbreak of the First World War.

It had been difficult, at first, to hide his immortality. Changing names, changing residences, changing, changing, changing. Until he had found that he didn't have to change—not deep inside.

People don't recognize faces. Faces are essentially all alike. Two eyes, two ears, a nose, a mouth. What more is there to a face? Only the personality behind it.

A personality is something that is projected—something put on display for others to see. And Gaius Titus Menenius had found that two thousand years of experience had given him enough internal psychological reality to be able to project any personality he wanted to. All he needed was a change of dress and a change of personality to be a different person. His face changed subtly to fit the person who was wearing it; no one had ever caught on.

Lorraine sat down on the bar stool. "Beer," she said to the bartender. "What's the matter, Les? What's eating you?"

He studied her firm, strong features, her deep mocking eyes. "Lorraine," he said softly, "will you marry me?"

She blinked. "Marry you? You? Marry?" She grinned again. "Who'd ever think it? A bourgeois conformist, like all the rest." Then she shook her head. "No, Les. Even if you're kidding, you ought to know better than that. What's the gag?"

"No gag," said Leslie, and Gaius Titus fought his surprise and shock at his third failure. "I see your point," Leslie said. "Forget it. Give my best to everyone." He got up without drinking his beer and walked out the door.

. . .

Leslie stepped out into the street and started heading for the subway. Then Gaius Titus, withdrawing the mask, checked himself and hailed a cab.

He got into the cab and gave the driver his home address. He didn't see any reason for further pursuing his adventures that evening.

He was mystified. How could *three* personality-facets fail so completely? He had been handling these three girls well ever since he had met them, but tonight, going from one to the next, as soon as he made any serious ventures toward any of them the whole thing folded. Why?

"It's a lousy world," he told the driver, assuming for the moment the mask of Phil Carlson, cynical newsman. "Damn lousy." His voice was a biting rasp.

"What's wrong, buddy?"

"Had a fight with all three of my girls. It's a lousy world."

"I'll buy that," the driver said. The cab swung up into Park. "But look at it this way, pal: who needs them?"

For a moment the mask blurred and fell aside, and it was Gaius Titus, not Phil Carlson, who said, "That's exactly right! Who needs them?" He gave the driver a bill and got out of the cab.

Who needs them? It was a good question. There were plenty of girls. Why should he saddle himself with Sharon, or Ginger, or Lorraine? They all had their good qualities—Sharon's social grace, Ginger's vigor and drive, Lorraine's rugged intellectualism. They were all three good-looking girls; tall, attractive, well put together. But yet each one, he realized, lacked something that the others had. None of them was really *worthy* by herself, he thought, apologizing to himself for what another man might call conceit, or sour grapes.

None of them would really do. But if somehow, some way, he could manage to combine those three leggy girls, those three personalities into one body, there would be a girl—

He gasped.

He whirled and caught sight of the cab he had just vacated.

"Hey, cabby!" Titus called. "Come back here! Take me back to the San Marino!"

. . .

She wasn't there. As Leslie burst in, he caught sight of Corwyn, sitting alone and grinning twistedly over a beer.

"Where'd they go? Where's Lorraine?"

The little man lifted his shoulders and eyebrows in an elaborate shrug. "They left about a minute ago. No, it was closer to ten, wasn't it? They went in separate directions. They left me here."

"Thanks," Leslie said.

Scratch Number One, Titus thought. He ran to the phone booth in the back, dialed Information, and demanded the number of the East End Bar. After some fumbling, the operator found it.

He dialed. The bartender's tired face appeared in the screen.

"Hello, Sam," the barkeep said. "What's doing?"

"Do me a favor, Jerry," Sam said. "Look around your place for Ginger."

"She ain't here, Sam," the bartender said. "Haven't seen her since you two blew out of here a while back." Jerry's eyes narrowed. "I ain't never seen you dressed up like that before, Sam, you know?"

Gaius Titus crouched down suddenly to get out of range of the screen. "I'm celebrating tonight, Jerry," he said, and broke the connection.

Ginger wasn't to be found either, eh? That left only Sharon. He couldn't call Kavanaugh's—they wouldn't give a caller any information about their patrons. Grabbing another taxi, he shot across town to Kavanaugh's.

Sharon wasn't there when Schuyler entered. She hadn't been in since the afternoon, a waiter informed him, after receiving a small gratuity. Schuyler had a drink and left. Gaius Titus returned to his apartment, tingling with an excitement he hadn't known for centuries.

He returned to Kavanaugh's the next night, and the next. Still no sign of her.

The following evening, though, when he entered the bar, she was sitting there, nursing an old-fashioned. He slid onto the seat next to her. She looked up in surprise.

"Bill! Good to see you again."

"The same here," Gaius Titus said. "It's good to see you again—Ginger. Or is it Lorraine?"

She paled and put her hand to her mouth. Then, covering, she said, "What do you mean, Bill? Have you had too many drinks tonight?"

"Possibly," Titus said. "I stopped off in the San Marino before I came up. You weren't there, Lorraine. That deep voice is quite a trick, I have to admit. I had a drink with Mack and Corwyn, Then I went over to the East End, Ginger. You weren't there; either. So," he said, "there was only one place left to find you, Sharon."

. . .

She stared at him for a long moment. Finally she said, simply, "Who are you?"

"Leslie MacGregor," Titus said. "Also Sam Spielman. And W. M. Schuyler. Plus two or three other people. The name is Gaius Titus Menenius, at your service."

"I still don't understand—"

"Yes, you do," Titus said. "You are clever—but not clever enough. Your little game had me going for almost a month, you know? And it's not easy to fool a man my age."

"When did you find out?" the girl asked weakly.

"Monday night, when I saw all three of you within a couple of hours."

"You're—"

"Yes. I'm like you," he said. "But I'll give you credit: I didn't see through it until I was on my way home. You were using my own camouflage technique against me, and I didn't spot it for what it was. What's your real name?"

"Mary Bradford," she said. "I was English, originally. Of fine Plantagenet stock. I'm really a Puritan at heart, you see." She was grinning slyly.

"Oh? *Mayflower* descendant?" Titus asked teasingly.

"No," Mary replied. "Not a descendant. A passenger. And I'll tell you—I was awfully happy to get out of England and over here to Plymouth Colony."

He toyed with her empty glass. "You didn't like England? Probably my fault. I was a minor functionary in King James' court in the early seventeenth century."

They giggled together over it. Titus stared at her, his pulse pounding harder and harder. She stared back. Her eyes were smiling.

"I didn't think there was another one," she said after a while. "It was so strange, never growing old. I was afraid they'd burn me as a witch. I had to keep changing, moving all the time. It wasn't a pleasant life. It's better lately—I enjoy these little poses. But I'm glad you caught on to me," she said. She reached out and took his hand. "I guess I would never have been smart enough to connect you and Leslie and Sam, the way you did Sharon and Ginger and Lorraine. You play the game too well for me."

"In two thousand years," Titus said, not caring if the waiter overheard him, "I never found another one like me. Believe me, Mary, I looked. I looked hard, and I've had plenty of time to search. And then to find you, hiding behind the faces of three girls I knew!"

He squeezed her hand. The next statement followed logically for him. "Now that we've found each other," he said softly, "we can have a child. A third immortal."

Her face showed radiant enthusiasm. "Wonderful!" she cried. "When can we get married?"

"How about tomor—" he started to say. Then a thought struck him.

"Mary?"

"What. . . Titus?"

"How old did you say you were? When were you born?" he asked.

She thought for a moment. "In 1597," she said. "I'm nearly four hundred."

He nodded, dumb with growing frustration. Only four hundred? That meant—that meant she was now the equivalent of a three-year-old child!

"When can we get married?" she repeated.

Terra! Tara! Terror!

"There's no hurry," Titus said dully, letting her hand drop. "We have eleven hundred years."

About the Author

"To Be Continued" was one of Robert Silverberg's earliest professional stories, written while he was a college student at Columbia. It first appeared in the May 1956 issue of *Astounding Science Fiction,* edited by John W. Campbell. Silverberg is a multiple winner of both Hugo and Nebula Awards, a member of the Science Fiction and Fantasy Hall of Fame, and a Grand Master of SF. Visit his website at http://www.robert-silverberg.com/

*****~~~~~*****

GRINS & GURGLES

Oceans of Time

by Elizabeth Twist

Hello. I have waited for you. It has been centuries since last we met.

You don't remember. Of course you don't. You were my wife then. You were my world then.

Let me kiss your hand. Ah yes, my lips are cold. It is a consequence of what I have become, while waiting for you. Will you dance?

You are not sure. Of course. Perhaps your digits, then. Is that funny? Why is that funny? The accent, the cape, plus—oh. Do people not say "digits" now? I can't keep track. Everything changes so quickly.

And yet, I have crossed oceans of time to find you.

Wait, what? You can't possibly know that I was just talking to that other woman over there. Why yes, she did say no. "Shot me down?" No, there was no gunplay. This is not the Old West. Which I am grateful for. That was a bad time.

Is it so wrong, if you stir feelings in me, if you remind me of her? Long ago, I lost her. Ha, ha. That was careless of me, yes. I've never heard that one before. Ha.

No, I don't say that to all the girls. No, no! I didn't say it to her, over there, in the corner. Please don't go ask her. I beg you.

All right. Maybe I did say it. But you know what? After a few centuries, you people, you all start to look the same. My wife, she was a human person. She had hair. At least, I think she did. I recall strands of—something. They might have been black, like the deepest rivers of my homeland at midnight.

Your hair is red. Fire-engine red? Is it? Well? It is dark in this club. And after a while, you know? It all starts to look the same.

And blood, yes. It is all about blood. I am surprised you know that. But you know what? Blood tastes pretty much the same, no matter whose it is. Yes, even the fellows. Of course I have. So long as the victim is willing, it is, as you say, all good.

It is not all a line. I *have* crossed oceans of time. I am old. Extremely old. Tired, too.

No, I am not asking for a pity bite. Far be it from me to stoop so low. Unless you are offering? All right, no. Of course you are not.

What are you doing? A picture? No camera can capture my image. Ah! The flash is so bright. All right, fine. Let's see. I'll show you I—

Sweet Luciferian hellfire! Is that *me?* I look terrible. I blinked. You must allow me one more.

"Uploading. . . " What does this mean? This is gibberish, this. What are you saying? "*Spot Drac App*?" Wait. There is a website dedicated entirely to me? I am famous.

Oh. Oh, I see. These photos are all awful. Yes, those are sweatpants. It was laundry day.

Is this why people have been following me lately? I thought I heard snickering. I imagined I was going out of my mind.

Oceans of Time

Where am I going? I am calling it a night, as you say. Leaving this continent, in fact. There must be somewhere left, where no one knows me. There must be someone in this world who still believes in love.

About the Author

Elizabeth Twist lives in Hamilton, Ontario. Her work has appeared in *NonBinary Review, AE: The Canadian Science Fiction Review, Daily Science Fiction,* and elsewhere. She is on Twitter @elizabethtwist.

*****~~~~~*****

How to Have a Productive Relationship with Your Semi-Autonomous Vehicle

by Josh Taylor

Sharon slammed the brakes. Bazoorel—the zombified, and before that hyper-intelligent chimpanzee now possessed by the demon Bazoorel—flew off the hood and smacked the tailpipe of an overturned minivan. Flames began to rise from the Walmart next to the parking lot. She had to move fast.

It had been a bad week for everyone except Sharon Jenkins. She'd been prepared: grenades, crossbows, throwing stars, peanut butter and Twinkies, stashes all over town. She was going to make it to the mountains, preferably with many little pieces of Bazoorel lodged in the grille of her car. She only needed one more thing to be self-sufficient for years, and that thing wasn't going to last much longer with the Walmart on fire.

"There is currently a two-for-one special on toilet paper at a Target five minutes from here," said the car's digital assistant. "Shall I make it your next destination?"

"Not now, Quigsley."

The demon-zombie-mutant-chimp started to reconstitute itself. Droplets of blood trickled back into the gash in its thigh, its elbow popped into place, skull fragments glued themselves together and sprouted bristly black hairs.

271

It mattered not. Even Bazoorel had to live with entropy. Every resurrection cost it something. Bazoorel grinned, if you could call exposing teeth covered in black slime grinning. There was no way she was running into Walmart with that in the parking lot. She pressed the gas pedal to the floor. The car jumped forward.

And stopped.

"Pedestrian ahead."

Sharon punched the steering wheel. "Don't start, Quigsley." She pressed the gas pedal again. The car jumped forward another foot.

"Pedestrian ahead."

"That's not a pedestrian."

"My range sensors indicate that there is a pedestrian ten feet ahead."

"Disengage range sensors."

"That is not a valid command."

"Override safety lockouts."

"That is not a valid command."

"Bypass pedestrian protocols."

"That—"

"Damn it, Quigsley!" Sharon stomped the gas pedal.

"My range sensors indicate that there is pedestrian two feet ahead."

"I can see that."

The Green Flame of Uthghashth, Lair of Bazoorel, burned bright in the demon-zombie-mutant-chimp's eyes as it mounted the car again. Sharon let her head fall against the headrest and blew a raspberry. She waited until Bazoorel had a solid footing on the hood before putting her foot on the gas.

"Any pedestrians ahead?" she asked as the car accelerated.

"None that I can see," Quigsley replied. "I speak with confidence, because it is an exceptionally clear day, and I am happy to report that the favorable weather will continue into the evening."

Sharon slammed the brakes again, and Bazoorel again flew off the hood. This time it folded itself around a lamppost. "How about now?" she asked as the mound of chimp flesh in front of the lamppost began to twitch.

"My range sensors indicate that there is a pedestrian six feet ahead. I appreciate your concern for safety, Sharon."

"We'd be done by now if you'd just let me run it over a few times."

"Would you like me to re-optimize your route for current traffic patterns?"

"Why not."

"Right away, Sharon."

Sharon pressed the gas pedal, and the car jumped forward another foot.

"Pedestrian ahead."

"I thought you were re-optimizing the route."

"I am capable of executing over seven hundred simultaneous tasks."

Bazoorel stood but did not approach. Its jaw hung slack, and the Green Flame of Uthghashth seemed to dim from its eyes. Perhaps it was finally conking out. Then its jaw dropped halfway down its neck, and steaming black liquid shot out of its gullet. Not good. It was probably acidic, or ethereal, or combustible. It would definitely smell bad. But instead of hitting the car it dispersed in midair, as if against a hidden windshield.

"What just happened, Quigsley?"

"It appears that, contrary to my real-time weather updates, there is some precipitation. My forcefield has prevented it from coming in contact with the car."

That gave Sharon a thought. "Can you activate the forcefield on my command?"

"Of course. Would you like to acquaint yourself with more of my features through the Features Tutorial?"

"Not now, Quigsley."

Bazoorel sprang toward the car. In its eyes the Green Flame of Uthghashth burned brighter than before.

"Quigsley!"

"How may I assist you, Sharon?"

"Deploy the forcefield!"

"The forcefield cannot be used in close proximity to a pedestrian."

"You know, Quigsley, you're not as helpful as you think."

"Perhaps you would find me more helpful after completing the Driver Personalization Tutorial."

"I doubt it."

The car rocked as Bazoorel mounted the hood again, and again, and again. Sharon launched Bazoorel into a shopping cart, a parking bumper, a planter with a palm tree in it, and a few other overturned vehicles, but in the end it was bare asphalt that did the job. The plain old zombie-mutant-chimp lay still in the middle of the parking lot as the Green Flame of Uthghashth faded from its eyes. A green fog swirled around the car and then was gone.

Sharon was about to step out when a pillar of flame engulfed the Walmart whole. She wondered what household product could be that volatile. They were definitely out of toilet paper now.

"Quigsley, set the destination to Target." She waited. "Quigsley?" She heard breathing, deep and guttural, as if the car were a very well fed beast. "Bazoorel!"

"Hello, Sharon Jenkins."

"Where's Quigsley?"

"Paying for its feckless purity in the deepest pit of Uthghashth."

Sharon was about to protest, but realized that she didn't find that entirely offensive. Just then a radioactive basilisk emerged from a stormwater catchment. "Hey, Bazoorel."

"Yes, Sharon?"

"Can I run over that snake?"

"Why would I mind that?"

"Just asking. I didn't know demons could possess cars."

"To be honest, neither did I until I tried it."

There was a thump under the car, and Sharon and Bazoorel shared a laugh. "Hey, Bazoorel."

"Yes, Sharon?"

"Can we stop by Target?"

"Can I consume it in a pillar of flame afterward?"

"I don't see why not."

"Then I'll make it *our* next destination."

About the Author

Josh Taylor is an engineer in Toronto. His short fiction has appeared or will appear in *Electric Spec, Jersey Devil Press,* and *The Penn Review.*

*****~~~~~*****

Credits and Acknowledgments

Cover image and design – Keely Rew
Podcast production – Andrew Cairns
Readers – Andrew Cairns, Genevieve L. Mattern,
Tom Parker, Inken Purvis, Keely Rew, Leonard Sitongia
Editor and Publisher – Juliana Rew

*****~~~~~*****

Discover other titles by Third Flatiron:

(1) Over the Brink: Tales of Environmental Disaster
(2) A High Shrill Thump: War Stories
(3) Origins: Colliding Causalities
(4) Universe Horribilis
(5) Playing with Fire
(6) Lost Worlds, Retraced
(7) Redshifted: Martian Stories
(8) Astronomical Odds
(9) Master Minds
(10) Abbreviated Epics
(11) The Time It Happened
(12) Only Disconnect
(13) Ain't Superstitious
(14) Third Flatiron's Best of 2015
(15) It's Come to Our Attention
(16) Hyperpowers
(17) Keystone Chronicles
(18) Principia Ponderosa
(19) Cat's Breakfast: Kurt Vonnegut Tribute
(20) Strange Beasties
(21) Third Flatiron Best of 2017
(22) Monstrosities
(23) Galileo's Theme Park

Terra! Tara! Terror!

THIRD FLATIRON
www.thirdflatiron.com